THE THINGS THOUGHTS FEAR
AN ANTHOLOGY

by

TOBY CRABBE

ISBN: 978-1-916551-07-7

POE GIRL PUBLISHING

EST 2023

Table of Contents

ACKNOWLEDGEMENTS.......................4
FOREWARNING.......................................5
THE FLIES...7
INTO THE WOODS 19
FANNY TALBOT 47
THE WORG 62
THE CATCH 80
THE WITCH GIRL.................................92
SUTURES 96
ELIZABETH'S LAKE 101
WILD THINGS 109
STILL HILL 117
ALLEGED DEATH OF ALBERT GREY153
SLITHER..156
THE BEAST OF SLEEPY WILLOW.... 158
THEY ARE COMING 164
RED RIBBON 173
REDBEARD...181
SNOWED IN 193
MUDBERRY 201
THROWAWAY....................................232
RODENTS..237
THE TROLL PAINTER 242
NO WAY OUT.....................................250
ABOUT THE AUTHOR.......................260

ACKNOWLEDGEMENTS

With thanks to all the frighteners that continue to influence my writing.

Thank you to the writing pack at the University of Wolverhampton.

Thank you to my friends (they know who they are).

Thank you to my family.

For Merlin.

FOREWARNING

In haunted houses, ancient forests, fly-infested churches. In gas-lit alleys, fog-veiled marshes, goblyn labyrinths. THE THINGS THOUGHTS FEAR conjures up fright through terrific creature features, weird tales, ghost stories, and grim fairytales. Read on, if you dare, to find the answer to an age-old question.

WHAT DO YOU FEAR?

‘The oldest and strongest emotion of mankind is fear, and the oldest and strongest kind of fear is fear of the unknown.’

H. P. LOVECRAFT

THE FLIES

They would come for him again tonight. The flies.

Father Henry lay still. Then, flashes of fear tossed and turned him in his crinkled sheets. A quiet flood of thoughts found their way in. They were larvae, planting pale eggs of horror in his sleep. It was night again in the church, a troubling night of irritation and soft nightmares. They always came at night, flies and other things. Threatening thoughts riled Henry's rest tonight. Thoughts that plagued his sleep. They were terrors, terrors that were not forgotten or ridden off. They teased Henry's faith. Roots of fear knotting and threading together to form a fouler thought. One after another, they gathered and harassed the old priest's sleep. Tonight, Henry testified to stay awake. It was a trying task, at that. A task that Henry found futile.

The night was bottle green. After that, it turned grey. It was wilting, moth ash flowering through the air like flaking skin, coating all it touched. The world was rife with scurf. Quick wind tore over the forgotten country church. It whistled through the rafters and raked against weathered stone. It carried out in gusts towards a quaint, gas-lit place. A quiet cluster of cottages formed a town out there. A town called Trifford.

Another gust.

Wind scratched at the church's windows and screeched through the shutter frames. It splintered the rotting wood, slithering by way of cobweb fractures in the stained glass. Painted saints pouted at the trespassing air. This was nature's teeth, thrashing with a terrific rhythm. It was a revolt against Henry's faith and the structure's stature. The gust found shelter through the narthex. The tall door of the church was torn from its worn hinges and crashed towards the flagstones, giving full entry to its formless intruder.

The racket caught Henry off guard. Trauma thundered through

his chest and punctured his heart. He shot up in bed. If, in a turn of fortune, the priest was sleeping, then the startle may have stopped his heart dead. Life would have released him from its cruel clutches. Yet, the outcome hung upon whether Henry was truly sleeping tonight.

Or if another terror had taken him.

The answer lay out there, in the night.

*

Henry woke up in a cold sweat. Saltwater trickled down his temple and touched the top of his lip. They were dry and peeling. He caught his breath and looked around at the familiar chamber, bristling at the thought of returning to sleep. Sleep offered nothing that any waking nightmare could not. Terrifying things gathered in the blackness of sleep. Always chattering, chirping, swarming; buzzing. He roused, tossing and turning in his nightgown. It was tan and dirty, like spoiled parchment. The moths had been at it again, eating holes into the fabric.

Henry loathed insects, always.

He rolled over. The bed frame creaked and the feather-stuffed pillows breathed. With a light flick and stroke of flame, he lit a candle. Then, he lit another, and another, and another. Four candles stood tall on their holder. The candelabra flickered in front of him, wicks waltzing and crackling together. Dim candlelight filled the chamber, brightening the gloom. Its strength struggled against the whistling wind. He could hear, feel it. It came from the narthex. He turned the doorknob and left to investigate the racket.

Henry stepped into darkness.

He slunk through the church's corridors, clutching the candle holder until his knuckles turned white. His hands were frail and trembling. Henry was far from young. Tremors were warranted, regardless of any festering night terror.

A jitter rattled at his left, around the corner. It was only faint. But he heard it. Henry turned with fright, brandishing the candles out in front of him to brighten the way. Nothing, there was nothing there. Of course, there was rarely anything in the church. The church welcomed few guests but for a host of insects and mice, a rat or three. One thing was for certain. Henry was alone in the church tonight. The way it had been for many years. The church was ancient and crumbling. It kept hidden secrets, memories, nightmares. It knew things Henry did not.

It invited *things* in.

*

The light of the candlewicks faltered, though they still lit the church's labyrinthine turns true enough to see. Not that Henry required it. He had committed every step and turn to his fading memory. The layout occupied a spot fought for by fond childhood memories and lost feelings. Henry lifted the candelabra to his forehead and looked up into the rafters.

Tracery ran across the stonework like fanciful netting. Henry was up there too, as a shadow. The candles cast his silhouette as a tall, lithe thing across the narthex walls. White cobwebs and stone dust choked them. Henry watched his shadow stalk through the church with a familiar gait until it fell out of sight. He rationed the light, covering the wicks with weedy fingers. If the darkness snuffed out too many, it would consume him. At the far-off end of the narthex, Henry noticed the fallen door. He approached it, feet bare to cold flagstones. The chill stung him.

The night crawled through the gap, intruding. It fed off the gloom, growing stronger and more confident. The night itself was flooding. Black tears wept from the gothic steeple. It brought with it a patient darkness. One that was watching Henry. One that was waiting for him. It waited for the old priest to shuffle into its cloak like a silken spider capturing its prey. To the night's webbing, Henry was a treat.

He was its prey: a fly.

*

Night found the church lonely, confined to the sanctuary. There was nothing there. There was no one within. The faithful churchgoers were gone tonight. Nobody sat with their hands locked in a late-night prayer. Not even the rats. They hid under the pews, tiny feet pattering across the stone floor. The tapping of Henry's bare feet followed them. It was in the narthex's dark quiet that he noticed something off. Something unfamiliar. A thin sheet of moisture coated the stone walls. It glistened against the candlelight.

A lifetime of rainwater and grime had stained the walls. Yet, they had not felt the touch of rain for a few nights. If not rain, then what? Outside, the wind gathered, then tempered. It slowed, and then, it stopped. The candles flared with new life. Henry was a statue of light, aglow amidst fathoms of nothing. What if he was still sleeping? What if this was only another nightmare conjured up to torment him?

Henry considered that thought. His fragile body may lay contorted under his quilt, and that nothing of tonight was true. He had to know for certain. Henry reached out to touch the nearest wall, running three fingers across it. He felt something tepid and sticky. Not rain then. Henry jerked his fingers back in revulsion. They came away with strings of frayed, yellowy pus that connected him to the narthex itself. No. Not pus, mucus.

Henry flicked his arthritic wrist. The thrash sent it flying like the hot drool of a sickly mutt. Something was not right. It all felt real. Too real. The stuff coated his fingers, trickling with horrid mucus. Henry steadied himself, then, he drew in a quick breath of dry air and pinched out a candle. It went out with a hiss. Henry recoiled at the sting. It hurt. True, then. This was all happening to him. He sucked his finger and felt comfort. Comfort at having steered away from another night of terror. And discomfort at what that meant for him.

Not too long ago, he had curled up in his cradle, foetal. There, he started at his resting place and fretted. To fall asleep was to invite the terrors in. If this was a nightmare, it would not be the worst in recent times. That was the worst part. Yet, Henry's memory was fading. It would not hold onto the terrors for too long. It was rare for any good thought to slip through without taint. Each terror painted its own colour of fear. After all, Henry was seventy-four, and he had known many of their ungodly shades.

He once longed to spend his senior years surrounded by family and friends. And now, he had neither. Henry was completely alone in life. He only had his terrors and only ever stirred in a state of pale horror, clutching his bed sheets.

Foetal.

*

Quite often, Henry would wake quarrelling with his fears. He would reach for the foul figures, fading into the air. Then, he would struggle to catch his breath. Boiling with damp fever and illness, it often racked him. Only after an hour of prayer would those *things* go away. Yet, some symptoms always persisted. The horrible, insect choir.

Chattering. Chirping. Clicking. Buzzing.

Henry carried the noises everywhere with him like a terminal tinnitus. It was quiet, but it was always there if he listened to it. Always on the verge of his hearing. A thick knot of fat, chanting grubs planted the noises in his ear. And when he laid his head to rest, he heard them.

Years. It had been years since Henry's last pleasant rest. These nights, he was grateful for three or four hours of uninterrupted sleep. But it was not getting any better. It was not healing. To his knowledge, there was no cure for it. Now, Henry was waiting for an end to come. That was his grim truth, his final acceptance.

Tonight, the taste of nightmares still lingered on his tongue and coated his teeth. The weather was purring over the olive valley outside. It had once been a marsh but had since dried up. Henry stepped through the open doorway. He crossed over the grey flagstones and out into the grey night. Ash garnished the grass out there. The valley was the colour of an unsuccessful harvest. Henry looked up and noticed a large, black cloud that promised rain. It tumbled toward the church and Trifford. That was a foul portent if ever he knew one. A lifetime of studying omens had taught Henry how to spot them. And that was the blackest of them all. What darkness awaited him, he could only imagine.

*

Henry strolled through the church cloister out into the garden. It was a garden surrounded by stone walls. The same yellowish mucus coated the walls out there as in the narthex. Yet, the garden soaked it up and drank it in. The vegetation seemed to swell with unnatural life. Henry should have turned away. He knew that. To return to his quarters and snatch away what sleep remained for him. But there was a black curiosity that whispered to him to continue. Something was on his shoulder. Whispering in his ear. Buzzing.

Henry massaged his brow, his expression troubled. This was foolish. He could muster the strength to reattach the door to its hinges. Yes, that was it. Henry could shut himself away. As he pondered, a new darkness descended from above. The clouds, for what else could they be, drew closer with uncharacteristic haste. They were swift and fuzzy. Henry had come to expect slowness from them. He had watched them drift by on green afternoons for years.

Then, Henry found himself strolling further through the garden. The earth resembled a tortoise's shell in colour. All green, olive, and riddled with rough patches. Brown flowers blossomed throughout the brush. The late change in seasons seemed to have forgotten about them. A hidden breeze haunted their petals. They crumpled beneath Henry's bare feet. No slippers, his feet were as frozen and pale as the moon. Topiary figures littered the garden. Some were shorter, some were taller. They were all pruned from thorny hedges into the shapes of men and young boys. They stood around the cloister like wardens. Nearly naked trees curled their branches towards Henry in threat. Their ancient roots felt far down and cradled corpses in their gentle repose. Corpses that were listening from below.

A sudden gust knifed at Henry out of nowhere. He recoiled at its cut. The strokes came cutting, again and again, from one angle or another. They lashed out like predatory insects. The black cloud was flowering over the church. The wind fled, only the frolicking of petals was left to tell of its departure. The remaining candlewicks snuffed out in its trail. The hedges, trees, and branches all fell still. The topiary figures shivered.

Quiet.

Only the chattering remained in the old man's ear. He started to wince. There was nothing to be found out there. Not yet. Nothing he saw troubled him. It was what Henry heard that stirred a fear within.

*

Another jitter.

Only this time, it was not faint. It was noisier and closer. Henry turned, but without any candlelight, he found nothing there. He was alone in the gloom. Then, a stabbing sensation ripped into Henry's heart. His lungs cried out for cleaner air. That god-awful fear that coloured Henry's nightmares started to taint the world around him. The church garden was transforming. It was then that he heard it. That irritating, buzzing choir. It started as a gentle flutter. Then, the chattering of insects. Not on Henry's shoulder, but right there in front of him. Henry looked up.

A noise like nasal thunder tickled in the black cloud. It itched. It yearned for scratching. Henry noticed something that unnerved him. The thrill of realization caught the lump in his throat. The chattering ceased in his ear, it was outside with him. He looked up again. The black cloud was hovering right there, right atop the steeple. It went no further.

Henry wanted to move. Yet, his feet would not take him. Nothing would, he was paralyzed with fear. The black cloud fell upon him. It fell quicker than anything else, but not as a cloud. It was fully coloured, furry, not fully connected. A great swarm of black moths and bottle flies flooded the garden. They ate plants and tore through the cloister. It was full in an instant.

Gorging gossamer wings, clicking mandibles, and fractious compound eyes.

They were large, larger than any insects Henry had ever seen. They ripped through the trees, splitting hollow trunks and releasing more flies. Green grubs and white worms slithered up from the fusty earth. Henry reeled. They were feeling at his feet, wet with strings of slime. The slime — mucus yellow as sunset — was the very same from the narthex. The flies were thrown through the returning gust on whirring wings. Hungry.

There were thousands of them. All of them were dark jade with yellow mouths. They had emerald eyes that caught and trapped light like tents filled with black mirrors. The flies flew at Henry. They struck at his chest and ate his gown, digesting cloth and skin. Henry dropped to the garden floor, testing a frantic crawl towards the church for cover. The flies gave him no time. They were entering him. All the while, they vomited up spouts of flaxen mucus. It burned fabric and singed wrinkled skin.

The reek of unclean flesh filled the air. Henry cried out in anguish. Tears streamed across his sunken cheeks. The cloud took to his open mouth, ripe for entry. They fluttered in on soft wings in their thousands. Scuttling across his dry tongue. Crawling down the back of his throat to nest and lay eggs in his gullet. Henry curled over in torment.

Coughing. Choking. Trying to throw them up.

He could not. It was too late.

The flies were within him.

*

Henry felt the swarm in his stomach.

They buzzed through his ears and filled his nostrils. He raked at his twisting torso and face with dirty nails, snorting, spitting out the smallest of the swarm. It was a pointless game. Finally, Henry clamped his mouth shut and covered it with trembling fingers. He sealed it shut. Locking away a secret that ought not to be told, or a riddle that must never be figured out. His eyes squinted into the thinnest of slits.

Henry continued crawling. His fingers traced through mulched earth. They tugged him through the garden towards the church. These were not flies. Not really. They were creatures of the night. Henry's terrors were created to torture and these were nightmare fragments hunting him into reality. Reality, yes. It must be. How could it not be? The pain was too intense, limitless; acute. Henry felt death lulling him into the thin veil.

With great upheaval, he gathered enough strength to stand. Henry stumbled up onto his feet. There was something strange about his stomach. He could feel it. It had a new weight. Henry's stomach was swollen and white. Fat pushed up against his skin like a pale balloon of whale blubber. Stirring, sagging with a host of festering insects laying their young. He cradled its heft like a child with frail, lacerated arms. Yellow spittle trickled out from between his teeth. It singed honeycomb holes into his tattered gown.

Henry tripped forward. He could not run, not yet. Then, he stiffened with the foulness of onset rigor mortis. All became numb and cool to the touch. Only the buzzing stayed with him. The buzzing and footsteps.

Footsteps?

They were light. Henry was not alone in the garden anymore. A cloaked figure shifted through the cloister, unflustered by the swarm of flies. It was only a silhouette, nothing more, nothing less. Henry wanted to call out for help. He tried to yell, but there was nothing he could say. Words left Henry's mouth as a thick, golden syrup mingled with grub juice and soft eggshells. His teeth were melting into his gums.

Henry crashed through the garden walls and into the cloister. It was knotted with thorns and bursting white bramble. They cut his face and palms open, pricking free streams of hot blood. He could still hear the light footsteps following him. When Henry freed himself and turned around, the figure was gone. It had vanished into the swarm of black moths and flies.

He kept running. Yes, running now, strength returning. The path rose and fell with tripping hazards and root weeds, snatching at Henry's feeble ankles. He wanted to fall and scream. Fear gripped his chest and nausea churned his stomach, silencing him.

Fear carved out Henry's soul and sat in his heart.

*

It was not over.

The cloud of flies continued hurtling themselves towards the old man. They were relentless. Henry turned to watch for a moment. The garden was gone, the trees were bare and split and eaten away. The trimmed topiaries were turning to white ash. They were wilting. The ground was dead and tough. The garden had become a graveyard. It was a sight of waste and ruin. The flies had left nothing alive. Their hunger was nearly satisfied.

Henry crashed into one of the stone turrets. At first, the jolt stunned him. He felt his collar crumple and his stomach's egg sack sway like pigskin filled with water. The effort to continue was painful. Henry wanted to fall. He wanted this all to stop. He wanted to let the cloud take him, to offer himself up to the flies in sacrifice, to accept the suffering. The intruders went as they came. With great relief, Henry flung himself at the church's front face. Then, he fell through inside.

The narthex stretched out before him. The only light spilt from the tall, glass mosaic at the end of the church. It was frowning, no rain, only spittle. Tears of mucus trickled from the corner of the eyes and spilt across the face. The Saint wept for Henry. She suffered him not to live. This was their final farewell to one another. The Saint, the only woman in his life, gone.

Henry stood, a slow and tiring action. The cloud of flies was growing larger, louder; stronger. It was following him in. With all the strength he could muster, Henry reached for the fallen church door.

It was already far too late. A string of hot mucus squirted out of nowhere, melting into his chest. Henry retreated, this time allowing for a wail of cold anguish. The flies took their opportunity. A cluster of them squirmed through his teeth and down his throat. Henry was gagging, coughing, and vomiting up all he could. They caught in his gullet, crawling around, mating, replenishing.

A nightmare. This must have been a nightmare, a new facet of terror.

The weather's wrath had ceased outdoors and it had gone quiet, too quiet. The cloud came no closer. The flies were chattering. They crawled through the cloister and across the walls, up into the gloomy rafters. They gave no thought to Henry, retching on the stone floor. Then, there was another tickle. It came from his fat stomach. Henry lifted his tattered gown to stare and inspect. What he saw grieved him. The writhing hurt ripped through his stomach in an instant. He had no time to process what was happening to him.

The tendons of Henry's stomach tore loose like stretched leather. His torso began to squirt juices as if it were a pustule put under the pressure of a fingernail. The flies were chattering, clicking, and chirping all above and around him. Henry could hear the footsteps again. They were the same light ones as before, in the dead garden.

Then, thousands of young larvae started working out from their burrows in his organs. Each one moaning, singing, and hissing to fill the church like a children's choir. The last thing Henry saw was the cloud of flies. They were fidgeting as they gathered together.

They formed a shape.

It was the shape of a tall man. His outline and contour were indistinct with gossamer wings. A pair of lime eyes lay in the nest of the forming skull. The fly figure paced through the narthex. His footsteps were feather soft and careful. A lithe set of fingers reached out towards Henry. Not just fingers, tendrils, dripping with filth. With what little breath he had left, Henry cried out for forgiveness.

Black. Then, candlelight.

He shot to his quarters. He shivered and boiled between his wet sheets. Father Henry was clutching his covers tight, curled up in foetal position. The figure was gone. The cloud was gone.

A lone fly tapped against the window.

INTO THE WOODS

The girl in the red riding hood ran. She charged through briar and bramble under the bent grin of an autumn moon. Her breath became heavy, a dog's panicking pant. No drool or spittle, however. Her mouth and lips were dry like wood smoke. A break opened in the path ahead and her feet caught on knotted roots. She scrambled beneath a canopy of oaks and pines.

The Black Forest. That was its name. A dark quilt decorated the bare, German wilderness. The forest reached out for the running girl. It wanted to keep her. Each bent branch longed to bleed her pale skin dry and drain her beauty. A hungry forest, one that tilted and tempted. It hid things in its darkness. Wild things.

The girl did not only run. She escaped. She was being hounded by the woman on the broom. But she was behind her now, gone in the dark. A wicked branch poked out from the woodland ahead. It slinked through her red riding hood and knifed it free of her skull. Her head was bare and exposed to the elements.

Never mind that now. Forget the hood.

The girl ran through the woodland. Her burnished hair danced about her back and rosy cheeks. Another branch whipped her across the right side of her face. Her cheek began to welt immediately. A pink rash blossomed with pinpricks of blood and white lumps. But there was no time to treat it. She needed to escape the woodland's darkness. In her daze, the girl without the red riding hood did not wipe her blood from the branch. It remained there, dripping. The smell of it became perfume to her pursuer. Intoxicating, irresistible, delicious.

Then, a nightmarish cackle echoed between the trees behind her. It disturbed the night and promised danger. And it drew nearer and nearer with each heartbeat. A shudder sounded. It conjured evil, dark eyes, broomsticks, and dishonest temptations of treats and candy.

Dark chocolate, blood apples, and bone sugar.

'No,' the girl blubbered. 'Leave me alone!'

The air in the Black Forest was cool and damp from rain. A mist was coming in and blanketing the undergrowth. Her plea for mercy was unheard in the haze. Her voice left her lips like warm pot steam in the woodland's chill. It mingled with the mist and disappeared. She continued moving. She remembered the way she had come, remembered her home. She remembered her family, her mother, her father, and her two younger brothers. One of them was nearly eight now. The other was only nine months old. The girl without the red riding hood longed to be home again. She wanted to be home and happy and warm. Warm around the hearth with a hearty plate of crusty bread, carved meat, and a bowl of pumpkin broth.

Those days were behind her now. She would not see them again. Not now. Not ever.

She began to pick up her pace. The girl had been chasing dusk for almost twenty minutes. And every step she took pushed light further away. Pink, purple, and orange gave over to blue shades of night. Then, the black closed in. The old forest lived up to its name, Black Forest indeed. Cutting thorns flicked out at the girl's bare hands and knees. They grazed her skin and opened it up. They dirtied the meat beneath with grime and splinters. But she did not scream. She could not give herself up. When the branches whipped out again with knuckled fingers, she ducked. The girl looked deeper into the woods behind her. The cackling was closer now. It was right there. Echoing down the path that was not a path. Then, the girl caught a glimpse of her pursuer. Her heart dropped.

There she was: crimson eyes, pinpricks of evil and bewitchment. The brittle noise of a broomstick filled the dark. All this and more. Beneath her black dress, nightclothes, and ragged riding cloak, she revealed her hand, bony, blue-veined, and pale. Her hand protruded from the sleeve and rubbed its fingers together. Pinched between her dirty, untrimmed nails was a delicious apple. It glimmered with moisture. And it shone with blood. The girl without her red riding hood clawed at her cheeks and screamed. Horror echoed through the woods.

And then, the darkness and cackling were all she knew.

Next, it was the darkness of her bedchamber.

*

'Bruno,' Mary moaned. A whimper, really. Mary, the village's amiable medicine woman, did not have the heart to shout for her dog's return. This game had become commonplace around the hour of eight o'clock. Bruno was a piebald dachshund, black and orange. The dog had not lived up to his breeder's promise of hunting down badgers on Mary and her husband's new plot of land. Instead, Bruno minded his own business by day and discovered a fancy for freedom by dusk. And each evening had become the same. Mary would follow Bruno with unfounded hopes of him coming home.

Dusk came again tonight, of course. And Bruno had wandered off into the woodland at the edge of the pasture. If Mary did not find the dog before nightfall, then she would not find him at all. She would return to her cabin in the woods and wait for morning to come. And she would do so understanding that Bruno had been taken by a fox, wolf, or another woodland bandit. But her chase was not over yet. There was still time to find Bruno. She hoped.

However, Bruno was unexpectedly quick on his tiny paws. Once he reached the Black Forest, a dense crowd of dark oaks and naked pines, Bruno vanished into the bushes and brambles. Mary followed, moving gingerly. It was difficult to track Bruno's impressions in the earth leading up to the trees. Mary passed through rows of dried-up cornstalks and pumpkin patches ground to mulch. Both were managed by chunky black and grey slugs that trailed foamy streams of silver slime.

A flicker of hope ignited inside Mary. She knew that Bruno could not have gone far. But it had been her fault for leaving the cabin door open. Bruno had already escaped twice since Sunday. Autumn drew over the Black Forest. There would be no food for Bruno to rummage for if he became lost in the woodland. Mary needed to find him. And she needed to find him soon. He was as much a part of her family as her husband, Hansel. Or the children she longed to have with him, one day.

Mary came up to a sloping mound. It led up to the treeline. Beyond that, the dark and deep woods began. It was a curling, gnarled, and bent wall of branches that were stripped bare of leaves. Now, they lay in piles of brown, orange, and black. They lay in the moist and misty undergrowth beneath Mary's feet. Pine needles and worms crunched and squelched as she moved. Some pierced her feet. Dusk was already robbing the woods of light. And, in a moment, Mary's world turned dark. She could only see fifty paces ahead. Beyond that: black.

'Bruno,' Mary muttered again. She was whispering now. Maybe a gentler approach would appeal to the distracted dog. 'Here, Bruno, come back.'

Mary did not hear anything by way of response. With Bruno, it was hard to distinguish his rustle from black squirrels and silver rabbits, the wild things. His fur matched the undergrowth he had ventured into, black and brown. Mary thought she had found Bruno a few times before reaching down into messy heaps of leaves. Her hands came away damp and empty. 'Bruno!' Mary shouted.

She was losing her patience now, barking hot breath into the mist. It dissipated in front of her. Mary's eyes were drawn up to the canopy above, seeing only a bent grid of branches and creeping tree limbs. Dark and heavy clouds were beginning to gather. Night's blanket would soon spread over the Black Forest and much of Germany that lay beyond. Mary needed to find Bruno before that happened. But Mary hesitated at the treeline. She had grown up reading grim fairytales about the woodland she now called home. There were many tales of pretty women and handsome hunters heading into the forest and never coming back out. Mary did not want to become another bedtime story used to frighten misbehaving children.

'No, don't be silly,' Mary said to herself. Those were only stories.

Spooks and scared made up for boys and girls who did not want to go to bed. Mary imagined her mother and father were reading to their other children right about now. Night was coming in, after all. Mary looked behind her. She saw her cabin, made of wood and stone. She had been lucky to have married her husband – a kind man – and come to live here. The chimney puffed smoke into the evening air.

Mary could see Hansel's shadow at the window. He was a dark phantom amongst amber firelight. She pondered calling for him and telling him to fetch his rifle or hatchet. But he had been working long and hard all day so Mary decided not to. She pulled up the hem of her woollen dress, fastened her red riding hood to her head, tied her hair back in a bow, and pushed onwards into a labyrinth of bare oaks.

Bruno was out there. And Mary would find him.

*

Mary followed Bruno's paw prints into the old forest. The path led her along an embankment of blackberry bushes and worm roots. Mary battled to keep her footing and balance. She could have easily slipped down into the mud. Leaves and broken branches were sharp, and one could puncture her throat and leave her bleeding alone in the wilderness. The woodland pulled at her dress and hood as she moved. It wanted to touch Mary.

It wanted to keep her for itself.

One lonely branch skewered her bonnet and dragged the red riding hood off her head. The bow came undone, and her hair tumbled down her back. Mary quickly retrieved her hood from a finger of pine. She batted it away with the back of her hand. The branch whipped back at her and opened her lip. The wood drew blood and Mary cursed under her breath. She refitted her hood, and then, she paced back a step or two. She halted in her tracks. She had lost her way. And she had lost Bruno too.

'Damn this forest,' Mary cursed. 'Damn it all!'

In her moment of anger, she grabbed the branch dripping with her lip's blood. She moved over the embankment, clambering onto a ridge. It was likely that Bruno had gone that way, chasing the scent of a badger or a shrew. Mary's dog always did its job at the most inappropriate moments. She placed her weight on a branch and tried to pull herself up. It broke away with a horrid snap and Mary was pushed down the embankment into a morass of mud and dead leaves.

'Damn,' she winced.

In public, she would never curse or profane in any manner. But it had become a bad habit over time after getting married. To curse in the company of the village people would deliver Mary into the hands of the Black Adders. Law-keepers who handled judgement, confessions, and punishments. Hansel did not mind. But out here, in the woodland, nobody could hear her. And no eyes were watching her. Or rather, that was what Mary thought. She scrambled around in her puddle. Her red dress was now dark like congealed blood. When Mary cursed again, she did not care who or what heard her.

The woodland was perilous. Mary coughed, hacked, and spat out a blotch of muck. It landed with a squelch in another nearby puddle. She dug her boots into the dead earth and put her hands against a pine. Slowly, she stood up on her heels. Meaning not to slip, Mary straightened for balance. She looked down at her bare hands. Both were cut open and bleeding. Much of the blood was masked by mud. Autumn leaves clung to her palms like limpets or leeches. Grey, white, and pink worms crawled over her forearms.

Mary flicked them off with her bloody fingers. Her hands were not trembling anymore. They had gone still. She could feel the warmth leaving them and returning to her heart. She pushed them into her pockets to heal. Now, she could not grab anything. With her hands warming up in her red dress, Mary called out for Bruno again. 'Bruno,' she whimpered, looked around. She saw nothing but darkness and heard only the coughing of crows.

Mary lamented her current predicament. She was happily married and had not thought that abandoning her family to move away with Hansel would lead to this. Cut up and lost in a big and dusky forest.

Part of Mary longed to return home to her family. But it had been their idea for her to marry and find a better life in the first place. Maybe she would meet them again, one day. If anything bad happened to her husband, she would have to return to her childhood home. There was no other way about it.

Mary wiped hot tears from her eyes. They carved clean streaks down her cheeks. She could not cry. She had not cried in months. Mary was not a little girl anymore. She was a grown woman now, by all accounts. That was why her parents had begged her to marry and move away. Mary was expected to begin her own life and start her own family. She was nineteen and nearing twenty by now. She did not dwell on her age very often, feeling that it did not matter anymore. She had become an adult and that was the very end of it.

The truth of her youth suddenly reared its ugly head. She thought about how she had been a child not long ago. And now, she had been married for nearly one year. Happily married, moreover. Mary had a loving husband, a dainty cabin in the woods, and an agreeable life ahead of her. It had come as a surprise to Mary that her arranged marriage to Hansel had turned out so pleasantly. She considered herself fortunate that Hansel had only been two years her senior. Mary had known many girls her age who had married widowed men old enough to be their fathers. The thought of it sickened Mary to her core. She had been promised to Hansel as a pious and caring young woman. And she was caring. That was no lie, although Mary had bargained with her piousness of late. Nonetheless, she had worn the mask of virtue on the day of her marriage.

Mary and Hansel had lived comfortably together in the seasons since. Though, even now, Mary was reluctant to drop the act and reveal the true nature of her personality to Hansel. She worried about him judging her and having married into a falsehood. Hansel loved Mary as she was. As she had been promised to him.

Mary did not want to jeopardise the loving relationship between them both. That was why she only ever cursed or blasphemed when alone. Hansel was a man of God. His family's heritage had been deeply rooted in the German church for generations. However, Mary did not care for Hansel's wider family. She had barely known his mother and she loathed his brother, Emmet, with all her heart. And Hansel's father had once patted her hind, and, with a gruff chuckle, had named Mary an "expensive beauty" and a "rare rose".

The memory of him drew her back to Hansel. Her husband was kind and handsome, and many women far prettier than Mary had wished to wed and bed him. Hansel was tall and angular. He had hard cheekbones and gentle eyes. His dark hair curled onto his shoulders. It was the subject of much gossip among the village's female churchgoers. But Hansel had not paid any mind to them. They were a disorderly gaggle. Weeping cats where Hansel longed to marry a lone doe. And he had found his doe in Mary.

Mary was quickly reminded of the deep and dark woodland around her. Suddenly, life was not too pleasant. She was not at home in her cabin. She was alone in the Black Forest hunting for Bruno. Nearby, the new smell of wood smoke billowed towards her.

*

Mary was no longer alone. But when she looked around the woodland, she found it empty. Empty as it had been when she stepped within. Mary placed both hands against the unearthed embankment. Worms wriggled out onto her hands and Mary threw herself back. Her red dress and riding hood were dirtied with mud and slick with burned leaves. She grabbed a long branch for balance and thrust it down into the mud. It sank a couple of inches before stopping. She could finally move around without slipping.

Mary searched around in the undergrowth for signs of Bruno's passing through. She came across a small trail that led around the embankment, not over it. And it led through into the heart of the black wood. Mary looked around and followed the path for quite a while. Then, she caught the whiff of a wet dog up ahead. In a moment, the scent faded, and Mary's senses were penetrated by a shroud of wood smoke. She breathed in and out. Something was burning nearby. It smelled warm. It smelled good. It was like nectar to her, irresistible.

Mary was unaware of any other inhabitants around these witch-infested woods. Maybe she had been wrong. Maybe someone was living out in these woods and had never managed to cross her path. She hoped so. Another man or woman living out here meant that Bruno may have been found. He may have been taken in for shelter and care. The path and smell lured Mary away from the dense oaks and dark pines. It led her towards a group of large stones that glistened darkly with rainwater. Mary inspected them. They jutted out from a huge mound of dirt and leaves. They appeared, to her eyes, like the petrified remains of a giant female hand. Four thin fingers and a thumb reached up towards the canopy. Crows perched atop its nails.

Just behind them, peeking out from a curtain of moss, was a house, a small stone and wood cottage. Mary could not believe her eyes. She had come this way before with Hansel, during his hunts or outings for firewood. But they had never found this cottage. The rocks and stones held the home together, weeping brown moss and wore autumn lichen. The house had no garden or gate. Instead, it was built into another embankment, and a door was built directly into the mound, a door with one round window was placed in the middle. A dainty chimney huffed and puffed wood smoke. That explained the smell. But that was not the only smell Mary caught. She could smell something meaty cooking inside.

It reminded Mary of her childhood meals. She looked around and felt a warm rush of relief upon finding paw prints in the muck. They belonged to Bruno, no doubt. They led up ahead to the cottage door and vanished at the doorstep. There lay a worn, black rug reading "Welcome". No light came through the window. And yet, smoke breathed from the chimney.

Mary knocked once and waited.

She knocked twice and waited a little longer.

When nobody came to the door, she tried the bronze doorknob.

The door and cottage behind it were unlocked. Mary breathed out and stepped inside. Upon entering, there was no light, and it was cooler than she had expected. This was no cottage. This was no home. This was only the dank and rocky interior of a cavern. The dark walls were wet, and Mary heard something dripping inside.

She could not see much. Dusk was setting outside as much as darkness did inside with her. The hollow looked like it belonged to a hibernating bear, a pack of wolves, or something else entirely. This was no human place. But why then did it have a door and chimney? Mary felt discomforted. She could sense danger and she regretted not having asked Hansel to accompany her. Nonetheless, Bruno's trail led right up to the door, inside the house.

'Bruno,' Mary murmured. She did not want to be loud, but even her murmur was enhanced by the extreme quiet. 'Bruno, where are you, it's me, it's your Mary.' Nothing came by way of reply. She heard no panting or barking. Only the crackle of fire sounded nearby. There was no light, however, to indicate that anything was being cooked, merely the sound and smell of it.

'Bruno,' Mary managed once more. 'Please don't make me come any further.' Her teeth were starting to chatter. She whistled for Bruno's return. Nothing came her way except hungry shadows and the smell of wood smoke.

Then, there was a new smell, a smell that Mary had not known since her childhood.

She smelled caramel, toffee, berries, and sugar. The mixture was pungent and almost overwhelming. How could such a sweet smell be coming from such a dark and empty place? What sort of place was this? A cavern with a cottage door, hidden deep in the woods. Like something out of a fairytale. One without a merry or bloodless ending.

'Please,' Mary said. 'Please...'

*

Mary did not move for a moment. She contemplated turning to

the door that had closed behind her. And she thought about returning to the dusky woodland. Running home to her husband, Hansel, and coming back with him later. But what if they were too late? What if, by the time they returned, Bruno had gone again or met a worse fate? Mary knew that she could not lose the dog. She had paid too high a price for his love and presence.

But there was more to it than that. This had not been the first time one of Hansel's animals had gone missing under Mary's watch. And she worried that, if she did not do something about it, Bruno would not be the last one they lost. Not too long ago, several chickens and hens had gone missing without a trace from their picketed coop, and now only the screeching rooster remained. Mary had suggested that a hungry fox had prowled down from the woodland and broken in during the night, but Hansel had disavowed that notion. There were no signs of brutality or savagery. If a fox had come, there would have been corpses and feathers flung about the place. And yet, there was nothing. Not even up into the treeline. The chickens had vanished without a trace or explanation, and now, it seemed the same had happened to Bruno.

But surely, Bruno was somewhere in this hollow cavern. She had seen his dirty paw prints on the rug outside the front door. Mary dreaded returning home to face her husband's disappointment without the dog in her arms. And so, Mary took one step forward, then another, and then one more. She was now in the cavern.

'Bruno,' Mary said. 'I beg you.'

Her words echoed off the walls and reached the back of the hollow. Mary's eyes had not yet adjusted. They had already attempted and failed to do so outside, in the Black Forest. Yet, in here, in this dark place, the blackness was somehow even worse.

Mary paced forward. Her footsteps echoed too loudly. She had dragged some of the forest's wet leaves in behind her, bringing feigning life to the cold cavern floor. She poked and probed ahead with the pointy branch she had been using for balance. She hoped to tap and feel her way ahead. Mary was blinded by the sightlessness of her surroundings. It tapped and tapped and tapped. The noise of it echoed further.

A new sound entered the darkness.

There came a brief rustle from ahead, further inside the hollow. Then, a low and unintimidating growl sounded. It was a noise that Mary recognized. She blinked hard. Relief tugged at her bleeding lips to smile. Finally, she had found Bruno. But then, the sound died out into a drawn-out whimper, as though the hound had been struck dead by a rusty knife.

Mary grabbed her mouth and caught her scream. Her entire body tensed up. She did not move further forward, for she knew that she was not alone. She understood that this den in the forest, this cave with a door, had not been as empty as she had first believed. Mary waited a moment before whispering again. She did not know who or what would hear her.

*

'Hello?' she said. 'Who's there?' Nothing came back. 'Bruno,' she continued to murmur, 'Bruno, is that you? Please come out. Come back to me.'

Mary had not realised the vigour with which she had been clutching the branch. Her knuckles were white with stress and the rush of blood. The splinters were digging into her palms like tiny, wooden blades. Her lip was bleeding again too. Mary sucked it dry and tasted harsh and bitter iron on her tongue. She knew she had to continue. If not for her own sake, then for Bruno's. With one anxious step, then another, Mary moved on through the cavern chamber. And then, she fell.

Mary slammed down onto the right side of her chest and felt her ribs twine over one another. Her breast pulled from the muscle beneath. She was dropping and falling, swinging and swaying. Mary threw her hands out as the branch dropped down beneath her into what could only be a pit, at the heart of the hollow cave. Her dirty hands scrambled at the stone walls. They gave way to wet and cold earth. Sliding downwards, she stopped with a snag as she groped and grabbed a cluster of roots. She clung to it and held it tighter than anything she had ever held in her life. If she were to let go, she would fall forever.

Mary looked down beneath her dangling feet.

There was nothing down there. It was a dark and empty hole.

It was from down there, down in the dark, that the smells came. They wafted up to her with heat like bread fresh out of the baker's oven. She inhaled the smell as she dangled. Her nostrils inflated. The sweet aromas of mead, berries, toffee, and chocolates made her eyes roll back. Mary shook and nodded her head. She could not give in to the temptations coming from beneath. Whatever was in that pit, down in the darkness, it wanted her to fall. It wanted her to give in to its sweet temptations.

Mary dangled. She could not hold on for much longer. She tried to pull herself up but felt the cluster of roots give way. Only a thread of rooted muscle connected her to the lip of the dark pit. She was breathing now, breathing hard and quick, just as Bruno panted. Just as he *still* panted. Mary needed to believe that Bruno was still alive. Hoping he had fled the terrible scene and avoided whatever awful fate lay down there. Mary grabbed for a rock. It came away immediately with a gush of water and grime, rocketing off the canyon's walls on the way down until it exploded in a heap at the bottom. It was a far fall, and the noise of it awakened something down there. There, at the bottom of the pit, amber light breathed.

Then, hot coals and fire.

At the bottom, Mary came to identify her fate. It was not a pit at all. There, at the bottom, was a cast iron pot or cauldron. It brimmed with boiling water that gargled and spat. Steam was flowing like gossamer over the hot surface.

'No,' Mary closed her eyes and shook her head. 'Not real, not real, none of this is real!'

But when Mary opened her eyes, not only was the cooking pot still there, it had risen higher. Something was pushing it upwards, towards her. Mary caught sight of dark cloth passing by the golden flames. She noticed the silken silhouette of someone, lurking down there in the darkness. Then, a bony hand cast spices into the pot. It erupted with bubbles that burst and screamed in the voices of one hundred stolen and boiled babies.

Mary screamed, and for the first time in four seasons, she began weeping. Her tears fell to the rising cauldron, some ten metres below her. She could feel the heat of it pressing closer. The smells were now overwhelming and had become too sweet. Her body threatened to give up. To let go and cast her down into the cauldron, to boil along others who had met a similar fate. There was no sign, sound, or smell of Bruno down there. Not anymore. He had escaped. Or he had never been here in the first place.

Mary opened her eyes. And there, in the sweet-smelling darkness, an old woman's face appeared. Gaunt, crimson eyes, rotten teeth.

'No!' Mary wept and screamed. She kicked out her feet in a flurry of helpless blows before reaching up on her side for the pit's lip. She felt her bruised ribs complaining and the meat on her bones mash together. The woman cackled and licked her teeth.

*

Mary winced and whimpered like an injured sheep, bleating for its owner to put it out of its misery. Nobody was coming to save her. Not here. Not now. She knew that, and she had to move quickly, or she would boil to death. Mary thought of those babies and her brothers.

New noises came from beneath, like a choir. The voices of children, the screaming of babies, and the horrid, wicked cackle of a witch. That same cackling from her dreams. Mary did not look. Not this time. She knew what she would see and that nothing in her world or the next could rid her of that terrible image. Mary swung a leg up and it found purchase over the ledge. She pulled and tugged and heaved with all her might.

'Yes!' she shouted, willing herself on. 'Go, go!'

A hand grabbed her by the ankle. Her skin burned. Mary screamed — a bloodcurdling scream — again and thrashed out. She felt the heel of her boot crack into the face of someone or something with a gruesome and bloody crunch. A new voice, one of pain and anger, filled the hollow. Then, the pain became pleasurable. And the screaming became laughter.

'Leave me alone!' Mary begged.

She did not expect a reply and was grateful when nothing answered. Mary threw herself over the ledge. The boiling water of the cauldron started to splash at her ankles and sizzle her skin. She brushed her body off the splash and patted her red woollen dress down before it got caught in the flames. Amber light was beginning to peel over the ledge after her. Mary crawled backwards. And when she saw a spider of pale fingers snag on the rise, she stood and fled. Terrible and monstrous cackling pursued Mary until she reached the door. With each step she took, it moved further and further away. As though, once again, Mary was chasing the promise of light during dusk. No matter. Before long, Mary smashed into the heavy, wooden door. She turned the bronze door handle, flung the door open, and slammed it shut behind her.

She opened her eyes to the quiet and uninterrupted darkness of the woodland.

The Black Forest was as it had always been. Deathly silent, wooded, and devoid of burning leaves. Mary tried to run a little way away from the door, but she collapsed to her feet before managing to do so. She turned her head back to the door, brimming with the belief that the crone would be following her. She gasped. The door was gone. The welcome mat was gone. The chimney, puffing its smoke, was nowhere to be seen. There, in front of her, was a bunch of dark stones built into an outcropping of dirt in the woods.

There was no cottage.

There was no crone.

The smell of wood smoke and sugar had faded away. Only the vaguest impression of a door remained. In the embankment, there was only the dirty outline of where she had entered. Mary lay still on the forest floor amongst leaves and black crow feathers. Her hands bunched up brown leaves, worms, and dirty rainwater. She had not yet managed to move from her kneeling when a familiar voice called out from the woody darkness behind her.

'Mary! Dear Mary, there you are!'

Mary looked up and behind her. Her shoulders dropped. She began to cry even more when she saw Hansel charging from the trees, holding a rickety old lantern in his gloved hand, a hunting rifle flung across his back. And there, at the handsome man's feet, was a piebald, black and orange dachshund. There was the lost Bruno. Mary clambered up to her weary feet and, before she could try running, collapsed into Hansel's arms. The lantern wobbled with faulty light at her impact. Bruno jumped at her ankles, sniffing them, before whimpering and hiding behind Hansel's black boots.

'Mary,' Hansel began. 'Don't ever leave me alone like that again. What were you thinking?'

Hansel brought the lantern up to his wife's face. He was filled with dread at seeing the state she was in. Her lip was bloody. Her eyes were bloodshot with stinging tears. Her palms were bloodied and sheet white, and her woollen dress and red riding hood were filthy.

'God,' Hansel managed. 'What's happened to you?'

'Oh, Hansel,' Mary blubbered. 'It was awful, you don't understand. The woods, and Bruno, and—'

'It's okay,' Hansel comforted her. He brought Mary into an intimate embrace and kissed a clean patch on her forehead. 'It's okay, you're okay. You're safe now. Bruno is safe too. He was outside the cabin, digging in his hole.'

'No,' Mary looked Hansel in the eyes, and then Bruno. 'No! What? He can't have been, I followed his little footprints, and they went off into the woods, all the way here, I promise!'

'Maybe it was that fox you spoke about,' Hansel mused. 'No matter, you're okay now, Mary.'

Mary did not look at Hansel then. Rather, she looked into the dark and deep woodland around them. She felt as though eyes were watching them. She was still trembling from the cold and the sheer horror of what had just happened. She pushed Hansel away and pointed towards the embankment with its big and dark stones. 'You don't understand,' she blubbered again. 'Bruno was in there. He went in there!'

Hansel looked over Mary's shoulder, perplexed. He followed her finger to nothing, nothing at all.

'Mary, dear, there's nothing there. Come on, darling, let's get you home. You're freezing.'

'You aren't listening!' Mary slammed her small hands into Hansel's broad chest. 'There was a door, and a cave, and a—'

'Enough,' Hansel concluded. 'There's nothing to worry about. You're in shock, it's dark and it's late.' He rubbed his thumb over a heavy bump on Mary's forehead. 'And it looks like you got a bump. Did you fall over? It looks that way.'

Hansel pulled at her hands and rubbed them together in his pocket to warm them up. Then, he made some familiar whistles and clicks that Bruno recognized, and the dog followed him. All the while, Bruno sniffed at Mary's right ankle, but she did not respond, merely placing her head against Hansel's chest and walking with him through the woods, back to their cabin. She did not speak for the rest of their journey through the darkness.

She could not think of anything to say.

Her mind was dancing, alive with a black memory. She thought of the crone who, when she sleeps, leaves her body and dances naked with the Devil. Mary thought of her cauldron. She thought of the inhuman screams of the babies put to boil. Mary looked back at the ridge one last time. Then, she nestled her head into Hansel's chest once more. The wood smoke and sweet scents were gone. And all she could smell was her own blood, and the promise of new rain. When it fell, it washed away the dirt from Mary's cheeks and the tears from her eyes. But not the evening's malign portents. That Devil's brand of evil blossomed and nurtured in Mary's heart.

And there, it darkened.

*

Dusk dwindled. The black ashes of night rose from the cinders. The moon above was red tonight. It was an odd hue, a bleeding red reminiscent of the horrific events in the Black Forest. It shone amongst a starless backdrop. The night sky was a canvas. No shades, only black. The autumn crunch of the forest floor gave way to hard grass and bramble. The briars became smaller when the couple entered the meadow. There, they found their humble cabin. But it was only upon drawing in closer to it that they noticed something different.

Mary was the first to spot the hitched horse on the porch.

Hansel stopped for a moment and looked at his partner. He let out a long and heavy sigh. His eyes had been fluttering through the new rainfall. But here and now, he was staring out with wide eyes and a dour look. He started pacing forward and Mary followed him.

'Are we expecting company?' Mary queried. Hansel did not answer immediately. He waited until they were beyond the horse and up to their door. The key had been moved out from under the worn, red welcome rug. And only one other man or woman from the nearby village knew of the key's whereabouts.

'No,' Hansel said. 'No, we are not.'

Hansel pushed the unlocked door open and stepped inside, Mary following right behind.

Mary had met the man sitting at their dining room table a handful of times. He was shorter than Hansel, as many men were, but where Hansel was tall and ropey, the man before her looked like a bullish gundog. He had dark eyes, which was not uncommon around these parts, and the brows above them were as bushy as the Black Forest's briars. He wore a leather jerkin and knee-high boots full of grime. The world outside was turning into a murky morass in the rain, and those very boots lay crossed over each other as he rested his legs atop the table. An oilskin raincoat lay over the back of the chair.

He took a bite out of a leg of turkey and chuckled.

'Hansel,' he said brashly, still chewing white meat. 'Good to see you. It's been quite a while, no?'

'Yes,' Hansel said, 'it has. Hello, Emmet.'

Emmet was Hansel's brother, older than him by quite a few years. And it showed in the wrinkles and crow's feet, although Emmet was not an old man. He looked at Mary gravely, his eyes full of malicious intent. She looked at the dining room table. The plates had been entirely cleaned up of the food they had contained. Before running off into the wilderness to find Bruno, she had prepared a meal for herself and Hansel and now, their food was gone. Emmet had entered their cabin without permission and devoured it all. Did he not know their current predicament? Did he not know how little they could afford to lose? He did not care one bit for either of them. She knew that. That was Emmet, deaf to other people's troubles, a boar of a man.

Emmet's eyes turned to Mary, standing behind his brother. In an instant, he reeled back and choked on his meal. The rain had done away with much of the dirt and blood on her cheeks, but her woollen dress was still murky.

'God,' Emmet exclaimed. 'What happened to her, Hansel?'

'Dog went missing again,' Hansel replied. Bruno ran in on command after him and Emmet batted him away from his side with the back of his hand. 'She took a tumble in the woodland and hit her head.'

'Knocked any sense into her?' Emmet grumbled. That made Mary angrier. She clenched her fists. Then, Emmet picked up a bare and meatless bone. He wiped his mouth on his collar, and said, 'I hope you don't mind, old boy. I've come some way from the village on horseback. And riding is hungry work.'

'No,' Hansel managed, 'of course not, don't be foolish, help yourself, OLD BOY.'

Mary looked at her husband. Hansel had never been one for confrontation. And Emmet had stomped all over him his entire life.

Emmet had always got his way as a boy, and nothing had changed since. And *no*, it was not acceptable that Emmet had helped himself to their hard-earned bounty. What were she and Hansel, and Bruno too, going to eat now? Emmet knew full and damned well that they were not playing host to a plentiful pantry. Having to watch him lick the bones of his stolen meal clean made her angrier than she could express. Mary had half a mind to leap over the table and throttle him.

'Mary,' Emmet said, snapping his fingers at her. 'Be a good girl and fetch me my water skin, outside by my horse. Go on now, get going.' Mary did not move. She grimaced. She was surprised Emmet had addressed her. He never did that. Very few men from the nearby village did. She looked at Hansel, who in turn looked at Emmet. She was not in the mood, after the evening's events. Emmet clacked his teeth and bit his lip at her. He gestured at Hansel and said, 'What's the matter with her? Bump made her an idiot? Tell her to get on.'

'Mary,' Hansel pleaded. 'Would you please fetch my brother's water skin?'

'Hansel?' Mary said. 'Don't you think we—'

'I do,' Hansel whispered into her ear. 'But do it anyway, for me.'

All the while, Emmet watched their back-and-forth with bemusement. He was amused by her sharp tongue. Mary brought disobedience to their relationship. Emmet would never stand for it himself, of course. 'You ought to reel this one in, Hansel. She'll be having the run of this place if you're not careful.'

REEL HER IN. This was Mary's home now. No matter how recently she had come to it. Who was Emmet to suggest such a thing? Mary felt a flush of hot anger in her grazed cheeks. But she did not give it voice. She turned on her ankles, one of which was still burning, and marched back to the front door and out into the rain. She was thankful to see it had now turned into a drizzle that pitter-pattered off the eaves. She found Emmet's horse, whinnying there in the rain. She patted its hind and rubbed its muzzle kindly.

Mary could hear the brothers conversing inside. She heard her name spoken from Emmet's lips once or twice. And she knew then that she was the subject of discussion, for better or for worse. It was clear that Emmet was attempting to lecture his younger brother on how Mary should not disagree with him. Hansel neither agreed nor disagreed with him, trying as he was to move the conversation elsewhere.

Mary returned a couple of moments later and set the water on the far side of the dining room table. Emmet clicked his fingers. Mary hesitated and then pushed it over towards him, feigning a welcoming grin. But Emmet was an unwelcome visitor. He always had been. And whenever Emmet came to visit, he did so bearing bad news.

*

'I come here bearing GOOD news.'

That was unexpected. Hansel and Mary looked at each other, having braced themselves to hear something terrible. Now they were confused, although Hansel appeared relieved. Mary, however, was suspicious.

'Oh,' Hansel said lowly. 'Well, I'm very pleased to hear it. Well, go on, then, out with it. Do tell, brother.'

Emmet reached over into the wooden fruit bowl on the cupboard shelf. He plucked free a round and red crab apple and took a big, juicy bite out of it. 'Very good this,' he chewed, 'very ripe.'

'Emmet,' Hansel urged, 'tell me, it's growing late.'

Mary looked out the nearest window. It was more than late, it was very late, and it was very dark too. She did not doubt that, as usual, Emmet would be expecting to stay overnight and hitch his horse here. The horse was welcome, Emmet was not. He never asked. He just demanded and acted according to his desires. Hansel had never once put his boot down and told his older brother to leave. It was not that it was a long journey back to the village. But strange things happened in the Black Forest after dark and on the road too. Not a month went by when some child or merchant did not go missing. When the night was darkest, as it was tonight, and the moon the shade of dry blood, bad things happened. But Emmet did not care.

Mary had experienced bad things in her dreams of late.

'Take a seat,' Emmet said.

He kicked out one of the wooden chairs at the dining table and gestured for Hansel to sit opposite him. He did not offer Mary a seat. Not that it was his place to do so. Mary was disappointed to see her comfortable homestead taken over by a man such as Emmet. A reminder of the worst men of the village, the ones she had grown up surrounded by and which her father had protected her from. Emmet sat there ahead of her was a visual reminder that she was not living a fairytale.

'Like I said, Hansel, I have news, news that concerns you and your woman.'

*

Mary flushed and scowled. She was not Hansel's woman. Well, she was. But he did not own her. Theirs was a companionship and a loving marriage, and that was something Emmet had claimed to have experienced twice already. Mary had heard many stories about how those marriages had ended.

'What business of yours could possibly concern Mary and me?'

Emmet took another juicy bite out of the crab apple and threw its parts around his teeth. Then, after swallowing, he continued. 'I have been speaking with Father. And he has already given me his blessing. Hansel, I've decided to remarry. I'm marrying Emma Schwarz.'

Hansel could not believe what he was hearing. A third marriage, why? Emmet had decided to divorce his previous wife eight months ago. Mary's mouth was also agape. She knew Emma Schwarz. She was a year or two older than she was, but Emmet was still far older than her. Mary had never liked Emma. She was a dim-witted woman and had shown such a bearing since her early years. She was so caught up with the prospect of marriage that she had not considered her options.

'Emma Schwarz...' Mary said.

'Did you say something?' Emmet shouted across the room to her.

Mary lowered her head.

'Emmet,' Hansel said. 'Well, I'm delighted to hear it. Let's hope that this marriage is a happy one.'

'This marriage isn't about being happy,' Emmet admitted. The apple juice was dribbling from between his thick lips towards his jerkin. He grabbed one of Mary's crocheted napkins from off the cupboard shelf and dried himself. Mary was stepping forward to intervene when she noticed that Emmet had raised two fingers at his waist as if to say, 'Please don't.' So, she stopped and listened from the doorway.

'Then what is it about?' Hansel asked. 'Forgive me, but I struggle to see the purpose of a third marriage. One that promises nothing but one more hungry mouth to feed in your home.'

'I am marrying Emma Schwarz,' Emmet said, 'because it is expected of me. I cannot have five children alone at home without a mother. With two mothers already gone from the village, I need an extra pair of hands. And besides, Emma Schwarz is a young and beautiful woman. You should have waited, Hansel, you'd have liked to have your hands on her, I have no doubt.'

'No,' Hansel retorted. 'No, I wouldn't have.'

Mary had heard bits and pieces about Emmet's two former wives. Between them, he had five hungry children, three boys and two girls. Each mother had been cast out of his household. Thrown into the clutches of the Black Adders under suspicion of witchcraft. In all likelihood, these women had been medicinal healers or herbalists. Mary was not unfamiliar with those practices herself. Among the villagers, she had quite a reputation, and they saw her as a fair and friendly source of medicine.

Emmet remained motionless for a moment. He stopped chewing and Hansel and Mary were reminded of how quiet the cabin could be when he was not around. The fireplace was still snapping, sparkling, and crackling away. The black candles were burning in their holders by the window, as the rain fell. Emmet finished off his bite and set the seedy apple core down on the wooden plate in front of him.

*

'Forgive me, Emmet,' Hansel said to break the silence. 'But I'm confused.'

'And why's that?' Emmet queried. 'You've been married a year now, no? You must understand a man's needs and wants.'

Emmet smirked when he saw the expression on Hansel's face change again. He had suspicions that the pair had not yet shared bodies and their lack of children was proof of it.

'I understand what I need to,' Hansel retorted. 'The rest is none of your business. I'm glad for you, I am,' Hansel continued. 'But could this not have waited until tomorrow? Why do you come now, when it's dark?

'I wanted to see your home,' Emmet said, as though that settled the debate.

'You've been here plenty of times.'

'Then let me be more straightforward,' Emmet leaned over the table. 'I NEEDED to see your home.'

'What do you mean?' Hansel said. Mary was listening more intently now, her anger having turned into curiosity and suspicion. She was filled with the notion that, once more, Emmet HAD indeed arrived bearing bad news for her and Hansel.

'You see,' Emmet said. 'Here is where the BAD news comes in.'

There it was, as Hansel and Mary had already figured out. Emmet never visited if there wasn't anything to gain out of it and for Hansel and Mary to lose. That was the way of life here.

'Please don't,' Hansel begged. 'We've had quite enough trouble for one night.'

'You see,' Emmet began, ignoring his brother. 'It has become clear to Father and me that you and Mary don't plan to have any children.'

'That's none of yours or Father's business,' Hansel exclaimed. 'What is all this? What do you want?'

'THEREFORE,' Emmet went on. 'Therefore, Father has decided

that this cabin would be put to better use in the name of another. And he intends on handing it, and its surrounding pastures, over to me.'

'What!' Hansel exclaimed. This was the first time in many months that Mary had seen her husband flush with rage. And it had been the first time she had ever seen it directed towards his older brother. 'How dare you, both of you! You would have me and my wife robbed of our home? Under what right?'

'Calm down,' Emmet said. 'Don't raise your voice to me, Hansel. I won't ask you again.' Hansel clenched his fists and sat back down in his chair at the dining room table. 'Under the right of our Father,' Emmet continued. 'I hope you remember that the deeds to this land are in his name, not yours and not mine, not yet. You have no children. You have but one woman and a dog you cannot control. I, on the other hand, have five children. I am soon to be married. I will likely have more sons and daughters in the years to come. I need room for all of them. Too many mouths and stamping feet in too small a place, you understand?'

'No,' Hansel returned. 'No, I don't. Where are we to go, would Father have us left homeless or setting up shelter in the woods?' That statement made Mary blink. Her head still throbbed and thrummed with the memory of the hut, the cottage, or whatever it had been. But the memory of it was a blur at the moment. Hansel had been right when he had found her. She had bumped her head and she had been imagining the most terrible things what had followed. Nonetheless, she had no immediate wish to return there.

'Not the woods,' Mary murmured, 'please.'

'Quiet, woman,' Emmet barked. 'Do away with your wiles and witchery, won't you?' Mary watched Emmet stand up and walk around the dining room table. He fetched his oilskin and belongings as he did so. On his way out, Emmet cast his dark eyes around. The cabin was filled with herbs and spices. It also had spider-silk dream catchers, hanging feathers, pinecones, acorns, woodcarvings, and other valuables. Mary had found or made them from the Black Forest, but much of it was for display. Emmet picked up a doll with burlap skin, black-button eyes, and a mouth that burst open from its stitching.

'Don't touch that!' Mary said, reaching out for her childhood companion. 'Put it down!'

Emmet raised his hand to backhand Mary but Hansel stepped in, meeting Mary, and holding her still. 'Contain your woman!' Emmet cried. 'The Devil has his claws deep in this one, Hansel. It'd be good for you to do away with her. Believe me. All of THIS will go when the cabin belongs to me and my family.'

'Enough!' Hansel exclaimed. 'Both of you, I'll hear no more, not in MY home.'

There was a beat of quiet. 'But it's not your home, not anymore.' Hansel looked at his older brother, who towered over him in the doorway. 'Don't worry, Hansel, old boy. I won't be staying the night. I have paperwork and deeds to attend to. You won't have to leave immediately. I'm neither cruel nor unreasonable. My wedding to Emma Schwarz won't take place for another month. You've got time to gather up all that you own and seek out new property. I may stop by tomorrow with the paperwork and deeds. Sleep on it, baby brother.'

With that, Emmet turned from Hansel and Mary. He looked her in her eyes. Mary saw that Emmet believed that his brother had wed a servant of the Devil: a witch. Then, he bowed low. And with a whinny, a crack of the reins, and a clapper, Emmet disappeared into the darkness of the woods. Hansel watched him go. Mary fell to her knees and began to weep. 'Hansel,' she blubbered. 'What are we going to do?'

Her husband did not answer straight away. He kept looking out into the woods ahead.

'I don't know, Mary,' Hansel admitted. 'I don't know.'

Emmet rode off into the night. But he never made it back home.

*

'Mary, come back!'

Mary did not slow down for her husband. She had not yet come to terms with the events of the previous evening. The memories of the cottage in the woods were now but distant, mere figments. And she had put them down to the hard bump on her forehead. Mary looked over her shoulder and saw Hansel picking up pace behind her. Much of the Black Forest had given over to the morning mist. Mary slowed down, pausing for a few moments and waiting for Hansel to catch up.

'I'm not in the mood for waiting around,' Mary said. 'Not today. We've got things do.'

'Yes,' Hansel panted. 'Quite right, but the village isn't far away, we're almost there. You can slow down, can't you? You shouldn't be rushing along anywhere after what's happened. Besides, I'm not hearing any bells ringing. We've got plenty of time before the Black Adders will want a word with you or me.'

Mary conceded. Hansel was right. The Black Adders were the village's ruling authority. They handled all matters about the church, the law, and witchcraft in the Black Forest. As much as Mary loathed them, she knew that the Black Adders were their only hope of keeping their cabin. But that came later. For now, she just needed to walk.

Mary did not tell Hansel what she had dreamed about last night. She did not mention the cottage again. Hansel had already dismissed it as a possibility, because he had seen no cottage. He had seen no cauldron. He had seen no crone. But Mary had slept to the distant crackle and cackle of laughter and the scents of sugar. Walking through the woodland now, Mary could not help but look around her and wonder if it had all been real. 'You're right,' Mary said, 'I'm anxious. You know what the Black Adders think of me, don't you?'

'Never mind them,' Hansel said. 'We're meeting to discuss business and deeds, not personal matters.'

Mary agreed. Hansel walked up to her and grabbed her by the shoulder.

'You're no witch, Mary,' he said. 'You're my wife. No harm will come to you from the Black Adders.' Hansel thought his words had been compelling. Mary slipped away from her husband, brushing his hand away from her shoulder. Hansel inquired after her, but she did not reply to him. 'Mary?'

'It's nothing,' Mary said. 'I'm fine.'

'That never means you're fine,' Hansel said. 'What's wrong?'

'Nothing, I said I'm fine, didn't I?'

'You're still upset, aren't you? About what happened last night?' Hansel did not need his wife to answer that question. He knew it to be true. He had known it since they had stepped foot out of the cabin and made for the road to the village. Each time they left the cabin now, it felt unfamiliar and sullen, as though they were departing it for the very last time. 'Mary,' Hansel continued, 'you know I could not say anything to Emmet. Nor could you, and if you had, he'd have reported you to the Black Adders. You know that. I'm sorry, it's true.'

'That doesn't mean it's right,' Mary murmured. She stopped on the road and crossed her arms.

'No,' Hansel agreed. 'No, it doesn't. But that's the way it is. You knew that when you married me.' Mary did know that. And Mary also knew that Hansel was correct. She could not have stood up to Emmet's demands or lashed out in anger any more than she already had. 'I don't know what I'd do without you,' Hansel added. 'Really, I do mean that.'

Mary did not respond. She had stopped still on the road. She was looking at something. A pale horror dawned on her face. Hansel recognized it in an instant.

'Mary,' Hansel began, 'what's wrong?'

Mary lifted a trembling finger towards the path ahead. There lay the broken and twisted body of a man, crushed and mangled beneath the weight of his riding horse.

There lay Emmet, deathly still.

And in his mouth: a blood-red apple.

FANNY TALBOT

'It's haunted, you know.'

Tasha Cairn uttered those words upon first noticing the house in the fog. Her tone filled with the kind of innocent certainty that only the young can muster. Her youngest brother, Felix, started crying at the thought of it. He wept more upon spotting the tall, ugly structure.

'It's not haunted, it's just quite old,' Stella intervened.

She knelt by her children and tugged them into a tight hug. Though, the true nature of Stella's feelings was of worry and concern. There were no such things as ghosts or curses. That was a reassurance for her. Luther Cairn reached down and lifted Felix into his arms. The child nestled his face into his father's chest, listening to his thudding heart.

Luther's jacket was wet with stinging tears. Through the tears, Felix watched the estate appear in the fog. He continued staring at it with fear. No words of comfort could sway the boy. They could not change his mind about the setting truth that the Cairn Estate was truly haunted. What terrible things awaited him in there, he could not fathom.

Cairn House was a large, Victorian structure that had been in the Cairn family for generations. It was a staple of Trifford town. The newly arrived Cairn family stood at the wrought iron gates of their ancestral seat. It lingered in the distance, far away from its thorny fencing, sitting near the top of a great, treed hill. Though now the trees were naked, thrice knuckled, and crooked. The Trifford marshes spread around it forever.

The Cairn family noted all the features of their new residence. The structure was crude, with silhouetted towering slate eaves and sharp roofing. It was three-storey high, at least. There would be enough room for every Cairn that had ever lived to live there. Though, they would not find each other in its gloom. Luther and Stella Cairn could relate to their children. They felt the same utter terror upon closer inspection.

The grounds were overgrown and thick with roots and weeds. They invaded the gates and flowered across the fencing like travelling rot. But there was little sign of true life past the gates. No birds. No rats. No flowers. Only fog, and in the fog, trimmed topiary figures.

'You listen,' Luther said to Tasha and Felix, 'there are no such things as ghosts, haunts, ghouls, or any other night creatures. They are not real. They exist only in your sleep.'

Luther's words left his lips as a soft utter. Yet the intent was intense. The father required both of his children to understand that their new home and life would not be tainted by the things thoughts fear. He ruffled Felix's tousled hair and turned to Tasha. 'After all, you should not be frightened of anything here. The Cairn Estate and Cairn House have been in our family for generations. It likely will be for generations yet to come. Your grandchildren may very well run around these very paths. You'll make friends, too.'

There was nothing reassuring in Luther's words. The gates swung open. The family strolled through. Gargoyle statues grinned with streaking rows of jagged teeth. Their wings unfurled slightly, shaking out stony dust from their stiff joints. Their masters had returned.

The statues parted, allowing the Cairns to creep through, towards their family estate. The old house groaned at its latest guests, its latest victims. It was intent on its guests meeting the same end as the previous residents. That same, god-awful haunt.

Cairn House groaned in greeting.

It hungered.

*

Trifford was a lonely and empty town. Nearly empty. It sat central to the marsh, a flooded forest and reedy fen that stretched out forever. It was silent, still. The surface of the water lay without ripple and reflected what little daylight fell over it. Though, there was no colour to the light. It was bleached. Tomorrow only ever gave a grey and cobweb afternoon.

The dark was a sick, strange darkness. Darker in autumn and winter when things without life took over Trifford's outlying fastness. Then, only the corpse light of a full moon illuminated the town's mossy flagstones and thatched roofs. It was a town without truth. There was no true title for it, no true history there. The folk kept coveted secrets that they refused to tell. It sat atop a junction, a fork of three rivers that fed from each flood to the next.

The church was the largest structure in Trifford, other than the old house. Everyone was buried together in its cemetery, reeking with flesh turned to earth. Just past the cemetery was the old house, walled in by thorny hedges and trimmed statues. The one that had once belonged to the Cairn family. Further afield, a cluster of ill-lit cottages puffed trails of grey smoke. For each cottage there was a pool. For each pool there was a child at the bottom, sunken, greening; bloated. Not just a child. But children.

Too many children lost to the flood. The floods were growing larger and deeper each year. All the paths and causeways were swallowed up by the fen's ichor. Plenty had gone missing trying to find them. Trifford was crumbling in on itself. More than that, it was sinking.

The still nights were familiar. All that rustled bristled from the breeze blowing over the town's flat marshland. Though, where it blew from, nobody knew. Nor did they intend on finding out. They were all in quiet agreement that it came from a coast they could not see. One that lay beyond the thick fog. They had to believe there was a haven out there.

With a stoop and a slight, a flock of crows fettered the night air with razor feathers and coughing carols. They flew in atop a frail gust in thin air. The gentle wind threatened the coarse shrubbery, graveyard grass, almost-naked willow trees. Serpent roots coiled. The reeds in the water curled wetly. Things far worse than reeds slithered through the marsh.

That quiet gust grew stronger. It threaded through the thickets until it reached what few trees were left at the church. From there, it turned to the old house. A tall, crooked building, Victorian, with a steep roof, little windows, and large doors. The trees rattled and tapped their fingers against the fractured glass in greeting.

That night, there was nobody to hear the tapping. That night, the old house was vacant, empty. Its only inhabitants were spiders, moths, and the rats that had escaped the lure of tangy fen water. The water seeped through the floorboards. The old house would be the first to sink. Everyone knew that. Though, it was not as empty as everyone thought.

Only the quiet ones in their graves heard the wind. They never stayed still, under the earth. The flood spirited them away from the cemetery, out and away into the marsh. The children were told not to play out there. For fear of who or what they may find. A whisper filled the night, an utter from chapped lips. It breathed life into the emptiness. Life, or a thing feigning life. It was a rustle or a scratch, the scratching of white chalk across a schoolhouse blackboard. It turned three o'clock, the turn of night to the witching hour.

The cold moon rose to meet it. A full moon gathered behind black clouds and streamed pale light through the windows of the town cottages. It touched the old house. It felt through its locks and hinges. The wind waned before falling to nothing. It was as though it had never arrived. And all in Trifford slept without knowledge of what had arrived with it.

It slept, waited. It wanted.

*

Years later, one October afternoon, Fanny Talbot returned to Trifford.

It was just as Fanny had left it, all those years ago. Fourteen years, to be precise. Fanny was not shocked to learn that nothing had changed there. In fact, it was more as she remembered it than ever it had been. Though, in truth, one thing was altered. Trifford was lower. It had sunken quite considerably into the flat. Though, the flat was not there anymore, not really. Now, it was a fen. Grey, jade, dank. It was a corpse marsh, infested with fog ghosts.

The fork of rivers first struck Fanny with the sound of rushing. Other than the rain and gravelly rattle of tap water through the pipes, it was the only water that ran. All other sources were still and lay without rippling. Perhaps it was a product of her time away, or her growing up in that time, but the town had been drained of its entire colour. Life tended to lose colour with age. But it was too apparent in Trifford to put down to that. It was a ghost town now.

Everything pretty — the river, the rain — glinted as it splashed against the cottage roofs and windows. They were all squat and their stones were riddled with spongy moss and creeper vines. They had always been there, but they held the cottages stronger in their grip than ever before. The crows were in again. Fanny had not missed them a touch. Nonetheless, they were familiar to her. Ghosts traipsed through the thick fog. Haunting, strangers looking for what they lost. Fanny recalled those ghosts. She had seen them in her youth. In her childhood nights, the grownups had put them down to turns and twists in the wind. Yet, upon her return, Fanny felt no wind. Fanny felt nothing at all but for a touch of cool.

Fanny's old car struggled over the bridge. Yes, *the* bridge, for there was only one in the Trifford. Under it, the three streams mated with one another and rushed on by. Where much of the marshland was a filthy emerald, the fork there was glass clear and tempting. The bridge followed through onto a long and flat causeway that spat out gravel and weed tumbles. Fanny could hear both racketing against and knotting up in the car tyres. It trundled on tiredly.

She followed the path until it was not a path anymore. Passed by the locksmiths and the cobblers, and took out from Trifford into the marshes. Those marshes held terrible things. Things that floated and glided over the bog like white wraiths in the thick fog.

Fanny watched everyone frequenting the town's streets. She noticed some of them from unmistakable characteristics. When

Fanny had run through the streets as a child, she had been mortally terrified by many of the older Trifford residents. But it appeared that time and age had spirited them away or carried them off to their graves.

There was nothing for Fanny to fear in the town. Not anymore.

The car carried on chugging until it wanted for rest. It splashed into sequestered puddles and potholes, through the countryside, guided only by a lonely crow that flew onwards squawking. Until, eventually, the church entered her sight. There, it touched the low point where the clouds met the fog and the fog met the cold earth. Further than that, the cemetery, the old house. It faded in and out of the fog until it settled. It was starting to rain gently.

Droplets pitter-pattered off the windscreen, and between wipes, the structure came and went. There were no more trees out that way, only the ones belonging to the church, resting in the cemetery. Unattended willows, weeping, stood tall in the vast garden of the old house.

That was where Fanny was going, then, to the old house.

But first, the church.

She remembered it, vaguely, from her childhood. Old Father Henry had once lived here. Fanny parked up against the nearest wall, which sheltered her from the rain. The raindrops were light and clung to her hair in clusters. They fell like glass ball bearings to her shoulders. There were no other cars there. Not only at the church, but in the entire town. Fanny's car was the only one. There had been others, once, but it appeared that there was little point owning a car that could not travel through the fen. Others were on their way. Fanny knew that. She was early and would have to wait a little while for the others to join her. To pass the time, Fanny traipsed up to the nearest steel gate and pushed it open. It winced and let out a hurtful whine. She stepped through and into the church garden. The cemetery sat to her left, the old house beyond it. Though, neither were yet any of her concern.

Fanny made her way up to the church door. It was black and the wood was chipped and splintered. It revealed nothing beneath it that spoke of layered paint or a former colour. It had clearly been torn from its hinges before. The church had been cut off from prying eyes and intrusive crows by a tangle of wire and thorns that kept the crows out. When Fanny turned around, it was difficult to spot her car but for the canvas roof doming overhead.

Fanny took a deep breath. Then, she rapped three times on the door. There was no answer. She tried the copper door handle. It gave. Fanny twisted it, easing it open with an earthy groan, and tentatively stepped inside. It had been getting colder outside. The fen was always cool. It held the chill of too many bodies in it. Nonetheless, Fanny was struck by the drop in temperature inside the church. She drew a sharp breath and started to rub her upper arms.

She reached into her green coat pocket and fetched a pair of leather gloves. It was a struggle to put them on in the cold. They were tight and wet from a leak somewhere in the material. They slipped onto her fingers and over her hands with a wrinkle in the leather and a crinkle like stretched reeds.

It was little wonder that it was so cold in the church. It was large and it was empty. The pews were vacant, the altar was dusty. It was, in truth, forlorn. It appeared then that the townsfolk were not a religious lot. The interior was little different to the exterior. The stoney walls were threaded with green lichen and swamp moss. And, despite the cold, the air in there was heavy. It weighed down on Fanny's lungs with each intake. Centuries of life, death, prayer, and grief reached out for Fanny as she stood there, taking it all in again.

Fanny's memories of the church were vague. Though, she accepted that she must have been there before. There were celebrations, of course, for Easter, Christmas, and the odd ceremonial service or family affair. Weddings in Trifford were rare. But there were funerals aplenty. Fanny took a look around the church. She moved slowly, as a cat waits for springing mice. Everything was grey and lifeless. The walls were grey. The floor was grey. Even the wood interlocking in the rafters was rotten grey and splintered.

A spill of light fell through a hole in the roof and illuminated the altar. Moth dust and wood shavings drifted down through the light like snowflakes. That was a bleak beauty if ever Fanny had known it. The only colour came in the form of three or four stained glass paintings, saints and the sort. They were painted in hues of green, gold, red, and wheat yellow. They caught Fanny's attention for a while, until their faces turned a little too canny and she had to look away.

They were frowning at her.

As she investigated the old church, Fanny was half expecting to come face to face with one of the townsfolk whenever she turned a corner. But she did not find anyone in there. The only sound in the church came from her footfalls on the stoney flagstones. The wind outside was muffled against the thick walls. It entered through cracks in the door and roof, but only as a fraction of its full strength, a whistle at best.

Fanny found her way over to a light switch by the entry booth. That had not been there when she was a child. Yet, when she flicked it on and off, nothing happened. There it was. The only modern gift was out of use. Fanny smiled wryly, that was particularly befitting for the town. She had to wait there, in the church, sitting in the strained light of an October afternoon.

She waited a while, but no one appeared. There was nothing else there to look for. Fanny turned around and started out of the front door. The churchyard was as empty as she had left it. Fanny turned off for the cemetery on her left, following the thorny path until the church became little in the distance. She was struck then by a strange sensation as she walked down that way. A feeling that could neither be shaken nor explained. It was as though she should turn around. No. Not turn around. Continue forward, carry on into the cemetery to find someone, or something; what or who, she did not know. The anxiety grew in her like a black stain on a tablecloth. That anxiety was the first familiar sensation to re-emerge from Fanny's childhood. It was not a welcome feeling. But it belonged to her, nonetheless.

By the time Fanny was on her way out of the churchyard and towards the cemetery, it was growing dark, although it was not yet four o'clock. But October started late and finished early. And soon the grey sky was falling black. That very blackness fell over the cemetery.

A still wind rustled the graveyard grass. Fanny took it as the sign to take her leave. She stopped herself, watched it for a moment, and then turned away. She made her way back up the path without turning around and made towards her car, parked on the church's furthest wall. The ignition did not start on its first turn. The engine whispered. Fanny crinkled the leather of her gloves as her clutch tightened on the wheel.

She tried the key again. When it finally started, she hesitated for a moment before departing for her true destination, which lay a little way off from the cemetery, the furthest structure from Trifford to still claim affiliation. Starting off, Fanny drove towards the old house, vanishing into the fog.

*

Through fen and fog, Fanny set upon the estate attached to the old house. It was only a short way from Trifford to the church. Shorter still from the cemetery to the moss-eaten manor. Yet, as she drove, Fanny felt a lethargy tugging at her. Time stretched unhealthily in the fog. Three minutes felt akin to thirty. Surrounded by the grey veil, Fanny could not figure out how close night was to her. Therefore, she continued along the straight gravel causeway towards the old house without sign of turning. Until, eventually, it came into sight.

Fanny followed a stretch of hedge along the road until she reached the rear of the house. It was precisely how she remembered it, although far more overgrown. It faced out onto the long road back to town for ease of access. Not that anyone ever frequented the old house anymore. Fanny parked the car. The engine died with a dry whimper. It chugged once, gasping for life. Filled with worry, Fanny tried the ignition. Now, it would not start at all. The engine was dead or empty. It would not answer to her. She was stranded there, at the old Cairn structure.

Fanny got out and walked towards the nearest gate. There were a handful of them, each of them wooden – not metal – and rough with splinters. She remembered the gates well. From back when she had played there as a child with her friends. Fanny recalled the way she swung to and fro on their hinges. From there, she could make her way out towards the garden, the causeway, the scullery, and the outhouses with haste. Though, she was quite often warned against doing so alone. There were always warnings and frets about the fen and its flooding. Too many young boys and girls about her age had been caught up in the reeds and dragged under, gasping. If you timed the floods and rains wrong, the causeway would vanish.

Fanny reached to open the large gate. It did not give. She tried it once more. Nothing. She took to walking around the rear face of the old house. Fanny followed a lengthy and untrimmed strip of tall hedge, brushing the thorns away from her face. Perhaps she would come to the front of the building in time to meet the others. But they were already rather late, and Fanny heard no car and saw nothing moving in the fog but for the ghosts. Licks of night fog were curling, luring her back towards the church with wispy fingers. Through a parting, Fanny saw the church stoop up. It was close, the cemetery too, a little too close for her liking. The old house had been built many centuries ago, between the town and marsh. The cemetery was close enough to the old house that some of the gravestones were already intruding in on the estate. Cairn House was touched by the grave.

Fanny rubbed her shoulders for warmth. The rain was not letting up, rather, it was falling harder than before, a sure sign that it would settle in for the night. It did not really matter whether they arrived soon or not, if the road flooded, they would not be able to go anywhere anyway. Fanny looked down the road again impatiently: nothing. Then, she felt something pull at her coat sleeve. A slight tug, nothing more. Fanny turned with a jump and a sharp inhalation. Unwittingly, she had turned to face the church and the cemetery in the distance. Fanny felt the urge to return there. Something inside her longed to spend more time on the plot. Though, in her heart of hearts, she held no desire to do so. What was out there? What called for her to return? Had it truly been business that had brought her back to Trifford or something else entirely? Too many questions left unanswered.

Fanny followed the luring fog through towards the cemetery's lychgate. She stopped for a moment and looked further ahead. Something urged her to continue, away from the old house and back towards the church. What had she not seen? What was waiting for her out there?

Her grip tightened on the swinging gate. A couple of headstones rose out of the foggy earth in front of her, but not quite close enough to read. Fanny opened the gate and walked through them. Each one was wrought of a crumbling grey stone. The fog was working its way through the engraved lettering, feeling out every dead name and lost life. The gravestones became more numerous and tightly packed as Fanny continued. Until she made her way towards a cluster covered with wet lichen and moss. These gravestones were old, very old; ancient. Fanny went up to each of them and traced her fingers across their faces. Their leathery tips came away wet and cool. Many of the names, dates, and titles had been scratched away or filled in. Fanny knelt, wiping away a clinging strand of swamp mesh and mouthed something she read.

Nothing happened. Nothing moved. Not even Fanny.

The still wind had returned. It mingled with the darkness and cast chill shadows over the marshes. The darkness ate Fanny up. She felt uncomfortable, isolated; vulnerable. There was an immediate notion that she was no longer alone out there in the fog. Though when she looked up towards the church or back to the old house, there was no sign of any visitor interrupting her private time. In truth, she would have welcomed it.

Fanny heard the wind before she felt it. Yet, it was not blowing from anywhere specifically. In fact, it was whistling up from her feet. The trapped air was escaping from underneath one of the ancient gravestones. There was room beneath it. That, Fanny could tell. Still kneeling, she tugged away a tangle of reeds and thorns. One of them pricked her thumb and drew a pinprick of blood. It swelled into a globule, and she brought her thumb to her lips. The iron taste bred with the glove's harsh leather on her tongue. Then, Fanny listened intently.

It was not wind. Not really. It was a sound like crinkling, the rustle of paper; the starting of sparks. The noise was faint and soft, but it was there. It found its origin in the earth, beneath the graveyard grass. Then the rustle stopped before turning into scratching. Scratching like trimmed nails against the wood of a coffin. Something wanted out. Something was finding its way up from the dank, musty earth towards the surface. Fanny stood up straight. Her knees buckled and clicked with the startle of it. In truth, she had not been sure what she had heard. After all, the hour was late and the mind played foul tricks on itself in the darkness. It could have been anything. That was what Fanny told herself. Nonetheless, she stayed there for a few minutes.

Every so often, the noise came again, sometimes stronger and sometimes softer. The more she listened, the more she grew intrigued. It was a noise she knew, although she did not remember what it was or how she knew it. Yet it was familiar. The answer of it lingered on the tip of her tongue. She bit her lip and clenched her jaw, willing the truth to reveal itself to her. But no truth came that night. Instead, it hid from her. Fanny remembered one thing, however. The way it made her feel took her back to her girlhood, here, in Trifford. It was an ill, sickly feeling. Like some tragedy she had tried to forget. Fanny dusted herself off raindrops and squeezed the remaining blood from her gloved thumb. Without her noticing, that droplet fell down towards the gravestone and into the earth. Fanny squinted, tired, and started walking away from the cemetery. The still wind stopped instantly. Only a thin whistle remained over the fen.

Fanny returned to the old house.

*

The old house lay in darkness. It waited for Fanny to come to it. The still wind was rising over that way and rustling the creeping ivy that plagued the wood-and-stone walls. Fanny lamented at having not brought a lighter or torch of sorts with her. She only had a matchbox. It was getting difficult to see without the bleaching sunlight. Fanny had not thought to miss it until it was gone entirely. She walked with her hands out before her, feeling her way through the front gate and fingering a narrow strip of fence that guided her up towards the manor house. With each step, Fanny could hear thorns and bramble crunching underneath her foot.

In her pocket, she felt for the key. It was cold and heavy in her gloved palm, ancient and wrought from iron. The lock to the front door was vacant. Fanny slipped the key in, turned it, and drew it out. It came away covered with white cobwebs. She pushed against the heavy door and felt it give way more easily than she had expected. She stepped inside, felt around for a light switch. Though, she felt nothing on the closest walls but for frayed, floral wallpaper. It took a few moments of frantic feeling before Fanny's fingers came to a hard box. The switches were gathered on a panel, a little further inside. She kicked the latches up and waited for the lights to flicker into life. When they did so, it was an unhealthy light that struggled to fully get rid of the darkness around it.

The lights did not stay on for long. They shattered and bulb-glass littered the floor.

The dark returned.

*

The dark was complete. Fanny started into the claustrophobic gloom. Suddenly, such a large hall felt so small; intimate. She fetched a matchbox from her pocket and struck a light. The gentle wick flickered against everything it touched. Fanny took a look around, leaning in close against all she inspected. Oil paintings hung up on the walls flanking the staircase. It was a wide and ugly thing sweeping up to the upper floors, its steps dusty.

Fanny reached the landing, entering a room where the air was stale. Relics and trinkets lay under sheets of cloth. A series of cobwebs flaked from the rafters high above. As if some supernatural intent had disturbed the dust up there. Fanny figured it was not an uncommon thing. Old houses were long to be dusty. Though, this one did not feel very empty.

Then, something touched her neck.

The touch was as chill as the grave. Fanny turned around, startled. She did so with such urgency that her foot caught up on the rug. She hit the floor with a thud and looked up. There was nothing there, just as she had thought. The fog was crawling into the old house now. Fanny looked for the source and found it flowing through one of the fractured windows. It was only open slightly. But the fog flowed through like froth from a waterfall. Fanny, struggling to her feet, thought she saw something in that fog. She thought she saw a hand. She thought she had seen a face. Instead, she found naked willows shaped like fingers.

Fanny watched three fingers tap against the window. Tap. Tap. Tap.

She unlatched the window further and pushed it open. A quick rush of fresh air tore it wider. Fanny's hair flowed and shot in the wind. There was something out there. Fanny could feel it. She scanned the empty path up and down, as though expecting company. Nobody passed this way after nightfall. It was raining and the causeway was turning dark, drowning.

The light fog found its way in through the open window. It flooded the floor and breathed through the rugged carpet. Its wisps were cool against her feet and ankles. Fanny had forgotten what it felt like after so long. Yet, every October, the very same fog returned. Fanny let it in. The fog sketched snakes in the air with its fingers. It coiled and curled, licked and looped. A stroke of it caressed Fanny's face, a touch gentle on her cheek. The fog felt familiar. It felt friendly.

Fanny grinned. Then, she turned to the window. The fog was thicker out there. There was not much to be found in the shroud. The stars had gone and the moon was hidden somewhere in the grey.

There were no leaves on the trees. October had stripped them naked and collected them in untidy, leftover heaps. When the wind came, and the fog shifted, there was very little rustling. Only the clatter of frail tree limbs against one another. Fanny missed their leaves. She missed the green.

In October, everything was either dead or dying. The grey days and nights that brought the fog were an unwelcome addition. Quite often, the fog came and stayed for days at a time. And Fanny Talbot would sit at her bedroom window and wonder if it was there to stay.

The fog let up. But for Fanny, it lay in wait.

A slight opening formed from its wisps. Fanny took a step back from the window. Then, the wind thrust out from behind her, returning to the night. The force of it nearly caught her and took her out with it. Only by clutching the rail of the stairs tightly did Fanny steady herself. To her, the open window seemed a pouting mouth drawing in cool air from the world around her.

A raspy whisper slithered into her mind. Fanny turned to the doorway. It was tainted by a thin mist. Her lit match went out. The flicker of white light hissed and vanished. Quiet fell. Then, Fanny heard the hand. She turned around and looked at the foggy window. It was wet with condensation. The dark imprint of a hand and fingers moaned over the glass. Fanny screamed. She dropped her matchbox and fled out into the narrow corridors of the old house. A foul wraith wailed from behind her. It was following her.

Fanny was running then, running towards the end of the hall. There, at the end of the way, a horrific apparition was waiting for her. It lay there. Translucent, wispy, made entirely of fog. A mockery of the human form that shuddered towards her with great speed.

The last thing Fanny Talbot remembered was its gaping mouth and a howl of grief.

And the chill of an October fog.

THE WORG

'Even a man who is pure in heart and says his prayers by night may become a wolf when the wolfbane blooms and the Autumn moon is bright.'
– From 'The Wolf Man'

Legends are true. Monsters are real.

It started at night. It began with a tinny jangle of talismans: pentagram lockets and full moon necklaces. It started with the soft flap of tent cloth and the rattle of falling broomsticks. The faces around the night fire were smooth as candle tallow. Wood smoke and cinders fought away the thick fog and chill. The wagons were gathered together. There were more out on the North Proctor moors yet to arrive. They romanced hinges and formed a tightly knit, private circle.

There wouldn't be any more visitors, not tonight. This was a private gathering.

The racket started as a string of violins. Their chords were foreign, full of cheer and played with trice. Bows jutted and slid around with a flourish and flip. This was a painted place to disappear into the shadows or thrive in the lifeblood of laughter. A throw of echo salt and a sprinkle of wraith spice into the contained flames. The fire erupted with serpent tongues that flowered and flickered with heat. A spit of rum and further fire shot into the air. The encampment enjoyed itself tonight. It breathed with festivity.

Once again, it was an autumn night. Wind billowed and haunted the canopies of wagons, caravans, and carriages. The night fire dimmed gently. The flautists faltered, the strings fell silent, and minstrels stopped their murmurings. They mouthed nothing more and moved to trample the light and heat from their roadside campfires. They went out and darkness fell.

There came a frightened bustle and rush amongst the entire gypsy caravan.

The campfires cleared, the wine was spent, and there was nobody left then to listen for the whispering wind. Latches locked with crossing thuds and sliding bolts. Window shutters were fixed into their layered frames. Only the snapdragon crackle of embers sounded in the dark. Its light snuffed out too, just after the last. Then, a tent fold lifted in the stir, and the chill of night slipped through.

A man sat crouched, palms resting against a stand, nails grating into the hardwood. The cards spread out lay still and untouched. He clutched the five-star necklace around his throat. It swung like a pendulum over his chest and heart. The wind whistled through and flipped one of the cards face up. The tarot cut the face of a beast. The Worg.

The gypsy man stood and approached the tent curtain without a hurry. He tugged at the knot of his shirt and let the cream cloth fall away from his shoulders. Something woke within him, rousing as if from a lengthy, starving slumber. He looked out across the endless moors. Then, up towards the full glare of the moon. He licked his teeth. No. Not teeth.

Fangs.

*

The full, autumn moon hung on its thread. It was a frayed ball of cotton yarn. Bunched up and laid out across an utterly black canvas. It swayed and twinkled in the dark, shining over North Proctor like a foiled rosary bead or roasted garlic clove. It was a green moon. Glowing and glowering behind thick clouds of soot and night air.

Tonight, it cast fading light across the empty moors and rural pastures of Blackhurst. Towards the forest they called the Wald. Tonight, the green moon shone. Tonight, it gave cause for a wolf song.

Though, it wasn't the sinister shriek of a creature — prowling late — that woke the hunter, Rupert. For it was too far-off. Rather, it was the quick and painful nudge of an elbow, stabbing at his ribs. He felt it through his grey leathers and sage oilskin. Rupert opened his weary eyes to nothing. Then, shapes started forming into focus.

'Pete's sake,' Talbot uttered. 'Why won't you keep quiet?'

Rupert huffed and rolled over onto his shoulder, scratching the stubble of his cheek. 'Quiet yourself,' he said. 'I've kept quiet all night.'

'Quiet?' Talbot chuckled. 'You've been snoring all night. You're supposed to be keeping your eyes peeled, not latching them shut. You'll never make a watchdog, you know.'

'And you're not funny,' Rupert returned.

'Oh, what's wrong?' Talbot jested. 'Don't tell me you're frightened of the Worg.'

'There's no such thing,' Rupert said. 'I'm tired because we've caught nothing yet.'

Tonight's hunt had, so far, lasted for several slow hours. Time passed without a rush or trace. Each languid hour was growing longer still. Their game was becoming rarer and rarer.

Rupert and Talbot had started on their hunt at roughly six o'clock. Now, they were out deeper into that black time that settled near midnight. These were the lonely hours, cold and quiet. Their only light streamed down vaguely from the moon glaring above them. It was growing larger, stronger, coming closer. Nearing enough to reach out and touch. Hunting had been Talbot's suggestion, one that neither man was unfamiliar with. Everyone hunted here.

Together, the young pair had struck down a fine gravel path. Out of Blackhurst and into North Proctor's veiled greenery. They'd left Blackhurst to sleep quietly. They could still see it, flickering lantern wicks flowering in the foggy light of streetlamps. There was nobody in town that had seen them set off. Not that either hunter knew of.

They were alone in their task. To return to Blackhurst with a stag, a lone wolf, a prize. Thus far, they'd found little other than squirrels, fretful rabbits, and the rest. Nothing moved that they could see. That was all too fitting for North Proctor.

The only signs of wildlife traipsed through the undergrowth. Those critters were too small and quick to waste their lasting ammunition. The pair waited for a grander game. Conversation between Rupert and Talbot had been rationed. They kept their voices to a hush.

After taking their leave from town, they'd come to reach harsh hill country and grassy moors flooded with fog. There, they'd settled. Talbot had stooped low first, steadying his wood and iron hunting rifle against his left shoulder and clavicle. From then on, he did not move. Just as his father – Karloff, the chief hunter – had taught him. He lay there, rigid in hunting position atop a pastured knoll, waiting. Rupert lay there next to him. Though, he'd yet grown tired of waiting. His arms were tiring and starting to tremble.

The last thing he recalled was staring out across North Proctor.

That was when he knew he'd shifted off into a light sleep. It didn't worry Rupert. After all, this had become too pointless an endeavour to continue with. Rupert could've been fast asleep in warm bedclothes, wrapped up in tight quilts of comfortable cotton.

But no. There he was, anticipating the arrival of a creature that no hunter had seen for many, many moons. Let alone a green moon. It was rare for Blackhurst's finest to hunt under a green moon's grin. That was an old, local wives' tale. Though, lately, it refused to shine out in any other colour.

Rupert groaned, rolling onto his other side and gazing up at its face. The moon was featured amongst a completely starless night sky. He only caught glimpses of its full colour and starless stage through the fog. The moon lit up the clouds eating at it. Still, they remained thick, slow, and concealing. It was as if they were tucking away a guilty secret or foul omen. A foul omen, yes, Rupert was certain of that. There were plenty of those in recent times.

The clouds were feeding off the moon's hue. Many of them were now the gloomy shade of underwater algae and rooted pondweed. Strange shadows and silhouettes crept through the foggy moors. They moved silently under leafy canopies and the cover of night. There was nothing solid about the fog. Fogs were gateways to other, unknown places. To danger.

North Proctor was cruel in concealing its creatures and secrets. It was a vista of pine and evergreen forests, grass flats, and tumbling hills. Tonight, the hunters caught sight of one thing, one thing only. It loomed and lurched without care for sharing.

The Wald was the great forest dominating Blackhurst's outlying countryside. It cut a stark shape through the fog, cutting and gutting the thinning veil as if its leaves were shears.

'Can you see anything?' Rupert inquired quietly.

'Not a thing,' Talbot furrowed his brow and shook his head.

This continued quiet was starting to irritate them both. Waiting was always a tedious game. It was worse tonight. Nothing sounded but for the rustle of frail leaves and a stirring wind. Talbot caught the scent of rain in the air. Then, something pattered off his cloak.

A lone raindrop.

Talbot turned his head up – still lying flat – and felt another raindrop shoot down his collar. The rain started falling across North Proctor. It followed through, bulleting through the vapour. Talbot didn't move. Raindrops pattered off his shoulders like glassy ball bearings. He kept watchful, vigilant. Both his hands and fingers were starting to numb. He kept them still. Talbot didn't shift the long snout of his rifle from its perfect position. He couldn't. Not after hours of waiting there in the grass. Something would rear its head soon for him to shoot.

The rainfall lightened. It was only a passing shower. In its wake, the fog whipped up again. Talbot and Rupert were very aware that the deluge could pick up again at any given moment. The weather across North Proctor was often grim and toying. Tonight, it was no different. It was unwise for anyone, hunter or otherwise, to roam the countryside at such an hour and in such terrible conditions. The moors turned treacherous, with sink pits and traps.

Too long spent sopping in your leathers would strike anyone down with a chill. Later, a boiling fever. Rupert wanted nothing to do with any of that. Not again. He'd be turning twenty-three soon. That age tasted too serious on his palette to be true. Yet, true it was. Though, he'd not thought to do so whilst tortured to sniffle or whilst gravely ill.

Talbot nudged Rupert again and he looked over, following Talbot's steady aim out across Blackhurst. Then, he noticed it too. Talbot grinned and rallied a fierce shot, aiming. There it was. The game of which they'd been hunting for all night long. It was a Blackhorn. A sleek, black stag. It came closer, gingerly, with a powerful grace. It clopped over towards a fresh puddle, staring at its reflection. Its eyes were polished oval pearls. No true iris to be found.

The stag scanned the area. It saw and heard nothing at all, just tranquillity. It stooped its long neck to quench its thirst. The hunters studied it closely, taken aback, their fingers falling away from their rifle triggers. The stag sported a giant crest of ebony antlers. This creature was royalty amongst all other Blackhurst beasts. To think that such a magnificent creature had come from the Wald was unsettling. It'd feed their families for a time too long to pass up on. Talbot thought of keeping its raiment. His father would be awfully proud of such a great achievement, proud that his eldest son traced his footsteps into hunting.

Talbot watched the Blackhorn, Rupert too. The royal stag swivelled and twitched its floppy ears. Its large nostrils expelled hot steam. Glistening black eyes stared up to inspect the grassy hillock just ahead. Talbot lowered his head slightly. Rupert followed suit. Talbot counted each breath, managing a pant. He was caught in the thrill of the hunt, feeling the weight of the rifle fall perfectly into his palms. It was satisfying.

Talbot's trigger finger twitched with anticipation. This was it. It was now or never. Talbot tapped against the trigger, ready to fire. There came a roar. Not just a roar.

Howling.

*

Talbot was rocked from firing straight, triggering to shoot. The unexpected howl tore up the night air and carried out across Blackhurst and North Proctor beyond. It'd come from nothing. It'd come from the Wald. The hunting rifle flashed, temporarily robbing Talbot and Rupert of their vision. The ringing fed into the prolonged, animal whimper. All other noise was muffled and strained. The bullet echoed out and found nothing of its intended target.

The Blackhorn's head snapped up to attention. It reared itself from drinking and took off, darting away into a clearing in the fog. Smoke tethered itself to the rifle's mouth, trailing off. Talbot was blinking furiously, clearing his vision of muzzle glare and grey floaters. No time. He blew the smoke from his rifle with a quick puff of air. He struggled up from his stomach to his knees, crouching.

'Don't let it get away!' Talbot shouted, forsaking stealth. He tore a pouch and strained sooty gunpowder down the rifle's iron throat, readying another shot. It sounded with a flint-click. The ringing hadn't left his ears. His skull was still shaking, and his sight was starting to turn uncertain.

'I've got it,' Rupert returned. He crouched, lowering his own instrument. Rupert's eyes followed a shape in the fog. Then, he spotted a crown of antlers. The Blackhorn was galloping up towards a jutting rock formation. It was taken towards a sheltered nook. In spite of the stag's great size and heft, it was wondrously nimble, and elegant with its footwork.

Rupert focused. He tightened his grip and prepared for recoil. On an out-breath, he fired. He shut his eyes tight before the flash flooded them. He opened them a moment later to smoke and spark. And he listened to hear only terrible, wounded grunting. It was a true shot.

Just after, the injured stag struggled off into the hills. Rupert winced at its trail. The Blackhorn was headed towards the Wald for safety. It was too late for any of that. The Blackhorn would surely die from its wound. He was certain. It irked Rupert that the stag's death wasn't instant. No beast deserved to suffer.

The pair stood, patting themselves down of stalks, yellow gorse, and dead dander. Rupert reeled in his rifle and squinted out towards the Wald. It'd be unwise to pursue the stag into the old forest. However, the Blackhorn was marked for death no matter what now. If the hunters didn't track their game down, something else would. The wolf's bay supported that.

'You hit it?' Talbot questioned. Still, he was blinking hard and appeared unsteady.

'I hit it,' Rupert said.

If not for the formless howling, that godforsaken howling, the shot would've belonged to Talbot. It would have been his to bring home, skin, stuff, and mount in the town hall. That howl had robbed him of it.

'Where'd it get to?' Talbot continued, trying to stare out towards the sheltered nook.

'It took off,' Rupert started, 'went for the Wald.'

There was an awkward quiet. 'That howling,' Talbot spoke softly, 'a wolf, out here?' There was a strong hint of worry and confusion in the hunter's voice. Blackhurst's native wolf population rarely ventured out from the Wald's twisted treeline. They often waited for their food to come to them. Elk, hares, hunters.

Rupert shrugged. The howl hadn't sounded entirely wolfish in nature. Not any wolf that he'd thus far encountered in his hunting career.

'Forget the wolf,' Rupert said. 'That stag's as good as ours.' He turned, reaching out for Talbot's shoulder. He was shaking his head as if batting away a cloud of midges or flies. 'Are you okay? What's wrong?'

Rupert didn't require an answer. Not really. He could tell with one glance that his hunting partner was still reeling from the effects of a faulty shot. The glare still flashed in his eyes, the rifle's bark ringing through his ears and skull. 'You ought to head back to town.'

'I'm fine,' Talbot swatted Rupert's hand from his shoulder. 'I'm okay.'

'No,' Rupert said, 'you're not.' He fetched his rifle and a beaten satchel from the ground. Then, he slung it over his shoulder and started down the hillock into the fog. 'If you're that stubborn, then wait here a little while. I'll find the Blackhorn, meet me out there.'

'Meet you where?'

Rupert gestured with the snout of his rifle towards the Wald. The fog was thicker over that way. It only thinned out gently where the stag had passed through whilst retreating away. Talbot conceded. He nodded and fell down to a crouch, tucking his head between his knees. When next he lifted his eyes, Rupert vanished into the fog. He was gone. Gone for the Wald. He lay there, stiff. He clutched his father's old rifle tight and listened for howling.

Talbot heard nothing. Not until it was too late.

*

Rupert found and followed a trail of stag blood. There was little sign of the Blackhorn. It took the hunter a few minutes to trek the stag's route through Blackhurst's vast moorland. He followed stray rays of jade moonlight. For it was the only thing that lit his path further ahead. Not long thereafter, Rupert stopped at the foot of a gentle incline.

The flat turned upwards.

There, in front of him, was a gnarled and bent treeline with razor leaves and dark cones. Rupert stood facing the Wald. This was foolish. He'd half a mind to go back, return to town. However, the sight of congealing blood diamonds in the undergrowth confirmed his suspicion. The Blackhorn had fled into the old forest for safety. If Rupert was to find it and return its corpse to Blackhurst, he'd need to follow it in first. The notion of that unnerved him greatly.

Fog flowed out from between the tall trees. It was as if the Wald were breathing out. The vapour carried a light whisper and a harsh bite. Rupert inspected the treeline, up and down, left and right. There was no preferable point of entry. There were only thorns, twigs, bramble, and moss. Rupert gulped away his fret and felt it flower in his gut. He traipsed further up.

One foot fell after another. Rupert stepped foot into the Wald. The leafy canopy caught all rain; thus the forest floor was still rather dry. It crunched and snapped underfoot. Unfortunately, it caught the moonlight too. But for some rogue shafts shooting through, the forest was completely black, completely quiet. Anything lurking in the Wald would certainly hear Rupert's approach for yards and yards away. They would find him quickly.

There was nothing graceful about Rupert's trek through the evergreen thicket. Each foot fell carefully. There was thought and intent behind every step. There had to be, otherwise he'd soon find himself lost, prone, or tangled up. Lofty branches slapped out at the hunter as he progressed. Their leafage was rough and stung at his face with each swat. He felt pinecones, snail shells, and other crunchable commodities shatter through his footfalls. Yet, he couldn't see anything. The fog was up to his knees and his boots were gone from sight.

Rupert halted. Only for a moment. He studied the route forward, unsure if he was following the Blackhorn's path any longer. The trail of blood had vanished beneath the fog. Rupert shut his eyes tight and forced his wits into focus. His panting lightened. His hearing became keen. Rupert opened his eyes to assess what currently lay before and all around him.

A tangle of roots, thorns, and creeper vines felt up at the pines and evergreens. These trees were old, ancient even, there was no doubt. The ground was littered with clusters of purple wolfsbane and other misplaced, colourful flowers.

There was rustling too. Night birds and woodland critters peeked out and fled upon Rupert's turning to greet them face to face. The hoot of an owl could be heard up in the canopy. He looked for it. He looked to find its head turning and feathers ruffling. He looked for big eyes but found nothing.

Then, a ray of green moonlight lit up the route ahead. Rupert noticed a path. Though, truthfully, it was little more than a creaky archway of interlocked tree limbs forming a tunnel. Rupert huffed. Hot breath spilt out from his mouth and nostrils. The stag must've limped off through there. Where else could it have gotten to? The prospect irked Rupert. One wrong turning in the Wald, and he'd not return to Talbot, Blackhurst, or his family as was intended. It all came down to chance. No hunter had ever mapped the old forest successfully. The route ahead was the only one offering itself up to sight. That was that. Rupert continued forward.

*

Rupert started off with a stoop and a slow. He bent his lithe body over to move through the tunnel. Starting with what neared a crawl on his hands and knees. Something wet then. Rupert lifted his bare hand up from the undergrowth and found it slick with blood. That was it. His game had thought to escape this way.

Though, how it'd fit through the tunnel confused him.

After some time, Rupert's hunting instincts attuned to the forest's gloom. His night senses came to life. Now, he could see shapes clearly. The Wald's night often warped things that way. Something snapped behind him.

Rupert turned. There was nothing there. But it was clear that something was wandering around nearby. Badgers or hares, he hoped. The slightest sound saw the hunter teeter ever lighter on his toes, himself not wanting to interrupt the quiet. Further after, the quiet itself shut off. For an animal grunting filled the forest. It was the stag.

The transition out from the tunnel and into the forest's heart was stark. There was no short route out of the Wald for Rupert. Not anymore. Not if he'd urgently wanted to get out. All Rupert had with him now was his rifle and his wit. Both were worn out from years of use. The trees started thinning out. The fog was heavier and more concealing than before. It was there, stooped and slumped into its own great weight, where Rupert came across his trophy kill. The Blackhorn was not as he'd last seen it, not at all. Little of the stag was left.

Rupert came over towards the beast. It had been ravaged and thrashed at by some other hunter. No man could've inflicted such grievous wounds. Its stomach was torn open, guts out. Its hind legs peeled out like tanning hide, revealing layers of dripping, red flesh beneath. There were wounds to the stag's throat. Nothing of the roaring grunt remained. It only whimpered now. It was a wonder that the stag still lived. Not for long.

Rupert caught the agony in the creature's glistening eyes. The desire for it all to be over. Its chest barely rose with breath. Much of its body was already eaten up beneath the fog. Rupert lay crouched towards the stag. He lay a hand upon its head and shut its eyes gently. The beast complied, gratefully accepting its fate, willing to let go. With a slide of unsheathed steel and a sharp gasp of air, the Blackhorn was gone. Rupert wiped his long knife clean of the animal's blood and set it firmly to rest in its sheath.

Rupert lay low, tired. He patted the Blackhorn's corpse and felt at its great antlers. 'Poor thing,' he whispered to himself. 'What sort of creature did this to you?'

His answer came soon thereafter. It started with a fiery crackle. Rupert turned. Twigs were snapping. The hunter was no longer alone in the undergrowth. The Wald had sent unto him a visitor. It was a visitor to bid him welcome, and swift return.

Rupert stood up, slowly. No sudden movements. It was coming from the gnarled tree tunnel, the way he'd come through. Had something followed him into the Wald? What fool? Then, the thought occurred to him. Sickly saliva rushed to his mouth in concern. If the answer was not the one that he sought, then Rupert's troubles were only just beginning.

'Talbot,' he shot a whisper down that way, 'is that you?'

There was no reply. No words or warnings. Something was moving through the trees. Rupert could sense it. His heart was beating fast now, faster than ever. It threw itself against the cage of his ribs, begging for an escape. Then, a pair of eyes opened up in the darkness. Pale, yellow, and large. Rupert choked up with fear. Carefully, he took a step back, another.

He tensed up. Fight or Flight, the choice was his to make now or never again. He reached down to his waist to fetch his knife once more. His fingers stroked the copper pommel and worked down towards the hilt. Another snap, the thing was coming closer.

'God help me,' Rupert uttered, 'Christ.'

He readied to strike out. If this was to be his death, then he'd not go without a fight.

He started counting, timing.

The creature shot out from the treeline towards him and, in spite of his best efforts, Rupert found himself completely unawares and unprepared. It came by with a burst of colourful feathers. It crashed against his knees then trundled off with a frightened squawk, vanishing off into the trees. Rupert fell down, toppling over the ravaged corpse of the Blackhorn stag.

A pheasant, it was only a pheasant.

Rupert threw his head back in relief, staring up at the leaf ceiling. He grinned ruefully and started chuckling to himself, forgetting his whereabouts and the circumstances of his hunt. Rupert plucked a feather, brown and plum, out from his sage oilskin and flicked it away from him. A still breeze carried it off into the Wald. It settled somewhere in the fog with a touch.

Rupert turned over, knife in hand. No time to lose. He started carving at the stag's hide and carving out the antlers from their holster. They could be worked into pendants and tokens for the children back in Blackhurst. There was little harm in minor superstitions, after all. The stench that wafted up from the stag was awful. It reeked of an unclean death. What beast had savaged it after entering the Wald had clearly not done so thoughtfully.

Though, whilst skinning and carving, it left Rupert wondering. Why hadn't it finished the stag off? Why had it been both attacked and left here to rot in such a short time?

Then, it all went dark again. The moon above the Wald was eaten up yet again by clouds – stirred by changing winds. The rare rays streaming through the forest faded and everything disappeared with it. Rupert clutched his game by the antlers, tightening his grip. He reached down to his waist, tapping his pouch lightly. In his foolish rush to track down the beast, he'd forgotten his lantern and tinderboxes.

In an instant, the forest was not as it was before. It had changed. Things shifted, rustled, twisted, and gnarled. Branches curled like thrice-knuckled fingers. Crows coughed. Rupert felt a presence nearby. Though, he saw nothing further than a few feet in front of him. He stood up and looked around. Rupert listened for something, anything. Footsteps, creaking, or panting. He bit his lower lip. A passing moon ray illuminated the twisted tunnel. He caught sight of something. Not a pheasant. Not this time. What came now was far larger. It growled.

Rupert tried tracking its trail through the evergreens. He couldn't see. So he listened. Listened for falling pinecones where trees were disturbed. He listened for critters fleeing. There, he caught something. By the time he'd thought to study it, it was gone yet again. It sounded close, passing through with a strange, tearing noise.

Whatever it was, it was approaching. Feeling out what hunt lay ahead. It flared its nostrils and sniffed the air. Catching the scent of what naive prey had entered into the Wald. Tonight, its prey was named Rupert. He knew it. A grim acceptance started setting in then.

It rushed for him.

It slashed through the trees without form, only noise. The brunt force of its contact sent Rupert hurtling over. He turned halfway and veered on his ankle. Panic now, hard and fast. He didn't know which way was right or wrong. He squinted into the fog. The Blackhorn's body was gone, torn away by this new monster further into the trees. Rupert looked up, and something wet hit him square in the eye. The rain was returning. The canopy was emptying its reservoir to the forest floor, turning it treacherous and slippery.

The rain came then, not only from above but from below. Droplets of boiled ruby leaked out like bullets of dark rain. It was coming from Rupert, coming from his own body.

Rupert crawled away, rolling through sludge and coarse undergrowth. His hands were pricked at and stung by thorns and nettles. One of his boots was robbed from him, taken away by a slithering snakeroot. Rupert struggled up and started away. He couldn't run. Rather, he marched with a gait. He struggled off in the opposite direction to the creature hunting him down.

Crunching, wet and hard, sounded then. Heavy paws ground up ingredients of pinecone, acorn, and dead leaf. It was only too late, that Rupert noticed that the sound was coming from ahead. He stumbled over a split and hollow trunk. Beatles, ants, and slimy things scuttled free under his heft. Worms wriggled through the creases in Rupert's fingers. It was then that he understood he was oozing blood. There was an open wound, a horrific gash, across his abdomen. Thin and fat ribbons threatened to dangle out from his leather jerkin. Rupert had left a trail for the creature to follow.

It didn't need to. Rupert reached out to drag himself further through the undergrowth. His hand didn't find purchase on stone or soil. Instead, it found fur. He clutched a fistful. The fur was wiry and thick, thicker than anything he'd ever felt. This was not the Blackhorn.

Rupert lay still for a moment, grovelling. He looked to find what his hand had found. Planted there was a giant, lupine beast. Quadruped, muscular, covered with black-brown fur. This was not a wolf. Neither was it a dog nor a bear. This was a monster wearing animal skin.

Just as the old stories told, this was it, this was the Worg.

Rupert lifted his eyes to meet the beast. Those same pale eyes greeted him as before. Olive mist flowed from its tear ducts. The creature was alive with the very spirit of the Wald. Those eyes were as large and as colourful as the full North Proctor moon. Full as it was tonight. It licked, revealing its fangs, each one as long as a knife and the hue of dirty cream.

Rupert stared at it. It stood right in front of him. The creature glared back hungrily. Rupert let out a callow cry. He fell away and started running, knowing that the monster followed.

*

Rupert charged through the old forest under the moon's green glow. He was no longer the hunter. He was the hunted. He ran, paying no mind to his limp and the sharp things stabbing at his exposed, bootless foot. Rupert felt each footfall with a crunch that powdered ankle bone. Huffing, heaving, empty air tore through his teeth in a shroud of night.

Knotting and roping weeds tangled the ground beneath his feet, trying to ensnare him. He kept casting glances over his shoulder, then turning back to the unfamiliar route ahead. A crooked branch caught in his hair then, jerking his neck back with a fierce yank. Pricks and probes knotted up in clumpy lugs. Rupert tugged against the woody finger, freeing himself. He chanced to escape and a tuft of hair came free. Rupert grimaced and gasped in horror.

He was already breathless, short of wind. Salty tears welled up and sent trails down his dirty cheeks, cleaning them with streaks. A lupine call bayed from the trees behind him. It was gaining quicker still. It was the howl he'd heard with Talbot, out on Blackhurst's flat.

'Oh, God,' Rupert cried, 'oh, Jesus Christ!'

His words dwindled down into a rasp of innocent worry. He was starting to bawl and cry. He'd half a mind to curl up on the ground, foetal, with hopes that it'd leave him alone. It was his birthday soon. Nearly twenty-three, a grown man and hunter. Yet, there he was: lost in darkness, waiting for his parents. Rupert wanted to return to town, to his family, to know everything would be alright. He wanted to understand the confusion of what was happening. He longed to hear a voice affirming that all would be okay. Nobody was coming to save him.

There was nothing that could rescue him from the Wald. Barbed evergreen branches carved through his hands and drew further blood, hot and sticky. It wiped across green foliage as he ran. The forest lashed out at him with furious intent. Rupert turned again. He found a pair of eyes glinting in the black: pinpricks of lonely lime. He ran on into the knot.

Rupert's stricken stomach threatened to vomit. He could feel it swashing around his gut, mixing with pumping blood. His insides were now out. They were hot in the Wald's night air. He closed his fingers over the strings, holding them in tight. He was too frightened and adrenaline-fuelled for the pain to take hold of him just yet.

Therefore, he staggered further. He ran away from his pursuer, trailing gore. He couldn't stop. Though, he wanted nothing more. Rupert was starting to wane and slow. He'd lost a lot of blood and was feeling *wrong*. For a moment, he thought the creature had stopped following him. That or he'd started to lose his hearing too. Then, he understood. It was still there, following. It no longer needed to chase after him, or hunt him down. It stalked quietly, thoughtfully. It knew Rupert couldn't escape.

'Stop,' Rupert begged.

His voice was raspy, throat clogged with blood. Rupert chanced one quick turn, only one, to check for the Worg. It wasn't there, only trees, leaves; fog. The forest was swaying in the wind and rain. Figures formed in the fog like lost ghosts, floating. Rupert changed path. He couldn't feel his foot at all anymore. His guts, he could feel plenty. Quiet, complete quiet.

A growl.

Rupert dropped his guard. The truth dawned on him. The Worg was flanking him. It'd gone around, knowing the shortcuts and trodden paths of the Wald as no other animal could. It was taunting Rupert, toying with its food. This was hopeless. Rupert couldn't go any further. Lethargy was leeching at and tiring him. Rupert stopped still, looked up, and breathed out. That was the last pleasant breath to pass through his lungs.

Long claws flashed out, shockingly fast. Suddenly, Rupert was without a throat or tongue. His face lit up with untold pain, pain like white fire running through carves, streaks, and gashes. Rupert started to choke. His throat was open, though not deeply. It was a thin slit that wept red spittle. His face was ruined. Lips, tongue, nose – all ripped away and on the floor.

Rupert moaned loudly, for he couldn't cry out. Not any longer.

Rupert started to sway and stumble forward, away from the creature slaughtering him for food. His legs were anchored to the forest floor. He couldn't feel anything on his face except cool air and spouts of tangy, iron blood. Perhaps, he was already gone. Air slithered through his remaining teeth and forced itself out through his grinning throat. There was no agony. There was nothing, not really. No thoughts, no emotions, only acceptance of it all.

For the first time, the Wald thinned out. The hunted hunter waddled out into a clearing in the trees. At its heart, there sat a den. It was the barrow-mouth of a cave. It was sequestered through coverings of withered moss and lichen. The entrance of the rocky formation was jagged and pronounced. It was shaped like a wolf. This was it. Rupert had, rather conveniently, come to perish right in front of its lair. They'd never find his remains.

Rupert fell to wriggle through the forest floor. In his rain-polished coat, he looked like a slug bursting from its skin. Footsteps came from behind and above. Rupert didn't look. He couldn't bring himself to roll over. The Worg was standing right over him then. He could tell.

The reek of wet dog scented from behind – strong enough to catch with no nostrils to do so. He felt breath on his upturned collar.

Finally, moonlight. Ugly green rays lit up the Wald's glade, setting the stage for the grizzly event yet to come. Rupert's face was crumbling down onto the grass. He had no choice. He turned over onto his back. The Worg craned over him, back-lit by a full green moon.

Thick, viscous spittle sloshed from its teeth and further sweetened his wounds. It could taste Rupert's fear, his vulnerability. The taste was as intoxicating to it as fresh nectar. Rupert knew what was to come next. He was only grateful that he'd not feel any part of it.

Teeth like flat knives and shredding, crescent claws thrashed outwards, tearing Rupert apart. Piece by piece, he parted. Cloth ripped and oilskin sliced. Bones snapped through his skin into open fractures. Flesh ripped off in unnatural, flayed patches. The last things Rupert knew were fangs and howling. Howling that rang out across North Proctor for all to hear.

Rupert died alone in the Wald.

Eaten alive, thinking of home.

THE CATCH

It was the thirteenth of August, at the turn of the century, when Oldfaire flooded. Oldfaire was a quietly haunted place. A witch-cursed town that was subtle, fierce, and saturated with the tinge of rotten fish. It was a tight and cluttered place, dilapidated too. Its roofs were gambrel and sagging with slate eaves that shed rainwater into their runnels. Though, with the coming of the rain, the runnels were drowning.

The hour was late and the night had grown long by the time the investigator, Richard Reed, woke in his office. The tired radio was fried with static. The tunes that came out of it were strained and growling. Richard snorted, and then, he opened his eyes.

It was a trying thing, to wake up.

The office around him was black with gloom and quiet. All of the white candles had hissed out and only the foliate light of Richard's gaslight survived. Fog flowed in from the slack window and he breathed in its warmth and colour. Jungle light filled the office and ate up the carpet, drawers, and walls. Richard stared out the little window.

It was raining again. Always raining.

It had not stopped raining for six straight weeks. Oldfaire was underwater and its tall streetlights glowed in the depths like schools of anglerfish. Their lights lit the long and slippery silhouettes of the things that slithered in the water. They swam through the sunken streets of Oldfaire, fetching the corpses of drowned rats, seadogs, and cats. Richard did not know what they were. Nobody did. They had arrived with the rest of the rain and had crawled out of the storm drains when the flood was high enough.

Oldfaire officers were already evacuating the local population. Neither the flood nor rain showed any sign of letting up. The water level was rising every hour and the lights beneath were growing smaller. Soon, the flooded streets would be black and lightless. They all needed to be gone before then, Richard with them. There was no trial or error to be made against weather such as this. You could only flee. Flee or drown.

Richard stood and pushed his chair out with a scrape. He pushed the papers off from his desk with a sweep and watched them dampen against the sodden floorboards. The ink soaked in the dirty water and began to trail away. All of Richard's cases were already lost to the intrusive damp. The only investigation left on his agenda was this one. What had caused such a storm? What creatures were lurking in the water?

Richard fetched a flashlight and triggered it to life. When it faltered and flickered, he hit its head three times against the corner of his desk until it worked. He shone it about the room and then turned it off, fixing it to his waist. He grabbed the gaslight. It radiated a light and thin mist that was nearly as green as the water flooding up from below. The topographical maps on Richard's walls were wet too. Tears tore through their paper and peeled the material away like old wallpaper. His whole world was falling apart.

Watch light flashed through Richard's window from the building across the street. Another group of officers were shouting for him to gather his belongings and leave. Richard did not return anything to them. He did not have any belongings or keepsakes. They were either lost to time or to the flood. All he had now was his flashlight, his gaslight lantern, his wallet, and a packet of cigarettes.

He did not count the firearm under his coat.

That was a secret that he hoped never to share.

Richard took the key out from one of his desk drawers and shut it after. He took one last look around his office and thought for a moment about how many years he had wasted in such a place. It had robbed him of a family, and friends, of a life he had wanted to live. Richard took to the door and pushed it open. A steady rush of water flowed inside.

There would be more water coming. There would be more rain.

Richard turned the key until it turned no further. The door was locked. The office was shut away forever. And only the waters of Oldfaire's rain would find their way within. With that, Richard held the key out in front of him before dropping it into the shallows filling the corridor. He left his office and the building for the higher streets of Oldfaire and left his life and career behind him. Richard walked out into Oldfaire and disappeared. A ghost in rain.

*

Oldfaire's square was flooded too.

Therefore, the rest of its populace gathered along a steelwork bridge. There were too many of them on there for it to keep stable. However, the structure's stability played second fiddle to the drowning of Oldfaire's townsfolk in the waters below. There were one hundred of them, men, women, and children. For every ten, there was an officer frantically trying to maintain patience, protocol, and organization. There was little point in trying. The law was always usurped by people's will to live, after all. Control was an illusion, authority a lie.

Richard strutted from the far end of the bridge into the crowd. Worried mothers felt at his overcoat and tugged for him to process their leave first. Richard paid them no mind and made it towards a gathering of officers. Some were scratching their chins. Others clutched truncheons tightly. They were young and inexperienced. However, there were those of them who appeared old and capable enough to talk about the situation fully.

The crooning of the masses was drowned out by the coughing of grey seabirds overhead. They took out with dull wings over the flat flood to find a more appropriate home. They had the right idea, the seabirds. And Richard Reed longed to take away with them. Instead, he was brought to process and investigate the nature of Oldfaire's evacuation. Until that was figured, he would not be permitted to leave. He had to stay.

Richard started towards a younger gentleman he recognized from the officers. His name was Ryan Flynn. He stood just in front of Officer Marsh, who appeared completely detached from the situation. He was just staring out into the rain, across the flat flood. Flynn was small in frame and pale. His skin was polished with the rainwater that his flat cap could not keep off. He looked like the rest of them in Oldfaire. Those folk with large and flat noses, oval eyes, and that caught the whiff of dead fish. Richard held up a finger to catch Flynn's attention. Flynn nodded frantically and pushed through the sopping crowd towards him.

'Flynn,' Richard nodded. 'What's the news?'

'No news,' Flynn said. 'Too many people and not enough boats to take them all.'

'Not enough boats? We accounted for over thirty, what happened?'

Flynn turned and pointed over the bridge. Kayaks, skiffs, and other little trawlers were belly-up, splintered, or flooded. 'None of them kept in good enough condition, Mister Reed. We have a handful of kayaks and lifeboats left. But they'll only take two or three at a time. Let alone the rest of them.'

Richard scratched the stubble on his chin. 'I see.' He looked up into the stormy clouds and felt rain hit his face. He breathed out, exhausted. 'How long do you think we have?'

'Before what?' Flynn said.

'Before Oldfaire is underwater. Before *we* are underwater.'

Flynn shrugged and squinted. 'If it keeps on like this? Three hours? Maybe four?'

'That's not enough time to send for help,' Richard concluded.

'No, Sir.'

'What about Innsmouth or Kingsport, any word from either?'

'Nothing,' Flynn started, 'but if Oldfaire's getting this sort of rain, I dread to think.'

Richard turned and looked at the children shivering in oilskins behind him. They looked like cherubs in the rain with dark eyes and greasy hair. He could not look at them for long. He turned back to Flynn. 'Okay, Flynn,' Richard groaned. 'Find whatever you can.'

Richard walked away, past the officers fighting back and

threatening the careless and overly eager townsfolk. It would not be long before fighting broke out amongst them. Richard had seen it happen before. He found his way over to Officer Marsh. He was distant, a vacant and glazed look in his eyes. Those bulbous, pearly eyes.

And Richard thought he was uttering something.

Though, he could not translate what. Then, the other voices started. The crowd was chanting. Richard looked out across Blackwater, the great lake flanking Oldfaire. The fog was coming. The boats and crews out there would soon be lost. He turned to Flynn.

'Signal the lighthouse. Call everyone back, now!'

But Flynn was chanting too.

*

Floodlight spilt from Oldfaire's lighthouse.

It lit the great lake they called Blackwater. The waters were dark green, stained by mollusc ink. Eely tendrils slithered through the gloom. They were thin and slippery, the fingers of things under the water. Quay foghorns urged for the fishermen and frogmen to return to shore. The tinny toll of ship bells rang out in retort. Steamboats were starting to return home. Squat skiffs reeled in their trotlines, untangling their nets.

There was rarely a plentiful catch in Blackwater. The native fish were no larger than the leeches that lured them to hook. The great lake was empty. It slept in a fugue state. The black clouds fell lower, the squall settled, and the rain tempered. Thick fog threatened the outlook a few lengths away. Further off, the world was soft and featureless. It would not be created until the afternoon clearing. That was the way of things in Oldfaire, at the weather's mercy.

The fog wafted nearer still. Swallowing reefed watercrafts and crag-stranded wreckages. There were plenty of those. You could track your route by the age and condition of the wrecks and their relics. Splintered skiffs, ruined steamships, and more.

The canoes stranded there were narrow. They had not rowed far from Oldfaire. The tugboats chugged white smoke, those that had ventured too far into the Blackwater fief.

Far out, THE CONFLUENCE teetered on fretful tides. The trawler's crew stood in fish guts and filmy, white offal. The stench was rotten like foul quail eggs. The crew waded through the entrails. Their oilskins glinted with rainwater and sea foam. Itchy salt air tainted the breeze. From the aft and stern, they stared out towards Oldfaire. The tall lighthouse flared at its centre, the shanty town glimmering with nightlife.

The wharf was a smoggy silhouette. It had fisheries, rookeries, steelworks, foundries, and cast iron gaslights. The steelworkers often visited the harbour's bars. They fought nonstop with the sailors and with each other. The shatter of thrown bottles and fists filled the waterfront quiet. It was nothing startling. Nothing in Oldfaire was fresh, least of all the water. Therefore, the local salt beards took to drinking sharp alcohol instead.

The graze of grey barnacles had been unkind to THE CONFLUENCE. The trawler looked afflicted and ill. Its hull groaned from overwork and the latticework was fettered from wear. Soon, the crew would require a fresh net. Though, once more, there was nothing fresh in Oldfaire. Nothing worth catching, anyway. What little freshness remained would later spoil in the Blackwater juices. The crew gathered at the starboard side of their trawler.

They had stopped talking. They had stopped reeling.

'What's this?' Skipper questioned, calling out from the wheelhouse. Skipper was a clay toad with bulging, pale eyes. He was fat and sallow, like his very own grub bait. There was not a strand of hair on his smooth skull. That was why he covered it with a fiddler cap.

'You don't 'ear that foghorn? That wants that we get going.'

'C-can't, s-Sir.' The stutterer tried. 'N-n-nets are caught. S-something's s-stuck down there.'

The wheelhouse latch turned. Skipper strolled out into the open air, retching at the oily funk. 'Stuck?' Skipper clutched the railings and brought a tattered cloth to his nostrils. He flashed a handheld floodlight into the water. It illuminated nothing. 'Stuck on what?'

'Won't know,' another continued. 'Got us planted good though. Tried tugging, can't be light, whatever it is.'

Skipper gnawed on a roll of stress relief, thinking. To call it "King's Leaf" or "Kingfisher" could bring trouble from the authorities. Yet, there were many contraband goods traded in Oldfaire. These goods averted their attention, for the right price. And the officers were preoccupied, it appeared. Skipper turned to his first mate, Reeves. 'Got any thoughts?'

'Aye, one or the other,' Reeves replied, scratching his chin. 'ONE, you shout for a tow whilst us lot figure out a tip for the Lucky Larry who comes rowing.' There was a grumble of complaints from the rest of the crew. They grabbed their pockets, stinting. 'But, they're all off our chart, or cruising home for the night, can't see 'em turning 'round.'

'An' the other?' Skipper tagged.

'The OTHER is one of us goes for a little sink, takes a look.' There was no outcry from the crew. They stayed quiet. Reeves rolled his tired eyes. 'That's what I thought.'

'That's that then.' Skipper settled.

'Aye,' Reeves cast off his oilskin. He peered down into Blackwater. 'That's that.'

*

'Three minutes.'

Reeves slugged across THE CONFLUENCE. He felt too slow, too sloth. Turning slightly demanded effort. After a night of reeling without reward, he could not do it. The diving suit was a relic. The material folded like thickset cattle skin. A fastened corselet constricted the throat and collar. It was already waterlogged from sea spray and dank intrusions. It held Reeves's skull still for the lowering bonnet. They were worn cobalt and gunmetal, with weed green verdigris. The diving suit was too tight, too airless. If Reeves were to suffocate or sink into a watery grave, then his final moments would be filled with fear.

The moon lurked behind the clouds. Oldfaire twinkled far away. Blackwater grew darker, a turquoise soup. The crew's faltering flashlights shot to ripples that layered like coiling serpents. In the Blackwater fathoms, fish were the least of a fisherman's worries.

'You 'ear that, lad?'

The words were Skipper's. A fractured wrist-clock ticked across his gloved fingers. He squinted at it and listened for it. 'Three minutes, all you got 'fore we hoist you up.'

'Aye, Skipper,' Reeves uttered, 'ready on the line.'

The first mate was trying to steady his frantic breathing. It was harder to do in the cold. Precious breath slipped from his lips like kettle steam, lost amongst Blackwater's fog.

'Listen 'ere. One tug on the line's half-a-fathom's slack. Two's a kink or problem with the wire. Three, we hoist you up. If Blackwater floods your suit, you'll be a whale to lift. Cold will take your lungs out, don't fret. Won't pray for you, son. God's only up 'ere, with us lot, not down there. In Blackwater, there's only Leviathan.'

The crew were staring. They cut gaunt faces. Then, the stutterer, 'R-ready, Reeves?'

There was no turning away now. After all, this had been his "other thought". Without a volunteer, *THE CONFLUENCE* would be stranded out on Blackwater. They would tarry until the late afternoon. The trawler may have been found and towed home to Oldfaire. The crew might not. That was the way of the great lake. That was the way of the fog. People vanished when left alone on the waters. They became ghosts.

'Yes,' Reeves forced, 'I'm ready.'

The vintage diving helmet turned on the collar, rotating to lock. It was watertight and rigid. Flaking coral and crusted limpets clung to and felt at the faceplate. The grill caught Reeves's breath. It steamed temporarily, flowing through the tube attached to the top of his spine. If the crew wished him anything, he did not hear them. If they gestured, it was not caught. Only one thing repeated. The thought of what lurked in Blackwater.

What skulked underneath the surface?

No. Reeves tried to concentrate. Freeing the trawler, that was all. Focus.

Focus.

A hooked crane lifted Reeves off from THE CONFLUENCE. The jangle of angling wires and chains rattled through the night. They fed Reeves the crane line and attached it to his suit. Teasing tension, they lowered his bulk into the gloom. Without rush, Reeves vanished into the water. All that remained were ripples troubling the lake's stillness. The grim echo of where Reeves had sunk. The crew watched Reeves go. He was eaten up by the great lake.

At first, there were only bubbles. They frothed, obscuring Reeves' vision completely. They cleared. Submerged, Reeves floated through nothing. In an instant, Blackwater rushed to infiltrate his suit. It felt him like a parasite feeling for an orifice, finding none. Reeves fought to control his limited supply of oxygen.

Reeves could feel the current, the undertow. It tugged him further, quicker than he had thought to fall. It would spit him out far from his crew. Or carry him off to some black lagoon or forgotten cove. Reeves clutched the line tight. The watery world oozed terror. This was a world without air, without light. He looked up. He only noticed the twisted shine of *THE CONFLUENCE* and its gnarled underbelly. There, he dangled, bait in hungry waters.

One tug, half-a-fathom's slack.

The line let out further and something slithered by silently.

Reeves continued, following the wire until he saw nothing at all. However, there was something in the thick water that told Reeves that he was not truly alone. That there was something else, watching, waiting; stalking.

Only too late, Reeves witnessed what followed.

*

Something shifted the water's current.

Reeves floated weightlessly down through the Blackwater gloom. He felt the urgent tug of shifting water. It was lugging his diving suit towards the surface. And then, down.

Something was starting to tug Reeves down into darker depths. It was further than *THE CONFLUENCE'S* line could afford.

Three minutes.

How much longer was left? Two minutes? Half that? Reeves did not know. Time was starting to move strangely in the waters. He was lost amongst tides of time and space. Though, out there, Reeves knew that he was not alone. Just as Skipper guaranteed.

Reeves could feel eyes on him. The diver veered his giant, optical head. It turned as a desk globe spins languidly on its axis. There was nothing at all. No sight. No sound. Thus, Reeves started feeling his way forward. The line attached to his nape and waist was thin in his deep-sea gauntlets. It whistled through his fingers. If not for several layers of repellent leather, the line would have torn his fingers.

The line flew through his fingers and then snagged taught. Reeves stared out ahead of him, fighting the current. He pulled himself closer. The faltering light lit up the catch.

There, sunk and shattered: the remnants of a very old fishing tanker. The ruined vessel was ruptured. A great injury had hurt its wooden stomach. It was caused by something rather large. This allowed the Blackwater to rush in and make her sick. It brought her low to the sharp rocks in the water. Barnacles and tangled weeds were running across the ship's belly. Across its belly, there was a series of claw marks. They were no larger than a normal man's.

No. Not a man's. Not here in Blackwater.

In an instant, Reeves knew there would not have ever been any survivors from such wreckages. They would have all drowned. Blackwater would have filled up their throats and guts. Reeves shut his eyes momentarily. He gathered himself. Reeves did not wait for long.

Time was short. Soon he would feel the tug of *THE CONFLUENCE* and break for the surface. There was only so much air left. Panicking would only use up the remaining supply quickly. It would go faster than an actual break to the mechanisms.

Reeves counted his breaths.

One... two... three...

He could hear the breaths passing through his suit. Oxygen bubbles danced up and away from his round visor and took off up towards the surface. The bubbles cleared and Reeves saw something. There, peeking from behind THE CONFLUENCE'S rock-snagged fishing nets. Reeves noticed a pair of bulbous, bright eyes glinting in the darkness.

Reeves turned about and got roped up with the remaining slack the line could offer. Now, there was panic. He was upturned and rolling in the current. He only caught glimpses of the eyes in the water and the long ridge of fins on the creature's spine. A long creature, thrice as tall as a man with turquoise scales, webbed paddlers, sharp teeth, and gills.

What was that thing? Was it coming close?

There were too many questions for too little time. The air in the suit was thinning out. There was no time left to cut THE CONFLUENCE free. Skipper and the rest of the crew would have to forsake their fishing nets and lines entirely. Nothing was worth staying down here with that thing to drown, or worse, nothing.

Reeves turned and started following the line back towards the surface. Blackwater was trying to hold onto him now. Its current would not allow him to leave. A ticking noise filled the suit and Reeves' time was coming to a close. He could feel the line being heaved from the surface and the ship. He knew the crew were also struggling against the current.

Reeves' vision was failing now. It was filled with white floaters, black spots, and stars. It was only with the last few breaths that Reeves came to realize there were no stars in dark Blackwater. There were only eyes. They were everywhere. Hundreds of them!

The line was cut.

Reeves floated there, alone in the depths. He knew only fear. The olive eyes of the catch floated out towards Reeves. Blackwater ate up his screams. The crew of THE CONFLUENCE freed their tethering line. Reeves – first mate of *THE CONFLUENCE* – was gone. The Blackwater flood had taken him. The children of Leviathan feasted.

To the chanting, their father woke.

THE WITCH GIRL

The witch girl's eyes were shut. She was squinting so hard they almost trickled crimson tears.

She could not remember why she was there. Or what foul act she had committed to warrant it. The girl felt at her lips. Her mouth was sewn shut. A rope of frayed string was tied around her skull. It looped from the bottom of her chin where it had been sewn into her flesh. From there, it ran up her face, over her clean-shaven head, and connected to the other rope in a tight and painful knot. She had been found guilty. Her crime: witchcraft.

She was small of frame, gaunt. She lay still, nearly trembling from the cold. The smock that covered her face sunk in with each nasal breath. The gloom in the cell was complete.

There she sat, central to the cell, chained to the floor. The witch girl's little hands were clasped behind her back in prayer. Her fingers were tied with thorny cords in looping knots. They were bleeding her. The odour of blood filled the room.

In the quiet, there was little other to listen for than the dripping of unclean water and the scuttering of rats. The witch girl listened for their squeaking and nattering.

From outside the cell, other people could be heard groaning, shrieking, and crying in random conversation. They were terrifying. They were insane. Someone was cursing God. Others wept tears of joy for their curses.

The witch girl wept cold tears. They ran down her face as she struggled to talk. To call out for help as the stitches shutting her mouth stung with pain. From down the corridor, she could hear authoritative voices speaking primly. For a slight moment, the witch girl dared to hope.

She listened intently. The voices were growing louder. Someone was coming her way, to her cell. She heard the stamp of iron-soled shoes as they drew nearer. Her feeble and young heart hoped against anything that someone was coming to find her.

To rescue her from this nightmare.

She tried to scream. Only whistles of pain escaped her tethered mouth. The stitches granted pain like nothing else. Ripping. Flensing. Tearing. She was robbed of everything.

Then, there came a voice.

'If you wish to be fed, I must remove your stitches.'

The voice struck the witch girl. It carried authority. And yet, it was as soft and fatherly. Tears rushed from her eyes. Frantic fear overwhelmed her for what lay ahead.

The man continued talking.

'If you try to speak, or whisper your witchery into our ears, then my friend here will take your tongue. Talk again, and he will take your eyes. You will wander your beloved underworld blind, deaf, and dumb. Shake your chains if you can hear me.'

The witch girl rattled her black chains. Then, she felt a gloved hand grab her chin tightly in its grip. The dark steel of a knife sliced through her lip-stitches and crumbled congealed blood.

The man spoon-fed her.

The witch girl felt her strength returning. With it, the memories of a happier life that had not long ago been hers.

'You are a witch. This black cell is where you will live out the rest of your pathetic life, unless you wish to confess to us the nature of your sins.'

The man fed the girl another spoonful of revolting mulch.

The witch girl started to give voice to a question. She was interrupted by the chill of a blade edge against her throat. She shook violently with renewed fear. Then, she felt out with her thoughts. She sensed the malice behind her capturer's eyes. Old memories flooded her, those of pain, torment, and family.

The fear of the man behind her was intoxicating, filling the gloomy cell.

The smell of it was like that of blood. It was the blood of her mother, father and brothers. Those that had been put to torch and stake for concealing her from the authorities. The men they called the Black Adders. The townsfolk chanted around their sacrifice as though partaking in the flesh of her burning family.

The witch girl grinned. She recounted how she had taken revenge upon the townsfolk. That had led her here, no doubt. But it had been worth it. She smiled and opened her eyes for the first time in the dark room. She looked into the face of the man standing in front of her.

The man's face turned white with fright. Within the girl's thoughts, she was comfortable at home, standing in the fleshy ruin of the townsfolk who had executed her family. The witch girl's hatred of them filled up within her breast and sunk into her bones.

And then, she wailed.

The man began to convulse. He squealed and fell to the ground. One by one, the Black Adders' frail bodies began to contort outside the cell. Their intestines traded places with their fingers and genitalia. Bones splintered into mushy paste. Milky eyes burst in their sockets. Brain matter blew out from shattered skulls.

The witch girl reached and fetched the key from the man's belt. She unshackled herself. She waltzed around the trail of corpses whilst the man twisted and turned on the flagstone floor. The witch girl twirled, splashing through their blood puddles. Their guts and intestines slithered between her cold toes. The witch girl was ankle-high in vengeance.

Outside, Black Adders and townsfolk alike collapsed on broken legs. With a flick of her little wrist, others burst into emerald flame. Their flesh alighted like her parents' pyres and lit the cold, empty night.

The man in her cell had stopped moving. He still twitched, once or twice. Though, other than for what little clothing remained to him, he was no longer a man of authority. His smooth body was pink and wet. A new dripping filled the dark, dank cell. He was stripped bare of all flesh from his face and torso. The witch girl left him his eyelids. He could keep those. Then, she knelt down to him. He could not talk. No matter.

That did not stop her. The witch girl plucked free a long string of stitches from his waist.

She grinned before sharpening her nail and sewing his mouth shut. He would never tell any lie. Then again, no lie was ever told.

The witch girl threaded his lips together. She left him alone, skinless, shackled, and sutured on the cell floor. Though, he was not alone. There were still the rats, hungry rats.

The witch girl walked free of her cell and into the night. She started for the Black Forest.

Into the woods.

SUTURES

The first patient had been rotting for hours.

Fletcher caught the thread through the skin. Foul blood trickled off from the operating table. It frothed and foamed like corrupt algae. It trickled across the table and floor in trickling runnels. All that was left was its black-brown stain. That was all that ever remained where bodies once lay. Filth, dirt, grime. Not to mention the clustered tangles of matted hair and organ linens. It took thirteen minutes to cleanse and scrub the table. Then, the surface was clear again. Only then did they take the sutured corpse away.

'Another, quite gone, this one can go too.'

Fletcher did not utter the words to anyone specific. The coated figures at the doorway quietly prompted the other to take the corpse away. Wheel it off on a rolling platform. The cut across the boy's throat left little argument for the cause of death. Young gentlemen got into quite a lot of trouble in the streets beyond the cellar. Though, it was no safer down there.

Fletcher quickly shuffled onto the next boy, nestled up in his cot. The table and sheets were sopping with sweat. This one was still alive. Though, for how long, Fletcher was yet to determine. That was the fun part.

Lots of strange people came and went from the coroner's office upstairs. Fletcher could hear their footsteps through the floorboards. If only they had known the truth. You never quite knew what's going on above or around you. That part was true. Yet, nobody ever spoke of what occurred beneath their feet. They gave no thought to it.

That suited Fletcher rather well. Any guild of doctors who found out his true nature down here would likely lock him away for good. He would not see the world again but through iron bars. Of that, Fletcher wanted nothing.

*

There was a credit to be found in this sort of underground work.

You could sell certain organs and limbs to the local medical cults. Though, you would need to know how to use a bone saw and keep witnesses quiet. That was what all of those learned communities were, in truth: cults. They wanted to know how the body worked. They needed all the right bits to conduct their studies. Fletcher could make a fine living by providing them with such instruments. He knew how to use all his tools: the saw, the knife, the needle, the thread.

Fletcher fingered his radio to record, 'Thirteen hours, four minutes, another terrible shame.' A rare burst of static and a quick click ended the recording again.

Another boy, older now, stared up at Fletcher from a table across the cellar. This one had been waiting for a long time before being seen to for his stitches and advice from the man with the thread. Fletcher continued towards him, carefully snorting the thick cellar air.

The patient's eyes grew large with relief. He saw the caduceus loosely patched onto Fletcher's dark green coat. In truth, Fletcher had all but forgotten the presence of the talisman. It meant very little to him now. If anything, it was worn out of sheer irony. A product of black humour and grim nostalgia. The young boy reached out for Fletcher. He felt with trembling fingers, wafting unclean air.

'Wait,' Fletcher gestured to the figures behind him. They stepped back, allowing the boy some room. The boy was clutching at his collar with his free hand. The limb was poorly sutured. It was black with spilt blood and gutter filth. 'That needs to go, boy. Let me see it.' The boy did not allow him in any closer. Fletcher insisted when next he spoke. 'Listen, boy, I cannot help you if you don't let me look at it. Let me help you. Or would you rather I left you to suffer?'

The boy did not speak at first. His lips were quivering. Though, he let Fletcher in after.

A pair of ropey plugs was stuffed to fill Fletcher's nostrils. The stench in the cellar was not rank. It was far, far worse than that. The figures covered their faces with handkerchiefs. They did so for anonymity and health reasons. The smell of sewage could not cover the stench. It could only cover the sight that caused it. Fletcher had since grown used to the reek.

*

The man with the thread.

That was what they called him. Fletcher was a ghost in the city. People who knew the surgeon's techniques often desperately sought his care. He was an angel for the injured and a reaper for others. The knife angel. That was another name. Fletcher enjoyed that one.

He raised the knives high to the lamplight. They twinkled under its glare. Thoughts flooded Fletcher's brain with this boy before him. Was it worth it? Could he get away with it? The thoughts faded as quickly as they had sprouted.

Fletcher cut through the arm's trappings. He investigated the source of the boy's ailments first-hand. The cloth had been wrapped too tight out of panic and circumstance. They were nearly too tough to cut through without snipping one of the boy's veins in the course of it. At least the other boy's corpse was easily sutured, easily fixed. Granted, there was little complaint from the patient in that regard. That boy had died quietly. Nothing to complain for.

Fletcher cut through the trapping. Instantly, he noticed something familiar. Fletcher recognized this one all too well. The boy had been to his cellar before. Fletcher did not know the names, never the names, but he knew their parts. He knew what was right and wrong with them. Fletcher never forgot a good suture. Especially on the ones that got away. He did not donate them without consent to a medical practice. That would have been a waste.

Fletcher recognized his signature stitchwork running up the boy's collar. It had been an open fracture some years ago. An awful sight, that much was true. Though, it was not a wound serious enough to justify taking the boy's life.

This one had a family. If he were to vanish without a trace, that would raise questions. It would provoke an investigation. Fletcher could not afford the risk and had let the boy escape with his life. It would be too taxing to cover up. But the thread of his needle would stay with the boy, forever and always.

The boy was young, sixteen or seventeen. He was not yet a fully-grown man, far from the set standard. This one had been roughed up by thugs in one of the city's ill-lit alleys for the contents of his wallet. An unfortunate occurrence, yes, but nothing Fletcher was not growing accustomed to. It was turning out to be quite the common affair.

'Let's have a look at it. You're lucky my friends found you in that street and brought you to me.' Fletcher spoke gently to the teen boy. The two dark figures giggled behind him.

Fletcher did not want to startle his patient and potential victim any further. One ill-timed shriek and it would all be over. Fletcher's world would unravel. There was nothing in that outcome that Fletcher found interesting. The surgeon would have to start over if not caught. He could do it. He could restart. Stitch his world back together piece by piece.

Thread by thread.

Fletcher grunted with effort. He was cutting through the tightly wrapped cloth on the boy's injured arm. Whatever lay underneath was thick and crusty like a gritty scab. The effort of cutting through was taxing even for Fletcher, a lifelong knifeman. Finally, the trapping tore free. What it revealed repulsed Fletcher and the rest of the room to no end.

*

'God,' Fletcher whispered.

This was just starting to get interesting. The instant he peeled the veil of bandages away from the flesh, Fletcher knew the boy would not live. The stench of the injury to his arm was terrible. It was rank, rancid. Rot had gotten its way into the flesh of his limb and was travelling quicker than originally thought. This was a uniform infection. Fletcher took a step away. The boy's face was a reflection of Fletcher's fear. There was no saving this one.

However, every cloud has its silver lining. Fletcher's silver lining simply lay in the fine edge of his scalpel, needle, and thread. This one would fetch quite the pretty penny with the local bookers and sawbones.

'Please, Sir,' the young boy croaked like a frog.

'I cannot help you, boy, I'm sorry, I cannot.' Fletcher came in close.

His gentle grin was shadowed by the surgical mask slipping over his nostrils yet again. He retrieved a razor blade so sharp that the boy would not know that he had been cut. At least not right away. The last thing the patient knew in the darkness of Fletcher's cellar was the glint of a knife. He also heard the zip of stitches latticing his flesh.

Fletcher would construct another suit full of sutures.

ELIZABETH'S LAKE

There was something in the water at Elizabeth's Lake.

1972. The school holidays had come. With it, a young family started on another camping trip. They were headed to a familiar place, a remote location in the North Wales hills. The family had little wealth, though they lived comfortably. After all, a true holiday was crafted from the enjoyment of each other's company and character.

The mother, Alice, acted as secretary for the local primary school. Her husband was John. John was a civil servant for the village council. He had been since his early twenties. Then, there was the girl. Her name was Elizabeth.

Elizabeth: twelve years old, full of intrigue, trouble, life, and curiosity.

She was fair-headed – mousy blonde – with rosy cheeks. Her cheeks were shaded by too many hours spent playing out in the new summer sun.

Elizabeth's family had set up camp in the corner of a lightly sloping field. The tents stood in sight of a far-off farmhouse over the ridge. Arthur, a farmer and old family friend, had agreed to let them stay for the duration of their trip. Partly, it was because many years had passed since he had seen the family. They suspected it was also a test before turning the site into a residential campsite.

Alongside their little tent there ran a gentle stream. Alice and John were aware that the rush trickled down to a lake. It rested about a quarter of a mile away. However, they had never once visited the lake. There was something about the water that felt OFF.

The walk there was short. Roughly twenty-five minutes over soft grass and tree-lined riverbanks. After a few minutes, John halted in his tracks. He was staring closely at a torn, fragmented map. He traced a gloved finger down across the sketched trail and scratched his chin. He turned to his daughter, calling out in gleeful surprise.

'Liz, you'll never guess what,' John started. 'The lake, it's called Elizabeth, how funny! Did you know that, Alice?'

'Really?' Alice replied. 'How odd, I never knew that after all these years. Arthur never once mentioned it, funny.'

Elizabeth appeared completely unbothered by the discovery. What was in a name that compared to the sight it applied to? She wanted to get there even quicker now. Throughout the rest of their trek, the family did not pass a soul in the wilderness. They were alone amongst tweeting birds and small critters lurking in the undergrowth.

John congratulated himself for finding a secluded spot during the busy summer. However, he conceded that it was a rarity to not take lightly.

Soon after, the three of them came about a grassy knoll. There beyond it there lay a little lake. It was a balmy afternoon and everyone was starting to feel rather thirsty in the heat. Alice was certain that a family gathering and picnic would be a lovely treat. The sun was high in the sky, with rays of silver streaming down onto the water.

Elizabeth could not take her eyes off it. It was forcing her to squint and cast her cornflower eyes off to the side for a moment. Around the lake: beamy birch trees, heather, gorse, and thick vegetation. The lake was carved out in an oval. It was fed at one end by the source of the gentle stream they had followed down through the scenery. On the other side of the lake there lay a pretty, walkover stone bridge. On opposite sides of the water, the banks rose several feet on a steep gradient. The incline was darkened by more birch trees. They were sparsely rationed across the river's lip.

The valley created by such hillsides had formed a deep trench. It was a groove in the hills that had now become a sequestered lake. Walking over the small stone bridge, Elizabeth cast her eyes down across the water. Her hair was hazing with the aura of the back-lit sun. Her reflection waved off the water, caught amongst fish ripples and tiny waves. There was something in the water. She could see it.

Flashes of faint light glimmered beneath the surface.

'What's that, Dad?' Elizabeth shouted out. John came up behind his daughter and looked down towards where she was pointing in the water. Then, the lights broke the surface.

'They're brown trout, Liz,' he explained. 'They're only small. But some of them can be over twenty years old, you know.' Though, Elizabeth was not quite sure those were the lights she had just seen. Their scales were of a coppery hue. The lights had been silver.

The family crossed the bridge. They made their way around the lake to a place that Arthur had told them about. Just over the nook, there was a large stone, giant and flat. It had slipped down from the hillside many years ago, coming to rest just where the water met the bank. It was a stone table. Was it a table, or an altar? Arthur had mentioned it the night before with a strange lilt in his voice and a grin splitting his lips. More rocks littered the site. They were around the table like chairs, half-submerged in the water.

*

The three of them removed their footwear. They sat down at the great stone. Pebbles shifted under its weight. Alice started unpacking the picnic and they began devouring their dainty lunch together.

Elizabeth ate and drank. All the while she stared out across the water. She was thinking about and searching for the lights again. Instinctually, she caressed the stone table. Her three middle fingers fell naturally into three grooves in the side of the flat stone. Each one was about two inches in length and unnaturally rough compared to the rest of the smooth stone. The grooves in the stone were stained a harsh, gritty red.

Elizabeth found herself repeatedly stroking the three grooves in the stone. There, she contemplated her life and the many things that interested her and other girls her age. After a while, John spotted a figure enter the scene. It was an elderly woman walking an old dog – a doting black Labrador – across the far shore of the lake. She too came to cross the stony bridge and came around towards the gathering.

They exchanged greetings. She had been carrying an intricate walking stick in her right hand. It was crafted from whittled branches from the birch trees that surrounded the lake. She was a local woman. Alice and John figured as much from her accent and familiarity with her surroundings. She looked and sounded as if she had lived here, at this very lake, for much of her life.

They soon got to talking. 'Do you know why the lake is called Elizabeth's Lake?' John questioned. 'It doesn't sound much like a Welsh name if you don't mind my saying.'

'I do know,' the old woman said. Her voice was wise and full of flavour. She sat down with a creak beside Elizabeth and tapped the stone table with the pommel of her cane. The act caught the dog's attention. It came splashing over towards her. They assumed such warm water was pleasant for any arthritic animal.

'It's only ever been known as Elizabeth's Lake. Though, the true name is Llyn Elizabeth. Many years ago, a young woman from the village came down to the lake with her fiancé. They hoped to enjoy the tranquillity before he went away to war. I mean the First World War,' she remarked, pointing towards Elizabeth and then out across the water. 'The lovers spent many, many hours here during their courtship. This was their quiet place, their secret shelter. The woman's name, you see, was Elizabeth. Her fiancé was Robert. The two were later parted for eighteen long months. When he returned, it was in the softwood of a coffin. Robert had caught his death in the trenches, I'm afraid. Poor Elizabeth became inconsolable and distraught. Later, she vanished from the village without a trace. The locals gathered that she came here and drowned. She hoped to find Robert in the joy they once shared. Local superstition stated that any young girl standing alone on this stone table, if she casts a stone across to the far bank without touching the water, she will find eternal happiness.'

The old woman was tearful. John looked around guiltily. He had only hoped to make polite conversation with her. She was stroking the spine of her old dog, who was panting softly on her knee. Yet, the story had captivated Elizabeth. It had stoked the fires of her imagination entirely.

'What a sad story,' Alice commented. The old lady stood up slowly, plunging her walking stick down into the shallows. She stared at little Elizabeth for a few moments. Her wizened face was marred with a strange concern. Elizabeth looked elsewhere, uncomfortable. Her fingers still slipped through the stained grooves, unknowingly. They felt warmer.

*

The family spent the afternoon resting by the lake and skimming stones. They listened to the sounds of the trees. A cool wind blew through the valley. The sun began to sink behind grey clouds. The trout were jumping out of the water. They were trying to catch flies and skimmer bugs out of the air above the surface. Later, they found their way back to camp and settled down for the night.

In her slumber, Elizabeth could think of little else. She thought only of her namesake and the ill-fated Robert. The story of love that she had never yet known was lost to her. She felt sick at the thought of it, full of grief too. Once her parents had fallen asleep, she donned her coat and knee-high fishing waders. She slipped out from her sleeping bag and out into the night air. The young girl quietly gathered herself in the moonlight. Then, she started following her earlier tracks downstream towards her lake.

Elizabeth moved quickly. She made the journey in about fifteen minutes. This time, she did not have her mother and father to hold her up. Adrenaline coursed through her. The chilly air didn't bother her. She was wrapped up tight in thick, heavy clothing.

After that, Elizabeth reached the lake.

The little girl stood motionless for a moment at the bank. She was contemplating her next action. What could she do? Where should she look? What was here, what light flowered beneath the surface that she could no longer see?

Her eyes were growing accustomed to the night. Elizabeth could see all around the lakeside and the sparse copses beyond. There, close to the bank, she saw the stone table again. The grey colouration of the stone was in stark contrast to the moonlight. It shone down upon it, bathing it in golden-white light. The stone glinted, casting a reflection straight across the lake to a point a few feet in front of her.

Elizabeth's small heart was starting to pump furiously in her chest. Suddenly, she was realised she was completely alone. The excitement and adrenaline wore off. Fear set in. She started to walk towards the bridge, seeking to cross the lake. As she did so, she felt the gleaming shadow from the stone table follow her like a cloak.

The wind was starting to rush through the birch trees. The odd leaf skimmed towards Elizabeth's face as they blew past. She flinched when one sliced her cheek gently. Elizabeth covered her cheek and found it wet with her blood. The moon was passing over her head. It reflected her image across the undisturbed surface of the lake. There were no ripples tonight. The fish were gone from sight and the birds had stopped singing. Elizabeth stood alone amongst wind, water, wood, and stone.

She was afraid. Yet, she was completely entranced. Elizabeth was intent on completing the story. She wanted to cast a wish stone across the lake cleanly. Slowly, she made her way around the lake, taking care not to slip as she ventured closer to the water's edge. Finally, Elizabeth reached the stone table. She looked down at her feet. She kicked off her waders and leaned down, reaching her hand into the icy water. It was cooler than before.

Elizabeth felt for a small stone. She picked it out from the water, stood up, and assessed her finding. A pearly pebble. She placed a foot on one of the stone seats, stepping further up. The angle of the moonlight made the stony grooves visible once again. Elizabeth ran her fingers along them and wondered how old they were and how they had been made.

She was standing on the stone fully now. It was a clear night. Elizabeth looked up to the brilliant, star-filled sky. She gave out a short gasp as she witnessed the fleeting glimpse of a shooting star. It streaked across the sky, carrying her untold wish.

That was her moment, her sign. Elizabeth raised the white pebble in her hand. It had a curious, familiar glow in the moonlight, almost fluorescent. Elizabeth looked across the lake for a point that could be closest to her. She had not truly assessed the distance it was for a young girl of twelve. Finally, she chose her spot and reeled back her arm.

Elizabeth was squinting with determination. The moon beamed across her face. Her shoulder sprung tightly with effort. Her left arm was counterbalancing her on the stone table. She gritted her teeth and began to throw. As she moved, Elizabeth felt a heavy rumble beneath her feet. The shift shook her. A lone drop of blood slipped from her cheek into the grooves below. She jerked around. The pebble was still in her hand but she lost her balance. Something hard struck the table violently, creating a blue spark like flint on steel.

Elizabeth cracked her head as she fell. Her left hand reached out instinctively. Her fingers slowly slid down the grooves in the stone. They were warmer than before. Her frail body fell into the water with a quiet splash. She started to struggle. She was weighed down by the heft of her coat. It wrapped around her like crushing silk and dragged her further down.

Elizabeth floated, only for a moment. Then she sank. The moonlight slowly fell away.

Elizabeth was gone, disappeared into the quiet lake.

The moon shone.

The lake went still.

*

They never found her little body.

Divers in frog helmets searched the lake for weeks. The search was fruitless. Elizabeth's distraught parents moved to the area, hoping to be closer to her, wherever that was. Twenty years later. It was another summer, another holiday. Another family sat down at the stone table and wet their toes in its depths.

Mother. Father. Daughter.

The girl stared out across the still lake. Her fingers fell naturally into four grooves. The father – reading his map – looked up quickly and leaned over towards his daughter.

'Look, Elizabeth. This lake has your name too...'

WILD THINGS

A stiff wind took over a tangle of bogs, little streams, and forests. Rattling stick figures turned and twisted. They gestured their fingers at the dark crows that nested up in the trees. They were returning home for the night. It was closing in over the plantation where the tall and wooden gates creaked and opened.

Chill air whistled through carrying thistledown and autumn leaves. There was a smoky scent clinging to the air like moss to a wet stone. In the courthouse, a quiet gathering was seated on splintered benches and church pews. A tall man stood at the front of them wearing farm cloth and a grim expression. He gripped a pointy hat against his chest with both hands, fingers tapping, fidgeting. Work was worn into his features.

Nothing of worry was communicated to the tribunal looming in front of him. They were robed in black. The rest of the gathering wore brown. They stared down at him from elevated chairs, their eyes empty under wide-brimmed hats. A lifeless authority lingered in those eyes.

The Black Adders.

'Arthur Warren,' the first intoned. The name echoed through the cold and crowded courthouse. 'You understand your charges. You stand accused of conceit, taking it upon yourself to stain the word of God in front of his children. You have tarnished the respect and reputation of your brothers and sisters in this wilderness.'

Arthur's eyes flicked over the assembled faces. All of them frightened, judging, sorrowful. His family waited there next to him. Arthur's wife, Caitlin, clutched their newborn boy against her chest. Her face was ill and spelt out guilt.

Their other four children huddled together at her waist: two boys, two girls, a twin a piece. Their eyes fluttered with confusion.

'Your words of God are not those that were spoken of to me,' Arthur growled, 'or my family.' A rustle of whispers filled the room until the first tribunal lifted his hand. The courthouse gathering went quiet again after that. 'Rather you cast us out into the wild than inflict on us your pretence and falsities.'

The tribunal traded glares. The whispers came again and then trailed off like falling leaves. The first of them thudded his lectern and tried to stand. He grunted to clear his throat. Then, 'Arthur Warren, henceforth are you and your family trespassed from our plantation. Take out to the trees and wilderness, and let *your* God go with you.'

The first tribunal sat again. 'You must go at once.'

A foul quiet filled the room. It was only interrupted by the soft cry of Arthur's youngest. He wept in his mother's arms. She wiped the corners of his eyes with his torn and rugged cloth. Caitlin stood beside her husband true. Arthur fixed his hat atop his head and turned off to leave. The doors to the courthouse groaned and folded out.

The last, pale light of afternoon flooded in.

The Warren family took to their wagon and loaded their life in with them. Untamed, tangled wilderness quilted the world beyond the plantation walls. A vast and unforgiving forest stood still. Without another word, Arthur gathered his family. They travelled forlornly, wheeling out from their relative safety and into nothing at all. The plantation gates croaked shut, watched them go. Wilderness waited.

Their wagon rolled into the twilight. Until, eventually, the trees ate them up and they were gone without path or trail. The twisting woodland crossed and hatched over and around them. The faint sunlight faded. The air was given to thrum with a black and hurtful intent. The wind went the other way. Mother Nature would not follow them wherever they were going. The trees watched, waiting. The Warren family trailed where neither their God nor another's could find them, into the woods.

*

Time went by with a crawl.

The Warren family wheeled and crunched through tightly packed trees and over wet undergrowth filled with wriggling white worms. Dusk blurred into dawn and grey afternoons after another. Further into the woods and the hills, the air turned less smoky. Civilization was gone out there. It never existed and was never meant to. Rather, the air carried the odour of rot and flesh turned earth. Further on, they reached a quaint and quiet clearing. It sat at the face of giant and festering woodland filled with wild things. The trees there were ancient.

Their gnarled and ropey roots twisted out from the earth like sprouting fingers or interlaced serpents. A thin mist flowed over the ground and felt at those woods. It coiled around the Warren family's ankles as they halted their wagon and stepped foot into the clearing. In the heights, crows talked and the sky was a single falling cloud. It was grey and wilting fog. But it was empty out there. It was lonely, too.

'This, then,' Arthur whispered to himself, 'this will be our home.' His eyes settled where the trees parted, at a rootless patch that appeared less hostile than the others.

Caitlin slipped to his left. She was teary-eyed and tired, her spirit worn. Their newborn boy, Timothy, nestled into her chest. He let out a little, fitful whimper. The other children were called Tabitha, Jacob, and the twins, Faith and Freddy. They stood together, hand-in-hand, watching the forest. Their faces paled at the sight of tunnels of twigs and trees before turning back to their parents, to the clearing. Yet, none spoke of the quiet terror or tension crawling in their throats or sitting in their hearts. An unforgiving way of life lay ahead for the Warren children. There was no turning back to the plantation now, then.

'Come, children,' Caitlin said. 'Let us make room to unpack. Jacob, you will help your father.'

Jacob, the oldest of the three boys, nodded. 'Yes, Mother.'

Arthur rubbed his eyes with his knuckles and squinted to survey the plot. 'We must construct some shelter before nightfall.' The others nodded and agreed. 'Do not start any fires,' Arthur stared at the forest. 'Not yet.'

With that, they started forth to clearing and cultivating their newfound plot. Arthur fetched a glinting woodsman's axe and it fell rhythmically as trees parted. The crack of timber splintering filled the clearing and shot through the forest. Birds took flight and scattered off.

Caitlin, still tired, started to assist him. She placed Timothy into a ramshackle cot or cradle formed from the folds of her shawl. The other children followed and started gathering stones and kindling. Tabitha, the oldest Warren girl and child, stopped for a moment. A strange and unsettling form of foreboding flooded her thoughts. She lifted her head up and watched the treeline, struggling to shrug the notion that something was watching her too. Though, by what or whom, Tabitha was uncertain.

The trees stood tall and large in the fog. Their thin branches reached outward with leaves green and cutting. The earthy air was tainted with an unnatural stillness. The clearing, though free from the forest's touch, felt no less unnatural. Through the hours that followed, the sallow sun fell away. Its wan light filtered through the clouds and cast the clearing in an eerie colour. Outlines and forest shadows stretched long over toward the Warren family. It delivered them a chill that chewed through their clothes and sank its teeth into their skin. Goosebumps rallied and tickled up their arms.

Later, dusk reared its dark face. By then, they had constructed a crude but sturdy structure, though utterly unfinished. It was a little cabin farmstead wrought of rough-hewn logs with a thatched roof. Rain was starting to fall and it collected on the roof like clusters of cobwebs. The house stood alone, nothing else there to be found.

Arthur stared at it with grim satisfaction. It would have to do, for now. That night, they gathered together by a little fire. The flickering light cast their tired faces with stark relief. Tongues of flame flicked, licked, and crackled. Shadows were sent skittering across the wood and dirt walls. Caitlin sat with Timothy in her arms, rocking him gently and humming an old folk tune. She found few comforts in the fire but for family and heat.

Tabitha rested near her mother whilst lost in her own thoughts. Jacob and the twins sat together and watched the flames waltz. Faith and Freddy were lit as amber cherubs, both chubby and gaunt in contrast. Arthur knelt in front of his family and offered up a prayer. His voice was gravelly and left his hairy lips as an animalistic growl.

Yet, even as they all prayed, wind howled through the trees. Their God and civilization was swept away by the reminder that, out there, Nature ruled. They were utterly alone in its twisted domain. Their prayer trailed off and the cabin went quiet. Outside, gusts touched the thin walls and whistled through the gaps. The fire waned and became small. The forest stayed still in the wind, unbothered by the falling rain. Night settled fully and the Warren family lay down to rest. The embers crackled out their last.

Tabitha shut her eyes, listening to her family's gentle pant and the structure's soft creak. Beyond the frail walls of their shelter, wild things watched from dark and thorny places.

They licked their teeth.

*

There were no stars that night. A strange tension hung in the air and the little cabin lay in an uncomfortable quiet. Tabitha lay still, her eyes closed, though, sleep eluded her entirely. Wind whistled through the cracks in the dirt and wood walls, carrying with it sounds from the forest. Unfamiliar rustles, curious growls, and the soft patter of feet that did not belong to any animal she could identify. Tabitha lay and listened for hour after hour. Nothing happened.

Tabitha opened her eyes, staring up at a roof so dark she thought she had been robbed of sight. Not sight, only light. The rest of the Warren family slept around her in cots and cloth. The fire had extinguished and blue cinders gasped in the ash. The corners of the cabin were filled with ugly shapes and intrusive weeds. Tabitha felt the pull of the outdoors. It promised fresh air and freedom from the stuffy, claustrophobic cabin.

Tabitha looked at her family. Her mother slept fitfully, her brow furrowed even in rest. Jacob and the twins were curled up together, their breathing soft and steady. Her father lay by the door, his axe within arm's reach, always. They were all here, all safe. They would never know she had left. Not until the morning.

Tabitha stood quietly, careful not to trip. Silently, she slipped on her worn shoes and padded softly towards the door. The night air greeted her as she eased the door open, touching her face, stroking. The forest stood still in the wind. She waited. But something called for to her from the depths of the woods. Something irresistible, ancient; wild.

Tabitha left her family in the dark. Into the wild.

The air was thin, though mist stuck to her arms and legs. She recoiled and shed the veil like snakeskin. The moment she left the Warren cabin, the sounds of the forest started breathing. Leaves rustled, branches creaked, and the earth beneath her feet squelched. It chewed and tasted the flavour of its latest visitor.

Tabitha found a path through the undergrowth with unnatural ease. There it was: just there. It had not been there before, she was certain of it. She ventured further into the forest. The trees knelt and gnarled at her height, their twisted fingers forming a canopy that blotted out the sky. It was without stars, just black. The mist thickened into tendrils. Tabitha's breath came in quick, shallow pants. Part of her wanted for a return. But something far stronger harried her to continue. She complied and crunched through the wilderness.

The trees parted. They revealed a little clearing flooded with pale moonlight. The ground was wet and mossy, and the air was filled with the sweet, intoxicating scent of wildflowers – snowdrops and forget-me-nots. In the centre of the clearing stood a tribunal of ancient stones, tall, weathered, and cracked. Tabitha could hear a whisper in the mist. It was wordless, though gentle and alluring. She felt their eyes on her, and the pull in her chest grew stronger.

Tabitha took a step forward, then another, until she stood in the centre of the stone tribunal. The moment her feet touched the moss there, the air around her turned. The voices rose up into a rough choir. Then, the things at the edge of the clearing began to move. Just in the corner of her eye. They started to appear. Coalescing into forms that were neither man nor beast, but something in between. Creatures of fur and claw, with eyes that gleamed like the stars stolen from the sky and teeth that shone like hunter's ivory. They emerged from the forest, patient and fey, circling her. Their movements fluid one moment, rough another.

The wild things.

Tabitha felt no fear as she stood there. Now, she was still. The wild things stared at her with knowing eyes that slit like crescent moons. They had been waiting for her. They wanted her. Tabitha belonged there, with them, in the heart of the forest. Her family forgotten.

One of the creatures, larger than the rest, stepped forward. It was covered in thick and dark fur. Its moony eyes lit with starry campfire cinders. It extended a large and furry paw towards her. It said nothing. The rest of them stopped still, holding growls, sniffling.

Without hesitation, Tabitha took it. The moment their hands touched, the forest started to change. The mist gathered into hard fog. The trees swayed as if in riot, and the air turned cotton with the tang of electricity.

Tabitha felt herself changing. Her body growing lighter, her senses sharper. The world around her was different now. It was heightened with colours never known to her or others from the plantation. These were the true colours of life, lost to the wilds. Where they belonged. Where *she* belonged. Tabitha looked down at her hands and saw that they were no longer the hands of a young girl. They were wild and free.

Tabitha took off into the trees. The wild things followed, their gentle patters filling the quiet. The clearing emptied.

At the Warren farmstead, the wind ceased, dwindling from a rush to a whistle. The night grew still. The Warren family slept on to the sound of it, unaware that they had lost one of their own to the wild things. That their eldest daughter was now a creature of the forest, forever bound to the wilderness. *Their* wilderness. When they awoke, Tabitha was gone. There, a silver-grey squirrel peered through the trees with star-lit eyes.

Tabitha lived out there.

Where the wild things are.

STILL HILL

As I recall, ghosts are real. I have seen them. My name is Charlie Sedgwick. This is my story.

When I first saw a ghost, it was winter.

She was not the ghost I was expecting. She was not a fair wraith or kindly spirit. She was a shade. Her skin was bruised and sunken. It was stretched across her skeleton as a consequence of black cholera. The hem of her latticed dress leaked a liquid as thick and dark as writing ink. She was a sutured slice of night that stepped out from the shadows. The tatters of her moth-eaten gown were scattered wisps. She was all smoky, loose, and curling off from her seams. I can recall it well enough. It was the ghost of my late grandmother, Wilhelmina.

The taste of that night's chill still lingers on my tongue and sheens my teeth. It was a black sight that saw me scarred and drained of all colour. The memory of it strains my soul. The story I shall regale to you does not concern that particular haunt. No. Rather, the focus of this haunting was found far away, in a sad and lonely place. Somewhere I shall not ever forget. It was an old church squatting atop a lifeless knoll, just outside of Oxford. I know it by one name, a name I shall not ever forget. The locals called it Still Hill. I find myself obliged to write down for you what took place there. There will be many questions surrounding the state of my death and discovery.

Yes, that is correct, death.

I have come to understand that there is no other way of releasing myself from the scares of Still Hill. So, before I go coldly and cowardly, I will detail all that occurred there. Once all is concluded and settled, I will raise the silver knife and search for closure. I shall start with this: my name is Charles Sedgwick, or Charlie.

Only my father and business superiors call me Charles.

You do not know me. Not yet. Do not worry, for we shall get acquainted soon enough. I will walk you through my ordeal, as it happened, as a nightmare come to life. Gather this if nothing else, the haunting at Still Hill was so ghastly, so utterly sickening, that simply speaking of it conjures up a fright that cannot be cured.

I know what awaits me at the end of our time here together. So, I shall breathe life back into the same scare that I cruelly witnessed. As I write these words, ink slides down my fingers. I cannot escape what I have seen. I cannot. There is something in my throat that I cannot swallow. Grief such as this is not easily absorbed. It is a grim, gullet-to-gut anxiety which still throbs on occasion. The sensation chokes and closes up, cutting off all air and sense of safety.

I once knew nothing of ghosts. Such has since changed for the worse. A sheer veil of spirit loosely connects the land of the living and the realms of the dead. Sometimes, the veil is sliced open, as scissors gliding through silk. The haunting at Still Hill details such an opening. I shall structure this account as plainly as I can. Some details may become lost along the way. From my understanding, the sightings are as fractious as shards of shattered glass. So, I ask you to excuse my brevity and all the loose roads I may stray from.

I often struggle to recall much other than the worst parts.

So, let us begin. It started, I suppose, as many great chills do. With an untimely death. With the suspenseful burial of my grandmother when I was a schoolboy in Oxford. Long ago, on a classically wintry morning.

A black Friday.

This is where we shall begin.

*

She was not a witch.

I was familiar with the whisperings surrounding my grandmother, Wilhelmina. But there was nothing solid to the gossip. They were rumours conjured from children's lips, spoken only to scare others on stormy nights. They were wicked lies. My grandmother's reputation was cruelly stained as a result. As usual, snow was falling that winter. It fell as sheets all across Oxford, the morning of my grandmothers' lowering into the ground. The funeral took place on a Friday, accompanied by cathedral bells.

The black dogs were barking again. The bitch had lost sight and scent of its game in the fog. Their search had unsettled the quiet. Elsewhere, cats were weeping like children from the gambrels.

The graves in the cemetery were shallow. The crunchy earth was difficult to soil up with shovels. Forenoon greyness was setting in. The firmament was pearly and grey. No clouds, only a single wispy quilt shaking off snowfall. The setting was characteristic of such grim gatherings. There was no colour. Only shades of black, grey, and white. The graveyard was a watercolour painting of blackthorn hedges, steel gates, woven latticework, and sullenness. It set the stage for the grim haunt to come.

I was a child. A whole twelve winters removed from my taking leave of Oxford and my return. We shall come to that later. As a child, I wore a fitted suit embroidered from black cloth and a small necktie which coiled like a worm around my throat. The constriction of it irritated me greatly. However, my father insisted I was not to make a fuss on the sullen occasion. I knew how ridiculous I looked, but I did not complain. I was only a child.

My face was pale and stricken with grief. I carried a guilt that I could not explain. I was feeling sick. My stomach was knotting again. This was my first funeral and I prayed that it would be my last. With the knowledge I now possess, I wish I could inform my younger self otherwise. You see, I would not only attend and oversee funerals, I would plunder them too.

My grandmother's burial had attracted a small crowd of locals.

They stood sparsely around the grave wearing cowls, crinkling gloves, gleaming jewellery, and weighty coats. As mentioned, this was my first formal funeral. I had not known death before. It was a completely fresh concept, one which I longed to never experience again for the rest of my life. However, the family business and generational trade of the Sedgwicks would compel me to doing otherwise. We were a funerary family, you see. I recall that my mother was dressed like a corpse bride. My father was a courtly gentleman sitting in on the council. Yet, I felt like a doll or toy soldier, dressed in a costume that I did not truly understand. I gripped my father's gloved hand tight as I saw the casket approach through the snow and fog. She was in there, my grandmother, cold and still.

I could see from the blankness of many guests' expressions that my grandmother's passing caused them little grief. Old people always died in winter. The local dignitaries of Oxford likely possessed entire trunks and closets filled with funeral attire. They would be dusted off and worn more often than one cared for — taken out to sprinkle soil on relative's caskets and let white rose petals slip down into the ground with them. I could still see the piled dirt atop surrounding graves yet to be shuffled down by shovelheads.

So shallow. The dead could almost crawl out and stalk the stones. So many graves. Right there in front of me. This was quite an introduction to death. Oxford's dead were sleeping beneath a sheer article of winter fog. I thought of them lying there, buried in the earth, cradled by constricting weeds. Were they restful? Or restless? I did not know.

My mother had commissioned a giant casket from Alastair Huxley, the local coffin maker. My grandmother wished not only to be buried, but to be buried alongside her late black cat and husband, so that they could sleep for all eternity in each other's fragile embrace. Word on Oxford's street corner was that the feline was carrying my grandmother along to an empty afterlife. I did not believe that. I did not believe in many superstitions back then. But I was glad that they were together in the end. Better together than to live and later die as two separate and solitary souls.

The large coffin was escorted across the cemetery by a procession of black-clad pallbearers. The crew ushered the hardwood casket across the frosted cobbles, towards its resting place at the roots of a weeping willow tree. It caressed a nearby saintly statue, a stone angel. Some generations previous, boys and girls my age had swayed from the willow's branched gallows under persecution for witchcraft. Though their bodies had long since decayed, some of the frayed rope remained. The willow was naked now, black, leafless.

With such rumours circulating about my grandmother, I considered it cruel that she and her cat be buried under such a grievous monument. But it was tradition. All of the Sedgwick family slept beneath the roots of the willow tree. One day, I too would be buried there. And perhaps I shall be, after our tale is concluded. Perhaps Charlie Sedgwick will also sleep in the shade cast by a winged, stone angel.

My grandmother's corpse had been completely withered. She was a husk. Her skin was shoe black and pulled tight over her bones. Whilst saying my last goodbyes, I had spent several minutes at her bedside, speaking to the thing that was once called Wilhelmina Sedgwick. She had been deceased for some days when they had found her, and her flesh was bruised blue and purple. Her body held pockets of ink. I could not look at my grandmother. So, I looked out the window, cobwebbed with hairline cracks.

I watched the snow come. I took her shrivelled old hand in my own and tried not to think about its rubbery texture. I had loved my grandmother dearly, more than anyone. Her cat had died two nights previous. I was further saddened but comforted in the knowledge that my grandmother would not be walking beyond the veil all alone.

My parents and extended family never discussed how my grandmother had come to pass. Black cholera, they suspected. All of the house's maids, menservants, and houseguests never once spoke of the tragedy. Only my father's butler, Sanders, paid her any real mind. I had started to suspect that something far more malign than old age was responsible for robbing me of my grandmother. Just as I suspected, my father and mother were keeping their employees' lips locked, for fear that I should find out. I knew of no death certificate. I knew of no coroner's report. And I was an inquisitive child in earnest.

Whenever my younger self entered a busy room, a quick hush snuffed all conversation. I shall never forget how people looked at me. As if I was a bad omen. I have never found out why. But to them

I was as much of a ghost as my dearly departed grandmother.

Quite often, I grieved alone. My private business became one of suffering and weeping, for I did not yet know how to grieve healthily. It was unfamiliar and unexpected. I needed someone, someone to love and hold dear. I longed to sleep to my grandmother's old lullabies and bedtime ballads, but I never had any comfort in that regard. My father demanded stoicism from me. And my mother obliged his demands. The burial marked the first time in many years I had held my father's hand. I treasured each moment in his grip, regularly squeezing his palm.

I was not entirely lonely, however. I had several close friends around my age in Oxford. At the graveyard, I noticed Wilbur Cape and his twin sister, Charlotte. They were both a year younger than me and had been born two minutes apart: before and after midnight. I had been surprised nobody in Oxford had mistaken their birth as another omen, attaching to their birth a hidden meaning worth pondering. Nonetheless, we were friends.

Both of the Cape children appeared to be far more comfortable during the burial than me. They had come to know death as normal, from an unfortunate house fire that had left them orphaned. They were fortunate enough to have been adopted by a childless couple residing in Oxford.

Loss of life was a common occurrence for Victorian children. It was a seasonal affair. A death in spring heralded a rebirth amongst the plants and animals. A death in summer saw the soul return to the sun and visit the world every sunup and sundown. Autumn deaths were celebrated, for they brought around a cycle of rebirth. And then there were winter deaths.

There was no charm to be found in a winter death.

Such a sensation was staggering to me. It was new and unsettling. Now, the mantle of the Sedgwick family had passed down to my mother and father. The weight of my grandmother's death had finally begun to burrow into my heart.

Not a moment after the giant casket was lowered into the ground, my heart broke. And I never viewed life or the inevitable promise of death in the same again. Hot tears welled at the corners of my dark eyes. I held them in for fear of causing a scene and dramatizing the undertaking. I doubted anybody — other than my mother, maybe — would have noticed if I had bawled out my sorrows. Victorian children were seen but never heard. And I rarely even felt that I had been seen.

I looked at the Cape children on the opposite side of the grave. Charlotte was completely disinterested in the event. But Wilbur eyed me, empathy shading his facial expression. He understood my misery and beamed to brighten my manner. I appreciated the gesture. But I did not show it. Nor did I smile back at Wilbur Cape. The dreariness of the burial was beginning to weigh on me. I began pulling at my necktie and tucking my black locks behind my little ears. I felt the cool breeze kiss my cheeks.

I kept looking at the Cape children. They were accompanied by their adoptive parents — the original Mister and Missus Cape. Distressed and overwhelmed by boredom, Charlotte began to kick into a clump of dirt with her boot. The motion sent soil down onto the casket before anyone else chanced to pay their respects. Rage brimmed inside me at that moment. I wanted to let loose of my father's grip, march over towards the disrespectful Cape girl, and wring the life out of her. See how much she would like to spend a night in a casket. Her time would come. We would all end up in a grave, eventually.

Wilbur pulled at Charlotte's wrist, making her stop. But Charlotte batted his hand aside like an invasive moth in her bedchamber. Missus Cape knelt, completely unbothered by Charlotte's mocking display. She reached down into one of her deep pockets and plucked out a boiled sweet wrapped in mauve paper. Charlotte calmed down in an instant and pried the confection out from her adoptive mother's fingers. She quietened down then. Wilbur pressed his palm to Charlotte's shoulder and murmured something in her ear. I did not know what. I could not read lips nor hear him from a distance.

Before long, Wilbur looked back at me. He knew from one glance that my heartbreak threatened to rip through my ribs at any moment. The offering of the sweet had reminded me of my grandmother, of Wilhelmina. No more sweets would come from her. Never again, she was gone now. That was that.

Wilhelmina Sedgwick had been stolen from my childhood like a visiting dream. She had died an unknown, horrible death which haunted me every time I closed my eyes and searched for sleep. I wish I could have spoken to my grandmother one last time, knowing what I now knew. But I could not. Still, I cannot.

The burial commenced. Prayers were spoken. Crows coughed their keening carols. And I knew of death and its heartbreak. My heartbreak never waned nor diminished. Instead, it developed and darkened inside me in the years that followed. I nurtured it and cared for it. I felt it mature, grief blossoming inside my heart like a black rose.

Before long, death was as much a part of my body as my own beating heart.

*

Old wounds do not heal.

My grandmother, Wilhelmina – and her black cat – were now two years deceased. The wound in my heart remained as raw as it had been back then, at the time of their drab burial. It still bled. I still hung a black-petal garland above my bedroom door and my necktie rested tilting atop a mannequin's shaven dome. Most of my room was black now. Curtains, furniture, and clothing. Sanders had offered on several occasions to refurbish my chambers, only to be greeted with a swift rejection. I wanted nothing to be changed.

Mister and Missus Sedgwick knew something had changed in their child on the day of the funeral. I had not known happiness – real happiness, that is – in the two years since. My mother was outspoken in her belief that I never should have attended the ceremony at such an impressionable age. I was too young to understand death.

I did not agree with my mother there. I was glad I had been there to offer my respects. Sometimes, during the winter months, I crossed the walkway to the graveyard and laid a bouquet of white roses atop my grandmother's grave.

One sleepless night, I lay flat on my back, gazing up at the ceiling of my bedroom. The quilt and cushions were soft to the touch, but they provided no degree of comfort for a weeping child. Weeping, again weeping. I had learned from experience to do so quietly, no more than a frantic pant in and out, in and out. At first, my cries haunted the Sedgwick family house like a wailing waif. My echoes rattled through the thin walls and disturbed paintings in their hanging frames. I had once believed my hurt would wane after a while. But my sorrow only grew deeper each night I spent alone dwelling on the matter.

Two years to the day now.

Snowdrifts mellowed Oxford's winter cheer. Shadows consumed the gas-lit streets. A thick layer of white dust coated the books, dolls, and trinkets which had been left to me by my grandmother. I had not touched them since acquiring them two years ago. I could neither stand reading, looking at, or cleaning any of these memories. To do so would be to ignite sad, candlewick memories or to polish away an impression of Wilhelmina's presence.

And so, they all remained untouched, unused, and unopened.

A decedent grandfather clock stood guard at the end of the hallway, beyond my bedroom door. I could hear its heavy, pendulous arms swinging over and over again. The clock clicked and clinked intermittently with my weeping. I rolled onto my shoulder. Staring too long at the wind chimes and stars decorating my ceiling had started whipping up a dizzy spell. I could see out my bedroom's patterned glass window now. I looked out across Oxford and saw an expanse of slate eaves, smoky chimneys; snow. The sight of snowdrifts made me feel cold.

I pulled my blanket up higher.

I was thinking about my grandmother again. I could not expel the ceaseless questions ringing in my mind. Was she at peace? Was she cold? Was my grandfather keeping her company in their shared earth? I had been assured by my father, my mother, and Sanders time and time again that I needed not be concerned. My grandmother was sleeping soundly, undisturbed by the underground world. I was still struggling to believe their stories.

So, I wrote my own. A creased leather journal rested on my bedside table alongside an inkwell and lofty quill. I used it as my journal, memoir, and art book for all of my strange and scratchy sketching. The contents of my journal did not amount to much. I was yet to scribble a story worth musing over. Writer's block was as real to me as the birds, the trees, and the snow. Surely there was a story out there worth telling? I was yet to find it.

I continued to lay awake, thinking of such things, throughout the low hours of night.

Sleep was stolen from me by the continuous ticking of the standing clock at the end of the hall. I always slept with my door open for fear of being alone in the darkness. No lights in my room. But the wall sconce in the hallway lit dim patches leading up to my doorway. Through it, I looked at the clock. Proud, antique; loud. The incessant mechanical clicking was starting to irritate me greatly.

Tick-tock... Tick-tock... Tick-tock...

I tried shutting the sound out. I wrapped a feather-stuffed pillow around my ears and counted sheep. The thoughts only dragged me back to evenings spent with her in this very bedroom. Wilhelmina would read me vignettes and bedtime spooks from old books whilst I hid beneath the embroidered blankets. I learned to tell tales of devils disguised as handsome men, old crones living in candy houses, and the lingering spirits of the dead.

Ghosts.

No stories were read to me that night. I heard no music. No supple kiss to my forehead or cheek and a promise of sweet dreams. My bedroom was barer now than ever before. My dolls glared at me in unusual and uncomfortable ways, peeking from behind corners and cloth. My wallpaper depicted woodland critters frolicking through windswept willows. Such decorations conjured up dark memories of the willow tree that lived on as a grim reminder of the graveyard's history.

Tick-tock... Tick-tock... Tick-tock...

The night dragged on slowly. I felt every moment, every waking second of boredom and lost sleep. The clock continued to click through the early morning hours, when the night was darkest above Oxford and its streets. I loathed such mechanical trinkets. Each and all of them were crude and gothic.

I veered onto my back once again and suddenly, I was no longer alone. A creaking groan echoed through the room like a roosting whisper. I shot up straight under the covers and cast a stare around my bedroom. I saw nothing. The black curtains undulated gently, stirred by a soft gale spilling inside. I listened again. An empty silence.

Tick-tock... Tick-tock... Tick-tock...

My heart was beginning to pound now. I could still hear a creaking. I looked around my chamber and saw the bedroom door swinging loose on its hinges — clock ticking some sixteen feet away down the hall. I cocked my head, listening again. No. Not the door, something else. Groaning, creaking; crying. It was a quiet whimper coloured by grief.

I slipped out from the covers.

My bare feet recoiled at the touch of the cold floorboards beneath me. Then I touched down with my toes and lowered my soul to the hollow floor. I started walking towards the open door. The floorboards creaked and spoke with each careful step. Now I heard something new: the rustle of frilly, silk cloth.

Sanders had told me, after my grandmother's passing, that she had been buried in the same frilly black gown she had worn in life. So that she may rest comfortably beside her husband, my grandfather, one grave over. I knew the gown well. Puffy shoulders, a wide hem, a tight corset. Sanders said that to dress her in anything too grim would circulate further stories of witchery. My grandmother had not been a witch. She had neither been a ghastly old crone. So she should be dressed like neither for her burial. She lay still, garmented like a corpse bride. I recalled the sound of its rustling and crinkling well.

I could hear it now.

It was not coming from my bedroom. It was coming from the hallway beyond my door.

Tick-tock... Tick-tock... Tick-tock...

I reached the door and wrapped my fingers over the polished handle. I stared across the hallway, deep into the gloom. Puddles of candlelight lit patches around the sconces hanging from the walls. I could not hear anyone else awake and moving around the house. Nothing moved, larger than small black spiders scuttling across the floorboards. I was thinking of the rustling sound again. Somehow, it was overpowering the clock's toll. I was thinking of Wilhelmina, thinking of my beloved and lost grandmother. And then, she was there.

Shadows slithered around the stairway banister. Pearly moonlight peaked through the peeling curtains. I looked down to the edge of the hallway. There stood the clock. It swung and swung and swung. It sounded once again, only once.

Tick—

The ticking tolled once, and never again. Now the house was quiet, truly quiet. I could no longer see the clock. The shadows had snaked around its wooden height and obscured it completely. I was no longer alone in the dark. Something stood there, conjured from nothingness right in front of me. The blood cruising through my veins ran chill as I witnessed a silhouette, wearing frilly black lace, standing facing the grandfather clock and starboard wall.

Not only a shape: the outline of a woman.

There she was, utterly still.

A shade, shrouded and cloaked, drifting off the ground at the end of the hall. It was the silhouette of a woman. An old woman. She had once worn clothes matching a black moth or raven. Fingers of shadow crawled off her. Now, she was a spider. I could not look away. I could not move. So, I gasped.

The sound echoed across the hallway like a rush of cool air. The shade slowly began to turn. I sprouted a cold sweat. My ears were chiming with the low, keening thud of my heart. This was the first time in two years that I had felt alive. The shaded woman's face was veiled. I knew the impression of it. It was my grandmother. She glided into a wide slice of moonlight. The silver lustre lit up her sheer veil, only for a moment. The spectre's eyes shot open, and I fell backwards with a startle. The woman began gliding down the hallway, away from the clock, towards me. I crawled backwards, whimpering.

I scrambled up to my feet and – without looking – shut, locked, and bolted my bedroom door. I had not seen the shade gliding towards me: reaching with skeletal digits, jaw agape, eyes wide and bright with deathly drear. The door shut, I dove across the mattress and buried myself under a folded bundle of weighty blankets and old quilts.

I closed my eyes. I started counting frantically. I whispered over and over, 'Not real, not real; not real.' My chanting was interrupted by the quiet fiddle of a door handle. I pulled my cover down beneath my eyes to the bridge of my nose. The bolt slid from its sheath. The silvery lock turned on its hinge. The door was creaking open again.

I did not watch the shade glide inside. I disappeared beneath my covers again, chanting incessantly, shaking through a pure strain of night terror. I could hear airy breathing. The shade was gasping. She was right there. I was sure the spectre was raking free its onyx nails to shred her quilt and carry her away to its land of living spirits.

Instead, I felt something unexpected. I felt a sunken weight fill the mattress beside me. Sitting there, just as my grandmother had. I did not peer out from beneath my covers. Instead I felt long, bony fingers trace up the quilt to where my face lay. The shade was caressing me softly. Wisps of shadow peeled off into the dead air and licked the quilt. The spectre was not harming me. She was cradling me. Rocking me gently, wrapping me up in a web of shadows.

I felt the press of immaterial lips through the cover above her cheek. I listened keenly to the whisper that followed. The shade spoke a sentence, a warning that I would never forget.

A single hush into the quiet.

'Sleep child. Sleep. Still Hill comes.'

I shrieked louder than I ever had before. My wail woke Oxford from its dispossessed slumber. Stars shot away from the shrillness of my worried cry. I threw off the covers with a flurry of little kicks. There was nothing there. My room was empty and dark.

A moment later, footsteps filled the doorway and candlelight peeked around the corner. Sanders came stumbling out from the servant's quarters, wearing a white ball cap and cotton slippers. He scanned the room and found me shivering in my sheets.

He inquired as to whether I was well, and what the matter was. I gave him no sure response. All I could hear was the grandfather clock at the end of the hallway. It continued to toll. And it never once stopped. I did not sleep that night. I only listened closely for any fresh creep or chill. The sound would continue to haunt me forever.

Tick-tock... Tick-tock... Tick-tock...

*

All bad things come around again.

So, now, let us leap forward some years. Let us come to a time when I am a grown and respectable man. Years later, though, not too far removed from where we first were introduced to one another. It was winter again, winter to the day.

Snow was falling. The nearest church started tolling after the rush of early morning. It had struck the hour and Oxford was coming to life once more. The bell chimed over the city and its surrounding landscape of cobblestone, chaff, and grey grass. The sound of it tore me away from my thoughts. It swiped me back to reality, where I stood, who I was, what time of day it was, and how I had returned home. I stood there, still, with memories of my lost childhood running around at my feet.

My bedroom was not quite an attic. It was not at the top of the house. But it was smaller than I remembered it. Nonetheless, it was my bedroom. Or, it was my bedroom as I had once left it to be. I took one last look at it. I spotted all my trunks, stuffed toys, sketching pencils, and books. The floorboards creaked just as they had all those years ago. There was a strange solace and comfort to be found in this groaning.

This quaint, small place had been my haven. It had been a place guarding me from the spooks of the outside world. And, after that cold winter night – when I had come face to face with the spirit of my grandmother – I knew that there was malevolence out there. It was real. And it was waiting for me. I continued to stand still and take it all in. Time had passed me by so suddenly. And yet, but for sheets of dust and gossamer cobwebs, the room had not changed. I had not seen any of my family or childhood home in Oxford for years. And now, it was work and work alone that had summoned me back. That was an unfortunate truth that I had come to accept of late. I felt guilt stir inside me and winced.

Work. Yes, that was it. There was work that wanted seeing to. And, though I did not know so then, the truth of my summons would soon see to something I thought I had left in my childhood. I never once thought that I would greet the dead again. And yet, I was wrong.

I breathed in.

I breathed out.

The air in my old bedroom was stale, filled with specks of floating moth dust and grey light from the curtains. The sun was still tucked away behind the sullen clouds and very little light reached the city below. The room was choked with cobwebs and their silk. Still, it was quiet up there. I allowed myself a couple of seconds to lament, just me alone with my thoughts. I was telling myself that I was ready for the work ahead. My family, the Sedgwicks, have worked in the grave industry for generations, quite literally.

It was, and still is, our duty to attend to the deeds and wishes of the dead. To see that the recently deceased are granted their final rites, wills, and demands. Such work had taken me all over the country. And it would soon see me spirited away to a new place. A place with one name.

Still Hill.

I cast my eyes at my stuff. All of my valuables and childhood belongings were caked with grime. Spiders crawled between the seams in their armpits. Their painted faces were flaking, and their rosy cheeks were as pale as salmon meat. Beneath all that, lay the boxes. Every single one of them stuffed full of books and old sketches. It had been a strange sensation, seeing my entire life packed away and forgotten about.

My most treasured possessions were left out on the bed for me to pick and choose from. The wooden figures struck stiff poses with crooked arms and fingers. Many of their eyes were only buttons, push-fitted into empty eyeholes. They were naked too, partly. Their clothing had come open and tufts of stuffing poked through like grooming dander or dandelion fuzz. I picked one up and turned it over in my palm. I ran a finger down its cheek, tracing a line bereft of dust like a tear. I set the miniature back down amongst the rest. Then, I thought to walk away. But before bringing myself to do so, I turned back to the bed and lay a feather-filled pillow under their backs for support. I tucked them up tightly in the threadbare blanket and thought of my childhood no more. I turned off and left.

There are those people who believe partings are upsetting. They cut away part of one's life as if it were infected with some spread of illness. That was not the case. At least, it was not for me on that sullen morning. And dreary it was. It was a cobweb arrangement, streaming down sunlight so cold it felt ill. It was the sort of sun that wanted for your squinting, to look down at your feet or hideaway. I had grown accustomed to such winter glares. Outside, Oxford was grey and nearly empty. The streets were strangely quiet and a thick fog was reeling through the alleys. It wisped. The air was filled with lamenting crow carols. I soaked up their singing.

Then, the urchins came charging down the street in tune, crunching snow underfoot. They were chanting an old Christmas carol that I too had choired along when I was their age. I watched the children charge past, flourishing bent sticks and steel rods like swords, vanishing into the fog gaily in play. Their footsteps echoed down the cobbles. The sound faded into nothing. I had played as they now did, once upon a time.

From a window, I watched Oxford waking up for work, shaking off the strain of sleep. The city was setting up for work, as was I.

Oxford was in the midst of preparations for the Christmas celebrations. The city had become a market. Food poured on to the streets, in for trade, from all of the surrounding towns. I could see the ugly prizes of their cultivation: grey potatoes, deformed cauliflowers, white apples, plums filled with ants, and broad beans that had turned turquoise. This year's cultivation had not been successful. The crops were ill and the food was foul. Nothing was warm. Winter's chill did not discriminate our supplies from, well, us.

Everything was cold. Everything was grey. The black gambrel roofs were dappled white with snow. Melting flakes drowned the gutters running up and down the old eaves.

I went to leave my room and heard only the house's quiet groaning. I shut the creaky door behind me, walked out, and folded up an old ladder that had fallen from the attic. I felt nothing of upset. I can honestly admit that I felt lighter and clearer of mind once the latch flipped up to shut. Being faced with paintings of your past does not appeal to everyone. It certainly did not to me that morning. I had been a grown man for some time and had not thought of my toys or bedroom for many years. To see them up there, all caked over with the dust of time made me feel something of guilt. No matter. Now it was done. My youth was shut away for the next Sedgwick child to find and treasure, for a time.

As for me, I was grown and gone.

As I walked around, I was greeted with hanging portraits,

landscape paintings, and marble busts. I was not quite sure whether I knew these people. Perhaps they'd been distant relations. Or perhaps my mother and father, renowned art collectors, merely enjoyed the style and brush technique. I stopped for a moment, halting in the hallway to stare up at them.

Each one of them was a frowning stranger. I could track the passage of time amongst their garments. The furthest away wore dirty cream rags and held four-forked rakes. The nearest of them wore buttoned-up waistcoats and tiny spectacles that sat at the end of their noses. There was a painted man, woman, and child for everything in between. However, one feature remained consistent.

I reached up towards one of the old paintings, then another. One by one, I brushed off the cobwebs and blew away what remained of the filth. I studied their faces intently. Their eyes were filled with grief. They were haunted in a way that I could not bring myself to try to understand. The most modern interpretations and portraits saw them holding rosary beads between their fingers or crucifixes dangling around their necks.

I continued down the hallway, taunted by the memories of my youth. Partway down, I caught the whiff of something cold, damp, and gross. What it was, I could not tell you. For I only smelled it. I tried ignoring it, yet it kept following me as though I were marked for its hunting. Eventually, however, I shook it. The foulness had left me. The reek of the grave.

Then, I reached the ground floor. The gallery was giant and empty. It looked as though nobody had lived in the house for many, many years. However, as far as I knew, my parents were a community mainstay and had never thought to leave to live elsewhere. They were very content in Oxford. The gallery was full of carpets, rugs, and tapestries. Every few feet, there was a tall door with a silver doorknob. Then, as I was passing one of them, I heard a voice call out from the inside.

'Charlie?'

The voice was my mother's.

She sounded worried, as though I had fallen and scraped my knees as I would, as a boy. Of course, she knew it was me. Nobody else lived here anymore, save for Father. Growing up, I could not hide anything from Mother. She found out everything one way or another. Therefore, I found my way of keeping secrets. I rolled my eyes, let out a deep breath, steadied myself, and pushed the door open on its worn hinges. My mother's private quarters were cramped and musty. The room was filled with old clothes, stuffed jackets, dirty aprons, torn flat caps, and a pile of outgrown leather boots for a schoolboy.

Now, she had no children. She only had men.

The room itself had always been off-putting to me as a boy. Nothing had changed. Perhaps those were the lasting effects of forbidden entry, but I did not feel safe in there. The place was incredibly cluttered, a hoarder's paradise. Yet, there was a feeling of vacant emptiness to the room. Upon stepping in to the room, I had to search for my mother amongst the piles. There she was: roosting in an ancient sitting chair, her eyes turned up to a window into the garden, the very small, round glass of which was riddled with cobweb fractures.

My mother had never been a particularly happy woman. Not that I could ever recall. She sat there, facing away from me as I entered. She was staring out the window again. Waiting for a change in pace that never came. She waited for a new life to find her.

'Good morning,' I spoke softly as I entered. Mother did not turn to me immediately.

'Afternoon, really,' she corrected.

'Why, yes. How silly of me. Can I help you?'

Then, she turned around. The grey light streaming through the tiny window lit up one side of her face. It was gaunt, creased with wrinkles. The other half was kind and gentle to see. Mother wore what she always wore now, a stained yellow dress with puffy shoulders. Around her neck: a cross. Yet, she had stopped attending church in recent times.

Mother reached for a light for her pipe. Her face lit up like a phantom and, with a huff and puff, dark smoke filled the room. The pipe she held was only small, but it was heavy. She'd filled it with medicinal herbs that kept her relaxed and staved off the tremors of ageing. The scent immediately took me back to the age of nine. It left me feeling nauseous. I had been trying to break my habit of smoking, up until then. But I did not say anything to stop it. This was not my home anymore. It belonged to her and Father.

'Charlie,' she said. Smoke trailed off towards me. I held my breath until it'd passed out through the door. 'Close the door, would you.' It was not a question. I could tell. When I turned around, she was looking me up and down, studying what I wore and how I wore it. 'You look well,' she said, 'very smart.'

I was wearing a black suit over a white shirt and a black tie. The boots were new, long and narrow. I was not used to them on my heels just yet. 'Thought I had to dress for Father, you know?'

Mother piped and nodded silently. Then, she said, 'You're the spitting image of your father.'

'Thank you,' I returned. The natural flow of conversation had already run its course.

There was movement in my mother's lap. One of her dogs, an ageing Jack Russell terrier. There'd always been dogs in the house, growing up. It appeared this was the only one left, a piebald brown and white. Its eyes were gone to cataracts, they were like tiny pearls. Mother stroked the dog along its back gently. It was panting heavily as if it had exerted itself.

There was a beaten collar around the dog's neck. Dangling from it was a tiny bell. I recognized it from upstairs as one of the bells affixed to many of my toys' ill-fitting shirts. It chimed when the dog shifted. Mother continued to scratch its scruff and loosen the tight collar. I had not seen such little bells in many, many years. But seeing it now, I felt jealous.

'That bell,' I pointed. 'It's one of mine?'

'It's one of yours,' she said.

'But,' I heard the pathetic disappointment in my voice, 'no longer?'

My mother turned the dog's collar over in her hand and fiddled with the tiny bell. Then, she looked back up at me. 'You won't need it any longer. You're all grown up, Charlie.'

'Yes,' I said. 'I suppose you're right.'

I usually tread carefully when conversing with Mother. She had never had the patience for riddles or emotions. Talking with her has always been like going through a tunnel of tripwires.

'Look at you,' she started and pointed towards a dirty mirror. 'Only yesterday you were just a boy. My boy, my little Charlie. How quickly time flies by. Now, you're a man. Just like your father.'

'Is that so bad?'

Mother squinted. Her eyelids fluttered. It was clear to me then that she was tired and that something was on her mind. Though, what that was, I had not yet figured out. Only then did I notice the hot tear stinging the corner of her eye. It fell, streaking down her gaunt cheek. My mother did not often show compassion, love, or anything else of the sort. But she cared. That was the way of all mothers, so I had always thought.

'Your father is a good man,' she said. 'But he's not one to follow.'

'I know.'

It'd been quite some time since I had last spoken with my father. I supposed he was somewhere in Oxford, tucked away in his sequestered office study. The question had been rhetorical. I knew what she meant. Father was a man of money and investment, working for a better life and choosing never to live it.

'Never mind that,' Mother dismissed. 'I've got something for you.'

She set the terrier down on the knotted rug and reached into her vanity table, fetching something out of a drawer. It was wrapped up in a white doily with gold filigree. 'This is for you,' she continued, passing it over to me. I went up and retrieved my gift.

I carefully unfolded the cloth, laying it out like a blanket. There, in my palm, was a crucifix and necklace of rosary beads.

'A cross?' I was not sure what to say.

'Do you know what it is for?'

'You know, I'm not a church-going man, not since I was a child. I don't pray.'

'No, but you should.' My mother wore a wry smile and then said, 'A cross, yes. I don't expect you to pray, Charlie. It's for when you leave again tomorrow. It was your father's idea, originally. But he thought it best if I gave it to you. He's at work, waiting for you. I'm sure he'll explain later.'

'I see.'

'Go on now, Charles.' Mother rarely used my formal name. It caught me off guard. 'Get to your packing. But remember, your Father will want a word with you before you go.'

I had been heading for the tall door again but stopped with my hand on the knob. I turned back to her, crucifix in hand.

'But, Mother,' I offered. 'I do not yet know where I'm going, or why?'

'Precisely,' she concluded. After that, I conceded, nodded, and turned away. I shut the door on my mother. Another door shut, another memory stored away forever and always.

I did not know it at that moment. But those would be my mother's final words to me. The last conversation held between a mother and her boy. Three weeks later, she was found dead in that very same rocking chair. She'd been dead a while, a husk in the winter sun's bleach.

I knew one thing, however. Something lay ahead for me in my travels, and somehow, Mother and Father both had a part to play. Every life came to an end. And it was the will of God that her time had come. My mother did not live to see spring arrive. She died in the heart of winter. In retrospect, I envied her for that. For I wish age and illness had carried me off before it was too late to turn back. What lay ahead of me was a fate much worse than hers. What lay ahead of me, was another burial.

The burial at Still Hill.

*

It was a familiar Friday. Another cobweb morning.

Greyness washed through the ill-lit streets of Oxford. It was fairly early, at that. Although the day was still young, the weather was already sullen. A thick fog settled across the flat and slithered through the alleyways. It could not have been any later than eleven o'clock. Yet, the fog sought to cloud all light with its gloom. What light remained slid through the firmament with the colour of a fisheye. This Friday was foul. I could taste it in the air. I followed the fog through the gaslight, spitting it out. The spittle vanished beneath the sheer article. There was something sinister in the haze. Of that, I was convinced.

The empty echo of my footfalls shot across the cobbles, giving life to an otherwise forlorn fog. It was everywhere. It felt against everything with wispy, curling fingers. Whatever it touched was swiftly swallowed up in smog. The fog was consuming Oxford.

There was little way of figuring out where things started and ended. This was making my morning's trek treacherous. Every so often, I spotted figures in the fog. Gentlemen, their ladies, and their children. All tightly clutching the steely railings flanking the river for support. I passed them by, flashing a grin. Then, I trampled across the steel-wrought bridge that arched over the river.

Halfway across, the bridge began to sway. I felt slightly seasick. A feeling I had not experienced for some time. I continued. The routine trek across the fog-shrouded bridge was getting physically taxing. The complete sullenness of the occasion, along with the strange quality of the weather, was soul-sapping.

It was only upon closer inspection that I realised something was not right. There was something *off* about the figures in the Oxford fog. For they were not walking, but floating. I could have sworn it. I stood utterly still, swaying left and right, to and fro atop the bridge. Families: ethereal, trailing wisps of ghost cloth. The fog carried them all across the bridge. It was a ghastly parade. A marching procession of the dead.

I stumbled backwards the way I had come, lost in the fog. The bridge stretched out across the river, forever it seemed. The figures in the fog were following me. But some moments later, I emerged. And the gossamer families did the same. Walking along as if completely confused by my state of shock. They pinched their hats in a manner of greeting and continued on their way. Not ghosts.

I stood up, brushed myself off, and again I was on my way.

Oxford had been preparing for the Christmas celebrations. Though, this year, the celebrations were marred by an increase of seasonal deaths that almost felt like a culling. The reaper was hunting for the elderly, the infirm, and the weak to add to his collection. In such a city as this, it had been uncommon to find a man, woman, or child who was not well-educated in their Bible verses. But those details weren't important to me. My mother had been right. I did have to pack and I did have some paperwork to tend to before taking my leave.

The air was laden with crows, clouds of them. The ground was wet from winter's melting. The seasonal greens faded into grey and the trees that lined the city's streets were stiff and bare. They had been beaten and worn down by the pale sun above them, though it gave out no heat in its light. A winter sun, glaring, never giving in.

I followed the cobbles through Oxford, past the church, down some slopes and tiered steps, and towards my father's workplace. As I was walking, something caught my attention. There it was again: that whiff. A terrible stink in the air that nobody, save me, seemed to have take issue with. That, or they couldn't smell it at all. I did not know which was worse.

It was an awful stench. It smelled like spoiled fish, flesh that had become earth, maggots, and unwashed skin. Though, everywhere I looked, I saw nothing but market stalls fettered with tattered bunting and weary-eyed traders.

Perhaps then, it had only been me.

I followed white tumbleweeds down the path ahead and into a tightly packed set of houses. Blown around, haunted by a hidden breeze that had arrived long before I did. The business down that way was sparse. There weren't any people. Not any that I noticed. Nestled between a few tall buildings and a few small ones was my father's workplace.

It was called *Sedgwick & Cooper's.*

But now, Cooper had been dead for many years. The sign swayed to and fro with a squeal. The shoddy paintwork had started flaking away. It seemed that many of my childhood memories had become dilapidated since I had left. Nothing remained but a sense of unease upon seeing the structure. Unease and grief.

My father's name was Ebenezer. Ebenezer Sedgwick. He and his recently deceased business partner, Cooper, had organised many funeral processions in Oxford, soliciting property deeds, and seeing to the wills and last wishes of the dead. He had done so for nearly thirty years.

My father was a good man. By that, I mean he was a good man of business. Though, I would not say he was a kind-hearted man. He cared for his family in a way he had never once admitted or outwardly shown. That was just his way. In truth though, I did not really know my father. He had been around, but never in the picture.

He spent more time in his office than in the family house. That had always struck me for it was quite the home to forget about. Ours was a true family house, passed down from father to son for generations. The family history was full of tales and yarns about how they had acquired the plot the house was built on in the first place. Many secrets, I imaged, were buried in the house. But the place had never felt like home for Father. He only ever seemed to be visiting us.

I walked over towards the front door of the office. Now, *this* was his home. It was there my father lived. And it was there I had come to speak with him, at my mother's behest. However, I did not know what to expect from our conversation, or whether it would be personal or professional.

The door was smaller than the ones at home. And the office behind, I knew, was claustrophobic, dimly lit by white wax candles.

I could smell the tallow from outside. At least it blotted out the unpleasant scent that had been following me all morning.

I stopped outside the door for a little while. The door had a polished knocker, shaped into the pouting face of a man — a dead man. I grabbed it by its silver septum ring, knocking three times, and waited for a response. But there was no answer. Eventually, a man, bald but for black mutton chops, came to greet me.

'Good afternoon, Clerk,' I said, pinching my flat cap. 'How are you today?'

'Very well, Mister Charles,' he spoke softly. 'Though the afternoon's a grey one. You're here to see your father?'

'That I am, Clerk,' I said. I tried looking over his shoulder to get a glimpse of the inside.

'Well then,' Clerk started, 'come on in.'

Clerk shuffled aside and I swept past him, taking off my flat cap and holding it respectfully against my chest. I still held my briefcase, stuffed with paperwork. The crucifix my mother had given me sat in my jacket pocket, over my heart. There, in the corner of the room, sat my father, Ebenezer Sedgwick.

It had been a while since I had last seen or heard from him. Of course, it had been a while since I had visited Oxford and this establishment. The office and the people working in it were as cold as I recalled.

I will not detail the meeting with my father. For it was not a happy one. In the interest of time, allow me to summarise and just tell you that it was during this meeting reunion that I was given the task of overseeing the funeral arrangements of a widow by the name of Augusta Spricket. And my heart darkened at reading her address on the paperwork.

For the burial was to take place at Still Hill.

*

So it came that Augusta Spricket was dead.

Quite dead, it seemed, dead as a doornail.

The widow had been struck down by a broken heart. She lay there still, within the confines of a casket garlanded with black roses and white petals. Such a cold image, so lifeless. The grimmest sights were often found in the search for grace.

Nonetheless, Augusta Spricket was a corpse now.

It had been a quick thing, the coroners asserted. Augusta's child, Wilson, a boy of six, had been carried off by pale sickness some sixth months earlier. Before Wilson, Augusta's husband had died no more than a sprinkling of winters prior. The boy had never known his father, not really. Augusta had conceived the child far too late in her sombre existence for it to be continually healthy.

Thus, it was the will of God that Wilson be confined to his mother's cottage for most of his life. There he was, a child, boiling away with a damp fever. He had never played in the snow, never known friendship or sunlight. The illness had seen Wilson wither into a gaunt and ghoulish figure.

Following the child's death, Augusta had become a recluse. She had allowed grief to carve through her chest and sit in her heart. It was Augusta's will and last wish that her coffin be laid beside that of her husband and her first and only child. There she would sleep, alongside a silvery locket with the faces of her husband and child. Oh yes, the locket: silver like starlight and just as valuable. But we will come to this locket later in the story.

*

The ceremony took place at All Saints' Church, on Still Hill.

A great wych elm curled up like a bat's claw from the church's yard. A giant, black gallows tree. Frayed strings and ropes fettered its limbs, a relic from the days when young girls had been tried for witchcraft and black magic. It twisted and creaked in the quiet of the night. I can see it more clearly as I write these words. It is like peering through a looking glass to sketch every aspect of that eerie gathering. I can see the whole, god-awful scene taking place before me now as if I were still standing in the cold. Grim carriages paraded down the cobbles from Still Hill, providing a gothic, pastiche impression of a corpse caravan.

The carriages sauntered sluggishly through the forenoon greyness. Each was pulled stylishly by a leash of Belgian Blacks, the strong equines strutting, sounding off with the tinny clack of steel horseshoes, down the church way. The dark road was piebald from a recent snowfall, white chalk on a blackboard. It was a common sight, yes, for those of us in the funerary business. However, the sight was one that never ceased to instil grievance in all of us all. All of the funeral attendees crowded around the carriage, all dressed in black. I watched on from the lychgate. I held my hat across my chest, keeping my other hand still against my waist. I often found myself looking away, casting my gaze into the fog. I stared across Still Hill and chose to focus on this landscape rather than on what lay before me.

I struggled to discern the vagaries of distant copses, gambrel roofs, and flocks of common nightingales in the mist. It satisfied, to some extent, the wish to tear the soul away from the business at hand. However, nothing ever blocked out the wailing grievances, nasal stuffiness, and the limp pleasantries of condolences. A service such as this – one in keeping with our customary cases – crawled through the early hours with little levity.

With our heads inclined respectfully, we waited for the ceremony to begin. The carriages passed us by. Everyone there looked lifeless, solemn. Soon thereafter, the cart came wheeling to the church. It trundled through the hoary fog that walled off the cemetery from the actual church. The carriages passed by. Above, crows croaked their death carols into the air.

*

The clocks struck eleven. Still Hill rang.

The mourners and grievers were garbed in suits, black-lace veils, and shrouding masks. They disembarked steadily from the black carriages, shuffling along, and crowding around a six-foot hole in the cold earth, circling around it like wolves. The clothes they were wearing struck me. They all looked like conspiring, nightly-feathered birds. Ravens, all blue, plum, and darkly regal.

Then, there was the hole. I had dug it myself the day before. Perhaps I should have led with this. This had been my role at All Saints' Church before I was dismissed due to fragile nerves. I could still remember staring upwards from the claustrophobic depths and muddy walls, and my unease at all these sad eyes staring down at me like some carrion corpse. If the dead had eyes to see with, they would likely feel the same too.

I was watching the gathering from the lychgate, recognising some faces huddled around the pit. Mostly gentlemen, the only women present wearing sheer face coverings and shielding their cheeks from winter's stroke. I spied Carlisle Chambers — a local dignitary and patron of All Saints' Church — and his wife Nina. Next to them, their girl, Evelyn or Emilie, I was struggling to remember her name. What struck me though was how the girl was stabbing her eyes down at Augusta's grave as the coffin was being lowered.

There were others too, of course, grief-stricken relations that had likely not visited Augusta or Still Hill in years. Yet, they appeared overwhelmed by a kind of wordless sadness that seemed to crawl up through their throats.

All those gathered were exhaling wisps of hot breath. I watched it, wafting up and away into the leafless hickory trees, fading into the cool winter drifts. Collected in council, the committal service of Augusta Spricket was set to commence. The choir sang with such sorrow that the hymns bore greater semblance to dirges than to heavenly praise. This sort of ceremony always conjured misery and an unsettling kind of melancholy.

This is where our story finds its ghastly origin.

*

The graveyard grew foggier.

The grievers chanted, circling the casket as it was being lowered. I glanced over to see the girl, Evelyn or Emilie, staring intently at the grave once more. Suddenly, she looked up, something askance in her eyes. She let go of her mother's hand, who did not notice her girl leave. The child's expression was wistfully aghast, her movements silky and graceful.

She turned and stepped away from the gathering, her whitish gown spilling from her black corset, licking and tugging against stalks of razor grass with each careful step. She was not looking at anything in particular. She saw and pursued something which others could not or chose not to see. It was as if none of them even registered her leave.

I strode after her, affixing my tall hat to my skull and fastening my coat. She had already sauntered off quite some way into the fog. As soon as I did, I was struck by the chill, not simply wintry, but deathly. My boots crunched on frost and snow loudly. Still, I struggled to track the young girl. There was neither sight nor sound of her. I continued walking for some time, searching, calling out names which may or may not have been hers. I was out of luck, being met with nothing but smooth silence. That was until I saw something manifest.

A shape. A silhouette beside a blackberry bush, still and small.

*

She stood still, facing a frozen sharpness of belladonna and nightshade. The child had her hands raised to her face, rubbing her eyes and wiping her blue lips. I walked closer, twigs snapping beneath the weight of each step. I called out for the girl to take my glove and follow me back to her family, back to the graveyard. She gave no response.

The girl did not move. She did not turn. She did not flinch. I used my silver tongue then, offering out hollow condolences to coax her towards me. I figured she was upset or overcome with sorrow. She remained still as a statue, utterly serene. I reached out to touch her shoulder and shake her out of her trance.

I spied a couple of black nightshade berries which had been plucked from their thorns. Some had fallen to the frosty ground below, colouring the grass in purple ichor. The realisation struck me, and my lip quivered as I turned the child around. I confess that, at that moment, my heart sank. She had eaten some of the berries.

I quickened to pry open the girl's mouth, wiping away the blue-black grit from her teeth and wine-stained lips. She was pale, her expression blank. I promised her comfort and guaranteed her that help was on its way. I held her, all the while shouting out into the thick fog. Her eyes were rolling back. Before that, she had been gazing into the fog, where the steeple of All Saints' Church, a very icon of death, loomed like a gothic spire.

I looked back at the little girl's face. There, in those streaming, round and black eyes, I witnessed the haunt that would follow me ceaselessly for the rest of my life. I saw the white silhouette of a face so feminine and skeletal that I cannot detail her image further but for a single point. She wore black lace. The girl opened her throat and shrieked. God, she wailed like a banshee! The voice was not hers, but that of a suffering old woman. A widow.

The image of the woman in her eyes screamed through her puppet, letting loose wails that carried shrill across the grey wastes. I fell backwards, gracelessly, and crawled a few feet away. I could feel the white space of terror eating its way through my chest and raking my spirit. The girl stood over me. Her black boots were beginning to rise off from the frosty grass. She started to drift towards me.

I covered my face and howled for mercy. She fell to the ground. There she lay, convulsing, scratching, and clawing. Only after a couple of seconds of agony did she grow stiff and still. The trickle of nightshade berries spilt from her nostrils and lips. Their essence wrenched the life from her cheeks. Her eyes never shut. With this, the girl was dead, cold on the floor. The widow's shadow crawled away from her corpse, towards All Saints' Church.

As I lay there, the congregation came charging out of nowhere, brandishing canes, accompanied by sniffing hounds. I was hauled to my feet in an instant and shaken to my senses. One look at me caused their faces to shrivel. I must have looked an oily picture of inexplicable fright. It only worsened when they saw the girl and the nightshade, easily understanding what had happened. I was not ready to tell the story anytime, not now anyway.

The tragedy of the child's death was the talk of Still Hill and Oxford in the next few days. Some called it a curse, Augusta's last spite. Soon enough, her corpse was laid to rest. I couldn't will myself to attend the service. In truth, I attended very few thereafter. I dug the graves. That was all. In the weeks that followed her funeral, talk of the child became scarce. Life returned to normality, as if the horror had never occurred. With that, I was expected to return to my station and profession with immediate effect.

I had started to believe in the comforts of everyday life. That the experience was one of early-morning madness and craze, and that the tragedy was nothing more than a terrible accident. Thus, I started up with life once more. However, throughout the winter there occurred very few seasonal deaths. I found myself penniless and downtrodden. I was stark out of luck and penny.

Therefore, I willed myself into committing a heinous crime. The crime of theft. I was set to reopen that weeks-old casket of Augusta Spricket. Therein lay a locket, silver as starlight.

*

I chose my night well.

All Saints' Church rested central to a scarce painting of leafless trees, frosted thorns, and cracked headstones. Night covered the world. There was no sharp breeze, only sad air. Those late — or perhaps early — hours came and went by slowly, with ease. I recall digging fervently. I was shovelling snow before sinking my shovel into winter's solid earth. Clumps of sallow ground flew over my shoulder with each heaving chuck. I usually committed such acts in solitude. For once, however, I was not alone.

My short-faced dog — Clive, a handsome, white gunner counting five years — rested guardedly at my leg. The dog was always alert to any enforcements wading through the night fog, searching for intruders, trespassers, and good-for-nothings. I sent the soil flying out of the grave like clouds of black dust. Clive shuffled elsewhere to avoid its choke. I struggle to recall precisely how long I dug before reaching the casket of Augusta Spricket.

The night grew stronger after a while and set in fully. Puddles of gloom were encroaching upon both me and my dog. Only a single, hooded lantern gave us light. Clive was wrapped around it in the shivering cold. I had laid my overcoat across his outstretched spine as a shawl. I was convinced that ought to keep the chill off him for a little while longer whilst I dug.

Finally, the sharpened head of my shovel plunged and stopped. It slammed against a wooden casket. I stood there, atop it, some six feet beneath the sheer article of mist flowing around me. I proceeded, wiping away dirt and debris with my gloves. The leather was dirtied with the crumbling pigment. With no small degree of effort, I lifted the casket's lid off its hinges. There, within, lay my prize. It was held in the blue-grey grip of a rotting corpse.

Of Augusta Spricket.

*

Augusta was repulsive.

The widow's cheeks were sunken. Worms had burrowed through the casket and made their resting place in the lining of her upper lip. A pair of grimy coins adorned her concave eye sockets. Her hair was darkly slimed with gritty grease, decomposition, and death. God, she smelled. I stayed the urge to gag by covering my mouth and nostrils with a thick tearing of cheap trouser cloth. Contrary to her flesh, Augusta's clothes and valuables were polished, gaudy; festooned. I spied her rings, necklaces, and coins. One by one, I took them and spirited them away into my satchel with hopes of hawking them off somewhere else.

Then, there was a bark. A singular bark, fading into a low-howling whimper.

I started up instantly to check on Clive, who snarled into the fog. I scanned Still Hill's graveyard for any sign of what had disturbed him. There was none. My stomach twisted at the thought of what the dog had seen out there. I urged Clive to remain quiet so as not to startle me in such a manner. I continued working my way through

Augusta's trinkets.

There, I saw it. The last talisman: a silvery, glinting locket, glimmering in the peaking moonlight. It illuminated Augusta's face, as if the place was getting ready for a cabalistic ceremony between the living and the dead. The veil was thinning around me.

The locket was steel, finely detailed, and fastened around her fingers. Augusta clutched the treasure tightly, but her fingers teased away without too much tension. I had expected a skeletal snap. Instead, her lithe fingers were rubbery and hard to snag. Taking the locket in my hand, I flicked its face open to reveal the other faces inside. There, I gazed at the scratchy portraits of Augusta, Wilson, and her husband — the old gentleman's name escapes me now. Now let me gather myself to recall the events that followed.

*

Clive shrieked.

I snatched the locket and started up, caught completely off-guard. The dog's cry was shrill. I rushed for the edge of the grave and clawed at the walls, crawling outwards. The act of it was so sudden and careless that I snagged my boot on a tangle of grave weeds sprouting from the ground. They lashed at my ankle and twisted the meat around the bone. I cried out in pain. I struggled out, panicking. Sweat spilt out from my blackheads and glossed my skin.

Clive's shrieking continued. It rang out longer, quieter. As if someone or something were dragging the hound away from the pit, further into the fog. I emerged from Augusta's grave and fell to the frigid undergrowth. Frost pricked my hands and drew hot blood, steaming in the night air. I cast a stare around the graveyard as far as I could see. Still, there was nothing. Clive was gone to the fog. There was no sign of struggle or any other creature's presence. I never saw the dog again. I miss him, even now.

This is where it happened. Out of the fog, I saw it. I saw her.

The form of something waifish and elegant appeared. It was spectral, a woman in black with snow-pale skin. She shivered out from the darkness and stopped. She stared. I could not move. I could not breathe. I tried to speak but the words left my teeth as gasps of sharp nothing. The black-laced widow shot for me, wailing bloody murder into the night. I sprinted for All Saints' Church. Each quick step crunched my ankle and powdered the bone. Her shriek was everywhere. I clattered through the church doors, slamming them shut. I locked them, bolted them, and started shuffling towards the altar before collapsing onto the floor of the narthex.

I thought myself safe for a moment, catching my breath.

I shall detail to you now the last moments of which I consider to be my life. My life as it was before cowering into a puppet of sullen haunts. I crawled for the altar, seeking shelter and mercy. I could still hear her shrieking. When it stopped, and I thought the ordeal finished, a slice of embroidered cloth rose from the cold flagstones.

The silhouette of black lace shuddered towards me. The widow's fingers were splayed out to kill. Her nails were sharp as ice, flakes of obsidian. I screamed out for help. I screamed out for my dog. I screamed out for God. I was met with silence and a single, cleaving cry. I took the locket out of my satchel and offered it up in my hands. The silver steel was dirtied with blood and grime. Augusta's shroud grew as she came closer. I flashed my mother's crucifix out in front of me. Then, all went dark within All Saints' Church. Augusta was gone.

When morning came, I was found in a paddle of my own making, sheet white, speechless but for the continual utterance of two words.

'Still Hill.'

*

So it is that I come to conclude this account. This last recollection of Charlie Sedgwick.

Now you know my name. Now you know my story, my nightmare, and my grief. I cannot attest as to whether what I saw that night was real, or rather if I am riddled with upset madness. I shall leave that for you to decide.

I am old now. Still, I feel her presence. A chill in the air, a bark in the distance, the unexpected waft of a curtain. It all reminds me of her. They all unsettle me greatly. I see her sad face under the veil and think only of the darkness that awaits me on the other side. I look at the silver knife. I hope that, upon discovering this account, you find no great deal of mess for my coming actions. I must apologize to you, however. For that trinket – Augusta's locket – was never returned to its grave. It was lost long ago somewhere in the church.

I scantly recall where it rests.

Word has it that the locals of Still Hill still hear her every winter's night. Some claim to have seen her. Perhaps if the locket were ever returned, her spirit may rest. I cannot be certain. Though, I can be certain of one thing. Those who have claimed to see her always have the same darkness in their eyes. And in that darkness: Augusta.

They never live out the winter months.

She is with me now. I will not look in the mirror. But she is there, behind the curtains, in a funereal gown of black lace. It is likely that whoever finds this summary shall scarcely live past a fortnight. That is a winter curse. You have my deepest apologies.

Lock this account away if it eases your worries. I confess that it has never eased mine. I judge that living to such a great age is a suffering of sorts inflicted by her memory. My soul has been allowed to live on in torment as penance for the theft of her locket. So, it has been. Too many years of suffering have passed under her watch.

This is the end, gentle reader.

Let it be said that, when I go, I wish not to rise as did sad Augusta Spricket.

So I raise the knife. So our story ends.

Goodbye.

– *Charles Sedgwick*

ALLEGED DEATH OF ALBERT GREY

A dark web of briars pulled at Albert Grey's feet. The cemetery about him was veiled by dense fog and decorated with bursting bramble. Albert had come for the whispers and hushed gossip of curses, death, and ghosts. And now, he was running. The world around him was hidden by a lilac shroud. The fog was full tonight and there was no sign of a moon behind it.

The purple haze drifted over headstones and caressed carved angels. It seeped down through the damp earth and cradled the dead in gentle repose. Hands pushed against sealed caskets and cramped walls of mud. Cavendish Hall lay just beyond. It was drenched in darkness – a darkness clawing at Albert's boots. No matter. He had many greater concerns tonight. Albert had disturbed a legend best disregarded. And now that it was awake, it was coming for him. *She* was coming for him. Inhuman, implacable, undead.

She was a memory born of love, death, and black desires. Desires that had claimed the hearts and lives of many young men who had come looking for her. And now she had chosen Albert. He would die in her dark embrace unless he acted quickly. There was no time to decide, he had to move. But Albert was already weak. A chill slowly crept up his body and drew numbness. He had seen it. Albert had seen *her*. And he knew he'd likely not live to tell the tale. She had already claimed braver and heartier men than him, no doubt.

Snow was beginning to fall and mingle with the grave chill. Albert was blinded by both snowfall and shroud. The dead, headstone beacons prompted his escape, guiding him. Snowflakes began to shed from the bleak sky in earnest, breaking and brushing against Albert's cheeks. Others caught in his black hair like cobwebs or cluster-pods of spider eggs. Warmth dribbled down Albert's cheek. He felt his face, white hands pulling away red. But Albert did not detect a gash or new wound. Rather, he felt tears. He was crying. He had seen his death at Cavendish Hall and was weeping tears of blood. Blood ate through his white dress shirt and bled the material until it darkened. Albert was already limping. He had lost his footing in the cemetery before and come crashing down at an irregular angle.

He did not loiter in pain for fear of what was chasing him in the fog. Albert veered and began moving in a circle. His movements were crude. This was a hopeless endeavour. Nobody could outrun death, never mind those consigned to meet it. Despite the coolness of the fog and December snow, sweat beaded down Albert's brow. His stomach wrenched and he bit his lower lip. His whole body ached, his head throbbed, and his vision was beginning to blur. His bloodshot eyes were riddled with black spots and grey floaters promising a daze.

Beyond the snow-packed cemetery, shadows loomed in the shroud. Even darker things disturbed the dead in the depths beneath Albert's feet. A new shade – darker purple – materialized and coloured the fog behind him. Albert did not look. He had already seen enough tonight. Would Albert die here? Would he join the dead and become one of the malignant spirits pursuing him? Would Albert's heart feed the curse over Cavendish Hall?

No.

He could not let that happen. He was not dead yet. Curses were real. Albert had discovered that much. But he knew much more. A brutal and bloody secret tormented the Cavendish family and their gothic abode. He could reveal it to the world. He needed only a few more blessings. Beyond snow and surety, Albert caught sight of her once more. His grip on his loosely-held lantern was clammy and waning. His impaired leg screamed agony up his groin and wanted for removal. Albert breathed out into the fog. He watched his hot breath dissipate in the morose December mists.

When Albert looked back, the silhouette of a widowed woman no longer loomed in the distance. She was right there in front of him. The curse of Cavendish Hall had found him, and she was ready to claim his beating heart. As she wailed, it stopped.

And the alleged death of Albert Grey bled into local legend.

SLITHER

Deep in the darkest descents and recesses of pleasure: a dining room.

'Don't touch anything,' her daughter had once pleaded.

Her words seemed so negligible now. How would she not be expected to do so? Once she had stalked through the curtains – claiming her invitation – Elaine perceived the domain personally. She knew it intimately. Elaine peered down a long, wide, and damp passageway. She looked up, spellbound, towards a painted ceiling. It was tiled with ancient mosaics in shades of purple, plum, and periwinkle.

Pillars held the ceiling up above Elaine. They were wrought from white marble, chipped out into curves of naked men, women, and cherubs. All of their extremities were laid out bare for her eyes. The marble people were crouched and hunched, crushed under the weight of the decorated ceiling they suffered beneath.

The floor was not so clean. It was slimy and carpeted beneath Elaine's feet like a grizzled tongue. And it was disgustingly moist. Liquid spilt out from the curtained walls like sweat seeping out from loose flaps of skin. The passage felt heavy. Its atmosphere was smothering and dank. Intermittent beams of light leaked through glass-paned windows embedded into the ceiling. They shone with error, blinking as Elaine passed them by.

She could constantly hear a heavy breathing in the distance, as if someone had been as deep in their sleep as to begin snarling. And with it, the subtle sound of slithering. Elaine shivered upon hearing the serpentine slide. Then, she slipped. Elaine would have dropped but for balancing out and managing her wobble. The noise never ceased. It accompanied her echoing pace and mingled with the distant breathing. She pulled the curtains apart. Elaine gazed inside. She marvelled at the banquet spread out before her.

Decadence: bowls of ripe, red fruits, and berries which burst beneath the pressure of her forefinger and thumb. Elaine plucked a lone morsel from a platter and placed it atop her tongue. She hollowed her cheeks, squeezing the delicacy harder and harder until it popped. Juice oozed from between her lips like a steady stream of blood.

A moment passed. A perfume filled up the chamber. The smell was sickeningly sweet. It penetrated Elaine's nostrils, apple bleach and grape. An immediate pain bloomed, became pleasurable. The initial sting faded into a more delicious breed of sensation. The food prepared for the banquet slept atop a long, oval table – devoid of diners – and had been untouched but for her prize.

Elaine's tongue began to sizzle. Her spit became venom and flesh-smoke billowed out from her teeth like a freshly boiled kettle. She fell to her knees, gripping her throat. Her hands were no longer her own. They were scaled, reflective, gleaming. She saw her face in those hands. Elaine licked out for air. A forked tongue whipped out into the dead air before sliding back between her fangs. She could feel herself growing smaller, diminutive. Her arms bound to her ribs, cobwebbed with membrane before absorbing inwards. Elaine could not scream, for her throat had become her chest, and her stomach, and her legs.

From the pile of clothing that remained, an adder slithered free.

Elaine had become the new guest for the banquet – a product of her own impulse.

When the next diner entered the hall, all they heard was her hissing.

THE BEAST OF SLEEPY WILLOW

Nobody had forgotten the curse.

'Eyes like night gems, I've heard, and massive. She's double a man's height and thrice as broad, with claws longer than any blade. I've heard it's the curse of Sleepy Willow come home.'

Jakob quivered in his black boots. His pale face was lit with nightmare imagery and grey light. It blinked behind dense clouds. Jakob knew the clouds, nobody better. A storm was brewing. Rain would soon fall, and the browsers in Sleepy Willow's market would disperse for cover. The storm was brewing and coming in quick.

Konstantin faked a cough of mild amusement while rearranging his market display. It was full of charms, trinkets, and dream catchers.

'Oh please,' he began, 'the beast is nothing more than a figment of children's imagination. Sleepy Willow's curse is nothing but idle gossip conjured up by fools, like you. Now, let's talk about something else before you frighten off my customers.'

Konstantin grinned widely. The women were old and walking to his stall through the market's bustle. He moved aside and allowed them a full view. They could see the silver charms, which lay on a luxurious blanket of mauve velvet. 'Come on, ladies. Fanciful new dream catchers direct from Blackhurst. Perfect for your bedchambers. Keeps away bad dreams and the like, you understand? Even curses.'

The elderly women suspected charlatanry and false promises. They gazed long and hard at the items on display, before looking at each other. Behind the women were the slate eaves and thatched roofs of Sleepy Willow. The eaves rose over their veiled heads. The quaint village was slanted and wrought out from black wood and rain-polished stone. Rainfall had always been abundant in Sleepy Willow, and the eaves glistened with the previous evening's moisture. Every cottage, cabin, and homestead was decorated with charms that chimed in the breeze. This was an old village, with old residents, old money, and old stories of evil.

Something darted from behind Konstantin's stall. It wound past Konstantin's pocket, and then went up into a crooked alleyway. Konstantin did not believe in curses, nor did he believe in the beast of Sleepy Willow. But the talk around town had become incessant, and unexpected bangs had made him jumpy and fearful.

Konstantin veered and gazed up the alleyway. It connected to bare woodland of willow trees that produced a sleepy mist. The movement had not come from the beast of Sleepy Willow. Nor did it come from an esoteric, lingering curse. It had come from a child. A roughneck local boy who darted between market stalls like a knavish rat or cat burglar. None of the market attendees had yet caught the street urchin. When they did, there would be a punishment which Konstantin was first in line to dish out.

*

'Don't move you little bastard! Why I'm—' Konstantin's bawling trailed off.

It turned into a weak, self-absorbed grumble. He had learned to acknowledge that he would never catch the child. There was little point now in even trying. The pickpocket stopped and looked back towards Sleepy Willow's market, and Konstantin too.

The young boy delicately dangled a silver locket between his gloved fingers. He dared a wink before darting further into the village's shadows. Konstantin usually lost some charms here and there in the normal business week. He had already accounted for that loss of profit before even opening his stall to the public.

'You know, Konstantin,' Jakob started prodding, 'I'm not quite sure I've ever seen you make a proper profit.'

Jakob did not wait for Konstantin's response. He knew it was unlikely he would receive anything other than a disinterested scowl of grim acknowledgement. Instead, Konstantin returned to his customers and put on a broad, welcoming grin.

One of the ladies looking at his market stall picked up an intricate brooch from the velvet cloth, an ornamental maple leaf that glimmered in the morning light.

'You've got a good eye, my dear,' Konstantin murmured. 'One of my best designs you've got in your hand. Catch the light with it as you are doing now and you'll be blessed with a fortnight of good luck. I don't make this stuff up, you know!'

Konstantin gestured to her partner to pick up one of his charms too. She plucked an exquisitely fashioned black-petal blossom. It had an amethyst at its heart. It was well made, evidently so. Konstantin's wares often attracted quite the crowd.

'You've got a keen eye for detail, madam,' Konstantin began. But his slick words were cut short by a loud howl, drifting through Sleepy Willow's market. It was coming from the foggy moors of purple heather and yellow gorse.

The moors lay beyond a bone yard and a gypsy encampment consisting of a caravan circle of brightly painted carriages. The dogs of Sleepy Willow began barking. But when the howl came again – closer now – they whimpered. They withdrew into their warm, stone homes. They could sense an evil in the air they wanted no part in greeting. Dozens of market shoppers became still and silent.

A pregnant pause passed throughout Sleepy Willow.

Nobody moved. Nobody spoke. Not even a crow.

Then in an instant, the village erupted into panicked commotion. People clambered over each other, vying down narrow passageways.

*

More howling.

Closer now, at the bare edge of the village.

'Konstantin, come on, we've got to leave!' Jakob called, abandoning the goods on his stall. He stopped after realizing that Konstantin had not followed. Konstantin had spent hours unpacking his market stall. He'd intricately laid out each locket, trinket, charm, and night gem. 'Leave them, you damned fool!' Jakob screamed. 'The beast doesn't care for your bloody brooches, Konstantin. It wants blood! Come on!'

Konstantin did not move.

Jakob grabbed a handful of goods from the market stall. He started to flee into the crowd of locals. With a backwards glance, he realised that Konstantin was far behind. And that he had left his friend alone in the market.

Nobody remained.

Konstantin stood alone in the market amid drifting dead leaves and fading mist. The village became closed. Doors were locked and bolted. The village children were hidden and wrapped in blankets under their parent's beds.

'No such thing as curses, no such thing as a beast,' Konstantin murmured. 'A black dog, nothing more,' he said. People had died. That much could not be denied. But Konstantin was deeply convinced in his mind and heart that it was only an animal. It was not a malefic, cursed beast. Konstantin was hesitant to neglect his livelihood. He only had rumours and whispers as evidence.

A new howl opened up in the darkness. It was close now and Konstantin was beginning to panic. It was nearing Sleepy Willow's market, nearing Konstantin. Eventually, once he could no longer burden the nerve, he broke from his stall and began running ahead. His home lay in the direction of the bloodcurdling howl, at the edge of Sleepy Willow, basing the heather moors. He could not go that way, not anymore.

*

Konstantin darted towards the nearest building. He began pounding on the heavy door. It was locked – bolted – and the candles had all been pinched out inside. The curtains were shut. The family inside were hiding, unlikely to open their doors to anyone with the beast on the prowl. His heart bloomed with hot panic and he began moving once more. Konstantin bumbled hurriedly towards the next building in the market.

Locked again. He began crying out for aid and refuge.

He found none. Not even a murmur sounded behind the door. Then a low, rasping grumble came from behind him. He did not look. He could not bring himself around to doing so. Konstantin convinced himself it was the deep rumble of new storm clouds. He looked ahead instead and began moving in that direction.

The heather moors looped around Sleepy Willow. They went up towards massive, naked woodlands. The new storm was looming high above the gorse. Konstantin began moving again. He slipped along the cobbled curb and dumped his weight backwards onto his right ankle.

Now, Konstantin himself was howling a prolonged scream of pain. He clambered up and limped on as effectively as he could. Rain was beginning to fall even harder as he moved. Konstantin lumbered through the deluge.

A shadow moved down the narrow alley ahead. It emerged from between two houses – the last pair before the moors began. Konstantin limped backwards slowly. He pushed the rainwater out of his eyes. Konstantin was panting heavily now. Then, he saw it.

Padding out of the darkness towards him, a beast. The beast of Sleepy Willow came into the light. Konstantin backed up, jumbling a mess of pendants dangling about his neck. The amulets were dead, cold, and metallic. The beast raised its brow and blinked its ruby eyes.

Konstantin registered every detail of the beast's muzzle. Its black coat was slicked back by rain, making it seem even darker than rumoured. A forked tongue slithered across two rows of jagged fangs.

It prowled forward several paces. Konstantin took many paces back. Its giant paws crashed down into puddles, displacing minor bodies of water with each step. Konstantin wanted to move, nothing more. His body, however, did not. Now, he only wanted one thing.

He wanted to live to see another day.

The beast of Sleepy Willow charged forward. And his last remaining want was diminished. Unable to limp away, the beast pinned Konstantin down to the ground. It decorated the cobbles with blood diamonds. The air shook with the wails of a dying man.

And the bestial roars of a cursed beast.

THEY ARE COMING

THEY ARE COMING.

A handprint brushed against the stone wall, leaving an impression behind. Perfectly painted, a handprint detailed by blood. The nails were clawed and dripping. That told Danika that her companion did not have much longer to live. Ahead, the man's mouth mumbled something noiseless. He was dying.

Hushed breaths passed through his wet lips. Danika had pressed him for a name. Which he had promptly given to her: Benning. His name was Benning. And Benning had known Danika. Rather, he had known the memory of Danika. She no longer knew anything of Benning or the thing that he was becoming.

Now, Benning was a body. A body balancing on the brink.

A noise rang in the distance. Danika peered down the corridor to investigate. She noticed the opening through which she had entered the old apartment building. Benning had informed her that 'they are coming.' And there was no time to explain anything more.

Benning was met only by measured silence.

Groaning leaked down the dark corridor. It was an unhappy noise, like that of a burst tyre releasing air or the moaning of an organ pipe. It became deafening. Danika did not note the sound alone. The odour discharging alongside it was disgusting. It was the smell of spoiled meat or an underground butchery. Men and women smelling of dead flesh came ahead.

Benning bundled in a heap on the hard floor before Danika.

'Move, quickly! Can't keep here,' Benning moaned.

Danika knew he was right. Nobody could be foolish enough to deny it. Not now. Medical amnesia had blasted her memories. However, even she caught onto this unavoidable truth. The coma had not been kind to Danika's memory. She knew her name. And she had been made aware of her predicament. She had awoken in a dead city populated by enemies. But what she did not know was who she was, or where she had been.

Perhaps Danika ought to put Benning out of his misery now before the worst part of his wound took hold of him. Before he became one of the Drab.

*

Benning had rescued Danika.

It was only right that she delivered him an equal kindness. Danika had awoken, limbs bound. Benning gnawing at her bonds with what little teeth remained to him. But they had come loose, eventually. And though she was without her senses, her strength had returned.

Benning had already taken an injury meant for her. Danika was certain it was a killing blow. She looked at him now: old, languid, grunting. Pain grew in his organs now as they hid. The two of them had already gone far down the corridor.

This was before she had fully regained consciousness. But where she had previously been, Danika had no memory.

Danika had ordered Benning to explain what was happening. Before she received an answer worth remembering, she was set upon by a newcomer. Benning fired his handgun twice. Two echoing bursts lit the dim corridor, giving flashes of the newcomer's gaunt mask. Those images haunted Danika, even now. The newcomer had pulled back like a wounded beast. The escapade happened so quick and sudden. Danika could not determine his character. She knew them to have been male. But the images that loomed in her mind — those quick, sudden bursts — she denied. They could not have been real.

No human man looked like he did. No woman either.

In the moments backing the ambush, Danika had noticed the gash grazing Benning's belly. The wound was wide and moulded like a bite. Danika believed the old man had been splashed with a horrid ichor. But she promptly recognized it as blood. A pound of flesh was missing from Benning's lower stomach. Something clotted in its place like a knotted rosebud, an organ. An intestinal worm dangled out from his potbelly like a baiting grub. The bitter odour filled the building as they moved. Benning was leading them to her. Blood in water.

'Can you walk?' Danika asked.

She knew he did not have much longer. But Benning nodded. The motion was heavy. He was dazed and battling off a coming disease. He could not walk. He could hardly move now. But the old man did not want Danika to leave him behind. He did not want to die alone. Here in the dank, dusty darkness.

Danika knew she had no choice but to leave him.

Benning's mouth began to move. His gums brimmed with gore. The same substance stained the walls all around them like gritty paint. It squelched under their padded boots and dipped the clear windows in ruby. It dribbled through the splintered hardwood to the floors and hallways below. They were in a converted apartment complex near Milton Peak. But the building had become compromised. It was no longer vacant.

Benning mumbled again. He cradled a chubby jumble of organs in his weak arms. The blood diamonds bubbled and popped beneath the dainty gas lamp dangling overhead.

No hope. There was no hope for him now.

Benning looked up at Danika blankly for aid. She honestly wished she had either for him in his dying moments. But she did not. Benning could not be helped.

Only death could claim him.

*

Bawling, inhuman moans came down the corridor again.

Whatever pursued Danika came closer. She could hear them louder than before. The noise of their moans was damp and tormented, as if they were drowning in blood or bile.

Danika looked down again.

Benning pressed his quivering hand to her knee. The old man's eyes were wide and dilating, delivering everything to her that his voice no longer could.

Benning dropped his guts down in a pile. He pressed into Danika's grip a beaten and battered handgun: a bullish snub pistol. He folded Danika's long fingers around it tightly, urging her to decide.

She could not let it go.

She *would* not let it go.

Benning had become so pale and lifeless. His face was sheet white and blue veins crawled under his skin like cracks running through marble. He looked like the "man" from before.

A Drab man: the very same as the newcomer from before.

A handful of bullets remained. Enough for Danika, Benning, and two mistakes. Danika's heart beat with an unhealthy pace. It bashed against her ribcage, campaigning for independence. The panic made her ill. Danika could feel a lump lingering behind her tongue, in her gullet. Saliva rushed to her mouth and slimed her teeth.

She handled the pistol and minded her breathing. It began to slow.

The bells chiming in her ears quietened for a moment. The bawling bumble of bodies neared the end of the corridor now. Contorted bodies broke and banded in the shadowed mouth of the hallway.

Danika aimed the handgun at Benning's head. He smiled, not broadly, and closed his eyes as if readying himself for sleep. He held his breath. It slipped out through his weeping nostrils and lips. It was warm on Danika's skin. She moved to pull the trigger and end the old man's silent suffering. He deserved this mercy. Nobody better.

A heavy moan echoed down the hall. Danika veered. She did so out of a primal instinct she had not thought she possessed. Then, she fired the handgun twice down the corridor. The shots echoed through the entire building, bouncing off the grey stone walls. The muzzle flash briefly illuminated the narrow passage before Danika.

Only two bullets remained.

The shots found a body in the distance.

No. Not distance, much, much closer than a distance.

The body: a bloated woman, round like a balloon, white as eggshell, and hairless. She had been as hairless as the raging newcomer that had bitten Benning. The odour wafting down towards Danika was sickening. It was the smell of copper pennies and pork. The pale, bloated lady toppled backwards into the encroaching dark. Her wounded moans were drowned out by more, many more. Danika knew this was only the beginning of her end.

And they were coming.

*

Benning opened his dilated eyes. He had expected death from the handgun. Danika knew he was wondering why she had not yet pulled the trigger. She would put one of the remaining bullets through his brain. He needed the pain to end. But he could not plead anymore.

The growling group was closing in on them. They were in the corridor with them and had caught a whiff of Benning's hot blood. Danika had only one answer for her companion. And she despised herself for it.

'I'm so, so sorry, Benning.'

Danika had not noticed the tears streaming down her dirty cheeks. She did not remove her eyes from Benning's when she spoke. She ate up every morsel of hate, remorse, panic, and pity in the man's vision.

Benning gripped the sleeve of her coat. He was frightened. He did not want Danika to leave him alone in the dark to his demise. Then the bodies came, more numerous than ever Danika or Benning had realised before.

Danika peeled the dying man's fingers from her coat. She bent them to snap before gliding away down the corridor, leaving him to die. The horde paused. It was only long enough for Benning to let out one final, bloodcurdling howl.

'Who are you? You bitch, you horrid, detestable bitch!' Danika cursed herself as she moved to escape. The body in which she had awakened bore a cruel mind.

Danika did not look back at the bloodletting in the hall behind her. Benning's screams were drowned by a louder ensemble of moaning grunts. Luckily, the noise was not prolonged. The further off she moved, the more drowned the noise became.

She did not stop. Danika could not stop. She knew the throng was coming for her. They knew her smell now and preyed after her like bloodhounds. The beasts were endless and bald. They punched through the floorboards, grasping for her defined ankles. But the question of what THEY were eluded her still. That was an answer she had not received since awakening.

Before long, Danika had broken out from the second floor. And the house became quiet once again. She came to the wooden door of a decrepit bedchamber that had once belonged to a child. A young girl. It was cobwebbed and piled high with dollhouses and rocking horses. It also had porcelain teacups, dream catchers made of spider silk, and more.

There was a cradle, a baby's cradle, marred by a puddle of dried blood. The image made Danika wonder and plunder for memories. Had she once had a bedroom like this? Had she owned a little woman with rosy cheeks and a bonnet? She knew she would not find answers. And now was certainly not an appropriate time to look for them.

Danika looked around and breathed. The air was old and dead. A window. Danika spied a window. It was circular and small, peeking from behind a pair of red lace curtains. The cloth was old and damaged, but still thick. It could block the door or be tied to a rope for climbing down from the floor. There would still be a drop. But she found the chances of survival much better. This was when compared to the pale crowd at the supposed "safe house".

*

No time to pad the door.

Danika bundled up the drapes and tied them together. The ease with which she did so came as a surprise to her. She harboured a subdued muscle memory.

Not long after, the curtains were roped together. They were thick enough to hold her body. She was neither hefty nor too light, either of which could have caused unforeseen consequences and would have seen her dead in any other predicament.

Danika could run fast, but not far. She could lift heavy, but not for long. Once the adrenaline waned, Danika dared not think of the toll it would reap upon her body. Danika held Benning's handgun in her palm. Perhaps she would not need to use it. Not on herself.

Two bullets remained. How pointless.

What good would two hard-edged bullets do against a Drab crowd of twenty? She pushed the handgun deep into her pocket, loaded and ready. Danika could hear murmuring and mumbling coming from behind the bedroom door. They were in the corridor. Not dashing hungrily and mindlessly now, but pacing. They were looking for her. She could hear the floorboards creak. A moment passed and she believed the copper doorknob would turn.

Danika held her breath.

She walked on the rug at the foot of the cradle, nullifying her footsteps. The floorboards were weakened from age. She could feel it. They were beginning to give beneath her.

Danika panicked. She pressed on for the edge of the room. It was made of grey stone and wood. The foundations would be stronger there if no place else. Danika placed a boot down. A rusty, upward-pointing nail shot through the rubbery sole. It drilled into the doughy meat of her foot. Danika narrowly caught her blasting scream of pain. She wrapped her fingers over her mouth and slowly eased her boot off the nail.

The nail was rusted brown and wet with her spilt blood. Danika squinted.

The adrenaline was beginning to wane. She knew this would be the end of her. This was her punishment for leaving Benning to die alone. He knew nothing but horror and crushed hope in his dying moments. Perhaps Danika would die knowing the same.

The Drab's pacing had not ceased. But it had dropped to a low patter outside the bedroom. However many of the Drab were out in the hallway, Danika did not know. Many, for certain.

A click came. And another a moment later.

Danika looked up, horrified. A smiling, pie-faced clock loomed up on the wall above her. Its fingers gently ticked, ticked, ticked, and then peeled over. The clock struck eight. The mouth opened, agape, and a lock ribbon tongue rolled out like a carpet in the air.

The clock chimed loudly. It dragged all silence down its throat and broke the quiet.

Danika dropped. The weight of realization rendered her both blind and dumb. In an instant, the building bawled. It became hostile once more. The Drab were coming in numbers. They cruised up and around in violent currents. They knew where she was. Dust choked the ceiling as they stamped from above. She listened for their craven crawl coming from down below.

No time.

Danika dashed for the window. She smashed it open with her bloody boot and knee. Shards from the pane embedded themselves in her muscles. Danika did not wince. She only panicked. The room closed in on her. The claustrophobic weight of the bedchamber stalled her descent. By the time she had dragged her body halfway out of the bedroom window, the door blasted open.

A dribbling, ravenous mass of Drab, bald bodies ran for her. They had bloodshot eyes and murderous intent. Their drooping maws were still chewing on Benning's wrinkled remains. Danika looked down at the junk heaps piled high in the streets below.

Could she survive the fall?

No time.

Before the Drab could reach her, Danika jumped out from the grey stone building. Hands peeled after her. She plummeted out from the second floor of the building. The Drab's skin sizzled upon meeting dusk's last sunlight. Danika crumpled upon the impact and immediately became passive to its monumental heaviness.

The junk pile began to move, dragging her under.

No point fighting it. Better to drown in its embrace than in a puddle of blood.

Dirty air began to fill Danika's lungs. The heat and weight of the pile thrashed her body around violently. They threw her until her skull crashed into a broken, bronze cog.

Danika's head cracked back and opened. She drifted into a dreamless sleep, violated by nightmarish images. Danika's body disappeared beneath the scrap. Her head wound painted the junk behind. Her body was found chucked against a collapsed engine. This was two days later. Once more, nothing of her memory remained.

But the Drab remembered. Danika was as alluring to them as any organ meat or ichor. Knowing Danika's taste and odour well, they moved on, blood drunk. They moved through abandoned grey stone buildings. They walked along cluttered passages under the humid darkness. They were an endless horde of butchery, primed and ready for one more victim.

Hunger consumed the night.

THEY ARE COMING.

RED RIBBON

A PENNY DISTRICT DREADFUL

Sunday became Monday.

Miss Brandie's purse had run dry. The weight had left the leather. All that remained in her mouth was the bitter burn of her evening's mistakes. Rum's burden was not one lightly managed. A new wobble embedded itself in her legs, weighing them down with ache. Darkness gathered. An eclipse thrilled the night sky. It had all the oily shades of premature dusk. Loose, black clouds circled above, obscuring the non-moon and its non-light.

The hot months had passed and autumn made its bed. In winter, blue ice floes would close off the market waterfront. Chilling fog would eat through the cobbled wharf.

Miss Brandie hauled herself down Penny District. She passed many taverns and bed sheds, noting that the buildings still bore memories of Old Hallow Night. Few hostels had any vacancies. She could tell from their dim windows and boarded doors. They only showed carved pumpkin heads and gossamer cobwebs. Miss Brandie had assumed as much. She had struggled to read any residential notice. They were pinned up against the broad boards and lamplights. Sloppy, black scripture had been scribbled all over the parchment. Only the boldest words could be read by the illiterate and the drunk.

Miss Brandie read several keywords: "dead", "murder", "prize", "predator", and so on. Most boldly, "BLOOD". Plenty of blood had been spilt during Old Hallow Night. Murderous deeds could be passed off as decoration during the celebration. No one had been alarmed to discover that the night had bred many murders. It was a commonplace discovery when morning came. The bodies. The blood.

Besides the empty barrels, Brandie saw a snub-nosed drinker. He leaned and smoked something spicy and eyed her up and down. He wore a crimson oilskin. Raindrops pattered off his shoulders like silver ball bearings. He eyed Miss Brandie like a bullish gundog, its attention brought to a meaty rib.

'Go home, Miss,' he pleaded. 'Bad folk about, don't need more blood in Penny District.'

Miss Brandie did not humour him. She merely cursed at him with a rude gesture. Then, she moved around the huddled buildings into the shade of a dank alley.

*

An autumn blow, cold enough to kill, burrowed through her cloak and chilled her bodice. The red cloth did nothing to battle the serrated edge on the breeze. Miss Brandie did not have any idea where she would sleep. In past autumns, she could have earned a bed by cleaning mugs or sweeping broken dishes in these very buildings. But she had been adamant not to stoop so low in what she considered her PRIME. Besides, she had only made a pocket's worth of copper. That would likely not even buy breakfast in the morning. Nowadays, younger and "better-equipped" people worked these jobs.

Miss Brandie might have presented a pretty twenty-something. However, she could not accept that her childhood had passed by like frames from a fever dream. She would wake up next week, somewhere and in who-knew-what shape, and she'd be fifty-something. Miss Brandie knew her life would go by in a blink and lamented that she had not spent her girlhood up with a degree more prudence.

Despite its state, she once praised the embroidery of her cloak. She once embraced the warmth it offered. A gentleman admirer named Conrad Murnau had given it to her. And Brandie had thought him to be quite a bachelor. He had hopes of warming her heart. The last two years had not been kind to the rosy material. And that made her question both the original worth of the cloth and Murnau's true intentions.

Presently, it was no more than a frayed, red ribbon around her neck.

In the beginning, many of her admirer's gifts had been given to her in the hope of one thing. Of this, Miss Brandie had no doubts. There were many beautiful necklaces, bracelets, jewels, and exotic perfumes. She had been given so many that she did not feel guilty pawning them off. Brandie had filed off their old owners' markings with her roughest nail files. What few pennies they had fetched had been spent long ago. Unfortunately, none of them had been worth much.

Her expenses had dwindled. Miss Brandie had taken to pawning off her own clothing. Most notably: her boots. None of them had ever been comfortable. They had either been too narrow, too wide, too gaudy, or too bland. Her feet had carried her through nearly every alley and backstreet Penny District had. And through their use and ruin, she felt a similar effect on her heart. Brandie had romanced a better life. The noisy journey through Penny District's winding roads irked her most. Now, Brandie's purse was empty, and the hole in her heart had been left unsatisfied. Perhaps, she would have welcomed a predator tearing it out.

*

In the distance, Miss Brandie heard music. She had always loved music. She noted a grand arrangement. It was a blend of an organ, strings, and a children's choir. It added deluxe flavours of luxury and dignity to the Penny District air. It also made the quiet around her clearer. Brandie looked up. Belgrove Bank rose above the highest of businesses and bed sheds in Penny District. The peak was lost amongst the black clouds. The amber impression of desk candles flickered in the darkness. There was warmth behind the brickwork. Of course, Belgrove was too far from Miss Brandie to be the source of the music. However, many noble places indulged in such opulence.

The orchestra dragged her back.

Miss Brandie had attended masquerades and balls in her better years. But, she went mainly as a show of her gentleman's pride and pomp. Brandie shuddered, as if embraced by the phantom memory.

In the direction she had been heading, however, no music was playing. Nothing was sounding, only the pitter-patter of autumn rain. It fell on rooftop canvases, crammed rookeries, and through the narrow lanes. Her only accomplice in Penny District was her shadow, cast against the path ahead, bending like a skulking street beast.

Brandie was ragged. She was lost.

Evenings such as this were often polluted by sooty chimney smoke. The metallic tang of new blood spoiled Penny District's low-hanging runnels. Brandie always assumed that someone somewhere was either dead or dying. She made it her business to never question, and never provoke. It struck her as poetic that Penny District was where the most coin was garnered, and the most lost. It was a pit of debt, deceit, and drunkenness. Perhaps, the Penny District Predator's bloody murders had been inevitable.

She had heard plenty about them. Nobody could live in Penny District as long as she had without hearing the stories. Only up until recently, she had pushed them aside as nothing more. But a cast of ladies had been disappearing from Penny District. Their shredded wardrobes were found days later with what remained of their bodies. Brandie had given in to the grim reality. And she knew she was no longer safe walking home alone after dark.

Penny District had a killer and nobody knew when or where he would pounce.

The black portraits showed the Penny District Predator carving a bestial grimace. He had claws like meat hooks. A devilish street demon with eyes of ruby fire born in a black cloak. A cloak that enveloped Penny District's lamplight like a wide slice of night. Sensible common folk had determined him to be tall and lithe if he were male. Others claimed he was no man or woman, but a monster. A monster bred from darkness and blood. Brandie prayed that she would never have the misfortune of being the one to end the debate.

Miss Brandie's head squeezed with the post-partum pressure of cheap booze. Her budget had taken over her preferences. She used to drink only the oldest red wines. Now, she only drank dirty rum –

often in a downtrodden locale. The wobble in her leg had not placated. Pain wove its way up her back and pinched her nape. The drink had burrowed into her brain and buzzed like a disturbed beehive. Nonetheless, she paid a pretty penny to numb the pain. It had been a shame that each dawn saw a new pain erupt in its place.

Brandie tried to remember when she had last eaten something other than damp, brown bread or bad giblets. She had mustered a few pennies from night work. And she had given them to the barkeep to please her addiction, not her belly. When no promised escape came, she would slip a contraband Queen's Bead onto her pink tongue. She would then anxiously await the pull of dreams. When – and if – morning came for her, it did so with the vengeance of a distressed parent. Although where Brandie's parents were now was anyone's guess.

*

Old Man Jacque, the barkeep at the Burning Brew, had described the murders as a dreadful business. Business in Penny District had dwindled in light of such evil. Vessels still visited the docks but did not stay long. The merchants rarely stepped ashore the cobbles.

Most men and women had decided that a blurry nightlife was not worth their heads and guts in payment. Miss Brandie had not received the memo. The predator would visit those found bumbling about Penny District after dark. Each had been ripped up and drained. Brandie had heard that whoever had been visited had not been seen again. One exception was Melanie Mace. She was a distinguished harlot who claimed to have seen the killer once before. He had been creeping over rain-swept rooftops. He was hunting a child heading home from her paper delivery. Melanie had claimed his eyes burned like hot coals. She said he could leap inhumanly far between rooftops, like some animal. Melanie, however, was no newcomer to the images conjured up by a bad batch of Queen's Bead. Her claims had been met with mixed reception. Desperate for information, the law-keepers had taken her words as gospel. And the law-keepers had taken particular interest in her imagination.

Miss Brandie did not divide between predator and prince. Most men she had known had been beastly in a manner of speaking. She deplored that she had ever believed otherwise. Coincidentally, the Penny District Predator was not alone with his "tools". Brandie carried a blade of her own. But for now, it hugged her bare thigh, waiting. She had half a mind to unleash it on several drunks. They thought it was fair to mock her bedraggled appearance.

Brandie needed a bed, a Queen's Bead even. An unacceptable number of nights had been passed huddled beneath a lamplight. It had been a miracle that she had not been bothered by drunks, law-keepers, or worse company. Brandie slumped down into the mouth of the back alley of an archway. Her body deflated from use. The aches were beginning to set in again.

The lights above her circled with languid motion. Beneath her cloak, she began to run her nail down the edge of her blade. It was maybe her only possession she had not considered pawning off for copper. She carried it everywhere but had not yet used it. Brandie may have been bottle-worn and bumbling, but she polished the blade with rainwater each night, maintaining its silver gleam.

Maybe that was it. Maybe that was her move.

Tonight would be the night she unsheathed the blade, and buried it in somebody's organs. She would collect the pennies her prize dropped. Perhaps she could get enough for a bed. Then, she would leave the blame for the Penny District Predator to digest.

*

An hour passed. And the dull buzz of rum had begun to fade. "Prospect" sounded better to Miss Brandie than "victim". THE VICTIM elicited more than one death. One murder was hardly unusual. She would merely be joining the league of a darker breed of drunk.

Penny District was a money lender's hole. Brandie noticed two drunken pinch-pockets fighting over their stolen belongings. An audience of drunks encircled the pair, punching the air and inciting more blood, and more rum. An hour ago, Miss Brandie may have joined in. There were too many people down that way, down Plinth Street. She had expected it to be quiet. Brandie did not linger. Any longer and it was inevitable that one drunk would bloody his knuckles on the nose of another. Soon, the law-keepers would arrive and break the rabble, and Miss Brandie's game would meet a premature end.

The law-keepers eventually came with leathers creaking and oilskins glistening in the downpour. Miss Brandie heard the audience complaining about the spoiled brawl. Then, they commenced one of their own. Fists flew, teeth were chipped, and hair was pulled.

Backing up from the upheaval, Brandie slipped down the shadow of an avenue. It was adjacent to Hack Alley. It was draughty, filthy drains were overflowing nearby. Goosebumps pricked her skin. She wrapped herself tighter in her crimson cloak and clutched her naked blade. Brandie veered. A black cat knocked down a potted plant from a balcony above. It shattered beside her and worms wriggled out from the dirt. She noticed a grimy stream pouring from the backdoors of a lodging house. Many such establishments littered Penny District, dens for deviants. The water was pungent and bodily. She smelled human waste.

Miss Brandie was not alone.

She rubbed the remainder of the rum-daze from her eyes and looked up and down the alley. The lamplight did not reach down here. Someone breathed in the darkness: a man. Brandie made out a black cloak, gliding from one pocket of shade to another. He put his head up to a similar flow of brown and white water in the wall and began to drink from the human waste. Perhaps, this was Miss Brandie's betting prospect. She only hoped now that the brawl would occupy the law-keepers long enough. She donned an innocent pout, covering her breath. Beneath her breast, her blade was drawn, naked.

Miss Brandie approached.

'Evening, darling,' Brandie mumbled. There was pretence in her voice, feigning innocence and vulnerability. 'I'm looking for a bed. Perhaps you could point me in the RIGHT DIRECTION?'

He looked at her.

Miss Brandie could not see what he looked like. But she heard him drinking, scoffing, and groaning. Brandie pulled the cloak from her chest. She hoped the skin about her collar and shoulders looked soft and alluring. She held her blade behind her back.

He heard.

His head snapped up like a startled beast. He moved. Miss Brandie noted the jingle of his deep pockets. He had a heavy purse. She licked her lips with the guarantee of Queen's Bead and a hearty meal coming her way.

He was near her now.

Brandie could feel intimate warmth brewing in the metres between them. She drew her blade. The man's breathing had become heavy, a pant. He had been interested in the heat her body radiated. He came in close, and Brandie jabbed out with the neck of her blade to open his throat and be done with it. Claws encircled her wrist.

Her bones snapped. Miss Brandie moved to scream in agony, but with a lash, he plucked the cherry from her throat. Night air escaped through the wound, along with pints of thin blood. All Miss Brandie could see, all that she would remember if she awoke on another side, were two eyes, aflame like boiled rubies. Her colour drained, and Brandie died alone.

The Penny District Predator dragged her into the darkness and ripped her up.

When Miss Brandie was discovered, it was as a decoration. A bundle of red ribbons.

REDBEARD

A PENNY DISTRICT DREADFUL

Blood and copper mingled in the darkness. The darkness belonged to the dungeon. It was all it knew. It was all it had. More darkness spread over the low ceiling, wrought from black marble. It drowned out what was left of the tiled floor.

This darkness mellowed – a brooding dark.

The air became heavier. It breathed in an absence of warmth, dense but cool. Cold and damp. It pulled breath from the lungs. An ambience of hidden malevolence dwelt in the depths of the dungeon. It bred and mated in the black. Malevolence with a name that must never be spoken. A name that pulls on heartstrings and rips horror from the heart.

Redbeard moved through the darkness. He was old and slow. He stumbled and breathed as though each breath might be his last. His frail and bent hands locked around the haft of a cane – a cane of beautiful, maroon wood. His vision had become bleary. When he looked about in the darkness of the dungeon, he did not know what he expected to see. There was never anything to see. But there are always things to be heard: things moving.

He could not see. But he listened. Redbeard's ears picked up each drop of moisture from the ceiling. He heard the rattle of heavy chains on each wall. He could hear the chatter and scurrying of mice down there with him. Redbeard did not know how long they had been down there. Or what they had been eating. But the crunch of an old finger bone beneath his boot gave him an unwelcome answer. He could not see the mice. But he heard them chewing. They were gnawing the caskets of dark sherry and red wine. These were kept down here to preserve their delicate flavours. Moisture again: drip, drip, drip...

But not water, blood. Soon, he would drink his fill. And Redbeard would be reborn. He breathed in and sniffed the air. A broad smile split his cheeks.

'She's here.'

*

Rosie Newman dreamed.

She came around, moaning through a daze. She woke, bare-skinned, beneath velvet bedding. Her hair parted over two piled pillows, curling down into cinnamon locks. The blanket's material was woven from night silk. It was black-laced and smooth. Rosie did not know this place. Her bedchamber was unfamiliar and unpleasant. Crimson drapery danced mockingly in the open wind. The breeze was hidden, but it slipped through the balcony. It whistled through the castle's baroque stone. A potted, dead rosebush crumbled in the window. Rosie did not remember much. Barely even an image, only an odour.

She had been in Penny District. Yes. Rosie remembered now.

A narrow back alley filled with shadowy puddles and lamplight. An odour had come from the dank passage, like a vintner's perfected brew. It was intoxicating, seductive, nauseating. Then, she knew nothing. Rosie had blacked out.

The scent remained with her now. It was indistinct and abandoning. She had awoken deep in its clutches. She did not know what had happened to her. She would discover the answer soon. For better or for worse.

Rosie cast her weary gaze about the chamber. Masks hung from each wall. They were golden, cherubic, like chubby babies. They possessed an ill innocence that lit the room, reflecting hearty candlelight. Rosie shuddered at the lie hammered into their expressions. She bristled more so at the daunting history brooding behind them. They were moulded and shaped by children for one purpose and one purpose alone. Rosie's bedside candle dripped pale wax beside her. It pooled in a burnished brass bowl. The wick flame chuckled and waned in the breeze, promising warmth. But it could not deliver. The flame was weak, much like Rosie. It danced like a strip of parchment.

*

Beyond the shrouded curtains in the chamber, Rosie found night.

She was high up, higher than she had ever been. Only married noblemen and beautiful ladies lived this high above the dirty cobbles. Their clothes and rooms were bejewelled and beloved. And their vows to Belgrove Bank had ensured they lived in opulence. That was how the charity was managed in Penny District. High above Penny District, bloodlines like those lived deliciously detached from the rest.

Penny District: an urban depression of gothic, black eaves and amber streetlamps. Penny District: a heinous pit of cutpurses, avarice, sin, and struggle. The district had most recently given birth to its first and worst killer, a beast, a predator.

Penny District was quite a departure from Rosie's current whereabouts. What unfortunate turn of events had brought her here? Until her predicament revealed itself, Rosie would consider its benefits. Perhaps, she would even indulge in a couple of them.

Beyond the billowing drapes — out in the cool, open air — a blood moon rose in the darkness, spilling through her balcony. It doused Rosie's new home in delicious, wounded ruby. Something had been sprawled out across her mattress. She had not noticed it until it caught the weeping moonlight and shone. It was a sheer nightgown, or maybe a dress.

The slip was woven from frosted silver. It glinted like a child's wish crystal in the leaking darkness. Rosie reached her long fingers out to touch it. She bristled at its brush. It was thin and icy. Rosie had only ever dreamed of owning such a piece. And now, it had slipped right out of her dreams before her. The nightgown appeared very valuable, worth more than anything her family had ever owned, twice over. It looked luxurious. It looked noble. More than both, it looked bridal.

*

Rosie stood from her bed.

Her silken sheets dropped and her silhouette danced in red light. The red moon eclipsed Rosie's beautiful, exposed body. She was pale, elegant, and ember-freckled. Her skin was like eggshell, porcelain. Rosie rolled her head around her palms. Bouncy locks of burnished ginger tumbled down her long back in loamy warmth. Rosie grabbed the nightgown. She slipped her limbs through its sleeves and slacks. Chilled prickles jaunted up and down her body as it embraced her intimately. The moment the gown touched Rosie's skin, it became warm. Warm as if hot blood coursed through the material.

In the corner of the room sat a mirror, peeking between piled-up furniture and covered with dusty cloth and grey cobwebs. Rosie eyed herself. The gown enveloped her body completely. But, it had one open cascade: a slit near her slim, defined ankles. She caressed the side of her head, rubbing her temple. Rosie was robbed of all memory from before her unexpected and uninvited slumber. Despite her lowborn heritage, Rosie wore the gown well. Where Rosie's old clothes were now was a mystery. She did not dwell on it.

'How beautiful,' Rosie mused. It was the first taste of wealth she had ever experienced. Her previous life had always kept her from handsome bachelors, noblemen, and a happier life. She veered and spun slowly in front of the mirror. And then, she spoke to the murky gloom eating at the walls around her. 'How ghastly,' she declared. Rosie did not expect a reply. But when one came, her heart filled with dread.

*

A new man's voice came from nowhere.

A booming, bass whisper filled the bedchamber. Rosie turned around slowly. She could not move much quicker. She looked deep into the darkness. There, she eyed an impossible doorway. By all reason and chance, she had missed it before. It was clouded, dark.

Nothing moved. Rosie's daring curiosity died in a moment. She tightened her throat and voiced her concern.

'Hello?' Rosie mumbled meekly. 'Who's there?'

A rasp raked through the air. The man's voice settled into its weight and boomed back through the dark. 'Rosie, my lady,' he bowed. 'Please excuse my manners.'

The man's voice growled from the darkness of the door. He paced his diction, purring over each syllable like a canny predator. She only hoped that she was not his prey, coaxed into his embrace. Rosie hearkened keenly. She had never before heard speech so beguiling and ambient. And she doubted she ever would again.

He was dressed well; a nobleman, no doubt. Immediately, Rosie Newman knew him to be of purple blood and pedigree. He paced from an inky puddle that separated the bedchamber from the great spiral staircase beyond. Through the door, Rosie caught a familiar odour, the same one as before, the last thing she remembered from the streets of Penny District. People were dining downstairs.

The strange man drifted inside. There were no footsteps. He had no physical presence past sight. His midriff was sheathed in black leather. A sharp, high collar emphasized his distinctive cheekbones. A heavy, brown fur coat was draped around his broad shoulders. It connected to an orange cloak embroidered by Penny District's finest tailors. Rosie could not see his hands under the long, wide sleeves. A copper brooch depicting a rose was affixed above his heart. Most distinctive, however, was his beard. Not red like fire nor autumn crunch. This was a weighty, dense beard the colour of spilt blood. The weight of it drew her attention away from his dark eyes, which twinkled like cinders. The man came closer. He paced through the bedchamber, towards Rosie.

The moon's ruby glow filled the space between them. Dust particles played in its light. The nobleman's entrance was marred by a moment of uninterrupted silence. All the while, Rosie kept her eyes on him. Her heart was beating fast now, faster than ever. Her waning dread was replaced with nervousness. The man with the red beard was devilishly handsome. No doubt there.

'Who are you? Where am I?'

Rosie's questions went unanswered for a moment. The man with the red beard tilted his head from side to side, pulled up and down by each new question like a curious hound. There was something rugged in his manner that completely contradicted his noble appearance.

He waded through the crimson moonlight blemishing the bedchamber. Rosie spied a curved blade clasping his abdomen, with a polished, brass pommel carved into a bestial face baring its fangs. It headed a hilt of pale elk bone. He patted the pommel softly with his palm. Rosie only heard him the second time he spoke.

'Do not scream. We have guests downstairs.'

Guests? Other visitors, perhaps. That confirmed Rosie's suspicions. 'My name is Redbeard, duke of this holding. And I bid you dearest welcome to my humble dwelling.'

'Humble,' Rosie whispered, 'how modest.' When next she spoke, Rosie declared her bewilderment aloud. 'I do not understand, Duke. How did I come to be here? I remember nothing.'

Rosie had many questions. She had been pondering each of them since waking. She wished to voice them vehemently from the gothic steeples until answered. But somehow, that did not seem a wise decision given her current predicament. Her vulnerability.

Redbeard's enchanting voice warned her not to interrupt. His words held sway over her in a way she did not and could not understand.

Redbeard, or so he had been introduced, paced around the wooden headboard of the bed. He palmed over the sleepy cradle with a courtly sweep. As he drew nearer, Rosie broke from her musing. She withdrew guardedly.

'Memory is a delicate thing,' Redbeard drew closer. 'Sometimes all it takes is the smallest stone to shatter the glass.' He grinned broadly, brandishing an array of perfect, marble teeth. The expression lasted no longer than a breath's sunken second.

Redbeard's voice was enticing. His blanket of seduction had barely been lifted. Redbeard continued, all the while eluding the neglected mirror positioned between them. Rosie's eyes bloomed and widened with misplaced glee. She took a step closer to him.

'That odour, I know it well,' Redbeard flashed his teeth once more. They appeared sharper now. Shining like pale knives in the blood of his beard. 'Indeed, my lady. Many feasts have ended. And many more may come.'

Redbeard pulled back into the dark doorway from which he had emerged. He enticed Rosie to pursue him into the darkness with a bejewelled hand, stretching out from his sleeve, a pale hand matted with red hair like that of an animal.

Rosie took his hand. It was warm. She looked into Redbeard's eyes. Dark things danced in the blood-laden blackness of his stare. 'Perhaps now, you will join me for dinner?'

*

Never before in her life had Rosie Newman known a banquet hall of such measure.

The dining gallery was peerless, both in its dimensions and adornment. This was a spectacle. This was the treasure trove of Belgrove Bank's laundered riches. She had never seen anything quite like it. Admittedly, Rosie had a bad memory. But a young woman from the streets of Penny District had likely never entered such a place. Not without due cause. The women who did were never seen again. It had become commonplace.

Before Rosie lay a monumental dining table, holding half-filled cups and a banquet of red meats and dark berries. Duke Redbeard hosted a cabinet assembly for noblemen and ladies wearing luxurious but gaudy outfits, many of whom had already sat down.

Candelabra chandeliers of pure star glass dangled pendulously above them, barely illuminating the dark corners of the dining gallery.

Rosie was directed to her seat by Redbeard. She nestled nervously between a pair of noblemen. He led the procession on a cathedral throne of old design and red, velvet leather. Already, the veil of seduction and enchantment was beginning to fade from Rosie's mind. She could feel more valuable memories returning to her.

Rosie paid mind to the dinner guests, gorging on bloody, juicy carcasses, sliding back mouthfuls of an unknown meat and washing down with cruor wine. A wine that smelled wrong. The drinks swirled tastefully in brass chalices. These members of the nobility disturbed Rosie profoundly.

Redbeard raised his chalice as if to make a speech. But Rosie could not hear him. Her ears were numb to sound. Her body was numb to everything else. She was frozen with fear. Her heart was crawling up the gullet towards her mouth. Rosie's entire body began to quiver with discord. Then, she looked at the people around her.

The charade was beginning to fall apart like shed skin. Despite their imperial attire, Rosie began to see them for who they were. Or rather, what they were. She realised with disgust that they were not quite human. The men and women of Penny District were never human, not really. They were all demons, in a manner. However, these noble people wore their wickedness openly, brandishing blades and vile insults at each other. Here, in this gaudy chamber of wealth, the denizens' falseness was revealed to her. Not quite human indeed.

Ghouls.

*

Ghouls. Rosie was dining with ghouls.

Elongated jowls and bladed ears framed grim masks. Corpse meat dribbled from their mouths. They were hunched like amorphous bats. Split tongues glided up and down the still-beating banquet with sadistic pleasure. Horror ignited in Rosie's heart alongside a primal need to flee. She needed to escape but she could not. Something held her motionless in her chair. Rosie spared a glance over towards the head of the gathering, Redbeard.

Redbeard was sitting comfortably on his throne. The velvet

rippled when he moved. He chewed and swallowed a chunk of muscle-strewn meat off a sharp, dirty nail. His hands had changed now. He was like the others. But his bloody beard was still as magnificent and well-maintained as ever. Each bite he took made it more beautiful. Blood dripped from his lips to his skin, colouring it with hot ichor and ever-darkening wine.

'Duke,' Rosie muttered. Her voice grew louder as the rest went quiet. The veil had been lifted. It was as if she had awoken from some dazzling magic trick into haunting verisimilitude. Now she could see things for what they truly were. Rosie was already teary-eyed before speaking once more. 'Redbeard, what, what are we eating?'

The banquet hall breathed. Everyone present did so. The cadaverous noblemen around Rosie were drooling once more. Penny District's nobility smeared the bleach carpet with viscous saliva. Redbeard beamed at her, his eyes ablaze. He remained silent.

He gestured an ostensibly dirty finger towards the guests huddled by candlelight. The thought was daunting. It caused warm bile to rise in Rosie's throat. It was what he had pointed towards. She was shaking, and reluctantly washed the bile back down to her belly with mellow red wine. Rosie bathed in the dining room's atmosphere. Not a gallery.

Neither carpet nor woven tapestry could be found. The banquet hall became a gruesome threshold. It was built of stitched abominations of swollen, sutured flesh. The blubbering, mournful faces had overlapping skin. They wailed loudly and drowned out the distant organ, playing discordantly. The wooden furniture blurred into bodily horror. Pale spurs of bone marrow had been carved into the crooked furniture. They formed the pillars, tables, and chairs. This was the same bone as Redbeard's blade. Not elk, it had never been elk.

Human bone.

Redbeard's hip brandished a blade hilted by human bone. The banquet: a partially-living mass of the stolen bodies of the Penny District lowlifes. Each one, young men and women, moaned and groaned for mercy. Rosie was not dining in a gallery. This was – and had always been – a flesh theatre, a bloody summer court.

Rosie screamed.

*

Everything changed around her.

Rosie flung herself about in frantic desperation. The muscle ribbons tore from the tablecloth. Rosie freed herself from her constraints. The trappings were slick and gritty, like congealing blood. Her chair hit the ground in a jarring crash. Rosie clambered on towards the grand double doors, only to find them locked.

The ghouls began moving. They raised their brows from the banquet to inspect the disturbance. Each vicious man-thing and woman-thing peered at Rosie with hungry eyes. Before they stirred enough to pursue, Rosie hurried back up the spiral staircase. It was the one she had come down with great urgency. Her nightgown was tight and wrapping even tighter. Rosie's nightgown – the one presented to her by Duke Redbeard – began to weep tears as red as his beard.

Rosie looked down as she climbed higher, recoiling at the image before her. What had once masqueraded as an exquisitely lucent dress had been reduced to its primal form. It oozed warm blood against Rosie's flushed complexion. She was wrapped up in a dress made of skin. The skin of Redbeard's previous bride.

Rosie continued spinning up the spiral staircase, climbing the heights of the tallest spire. She glided along. Before long, the ghouls were behind her in carnivorous pursuit. The beasts were gaining on her. They knew these corridors and passages better than Rosie ever would.

She could hear them in the walls. Their movements caused old paintings to rattle against their hangings. The walls choked up with disturbed dust. Her skin gown wept streams of blood. Its teeth were sinking into her skin. The remaining trails baited the ghouls. They also betrayed Rosie's position in the spire. Shadows blocked out the ruby moonlight. Then, she saw them. Redbeard's ghouls were outside in the night air now.

They were highborn cannibals who had developed pink, threadbare wings. Their wings blocked the stars above Penny District. Before long, Rosie stopped. The effort had slowed her. She crashed into her bedchamber ahead and clambered across the room, knocking the golden cherub masks off the walls. Rosie placed her arms on the frame of the balcony. She stared at the gothic silhouette of Penny District down below.

Penny District spread out and away, forever. The bells of Belgrove Bank were ringing.

The smell of blood radiated from the streets below like an overly pungent admixture of ingredients. Rosie turned around. She had left the door of the chamber open behind her.

A choir of whispers and greedy blandishments called out after her. They stalked towards the door. They craved Rosie's flesh. Then, the ghouls entered her room. And there, they stopped, they stared. Rosie faced them and backed away. She edged her heels along the precipice, almost stumbling over the black balcony.

An individual paced out from the monster's ball before her. Redbeard now looked the same as his coterie. His cheeks were gaunt, a sign of endless depravity. Sobs of nightmarish whimsy grazed Rosie's cheeks as the duke spoke.

'Do not fear, Rosie. We are family here. We are brood.'

Redbeard reached out and caressed Rosie's cheek. She could feel his diabolical enchantment weighing heavily on her heart once again. Redbeard attempted to bring Rosie in close for a deadly kiss. The kiss was broken in an instant. Redbeard felt a horrid pain in his chest. Rosie gripped him tightly. She buried the duke's bone knife deep between his ribs, meeting his heart.

Redbeard let out a violent wail of pain. His scream scraped the folding night with bleeding agony. Rosie detached herself from Redbeard's embrace. Her long hair waved in the Penny District's winds. Redbeard crumbled to ash. The ghouls shrieked and lashed out towards Rosie. She turned back through the drapes.

Rosie dove from the balcony.

SNOWED IN

The Carrington estate crept into sight through the forest.

I saw it as a shadow. A lump of coal amongst a bed of packed snow. The manor house was a large, sharp, and ugly thing. The uppermost windows were cobwebbed with hairline cracks from thrashing blizzard winds. Slate eaves struck out above the mountain woodland. Sombre and silent like gravestones. The rest of the house was wood, black wood. It was a marvel of sable construction out here in the cold, cutting a separate colour from the world around it.

The porch rose from an inching snowfall. The same snowfall coating the surrounding crowd of crooked trees. The Carrington estate was a work of absolute contrast. Dark in light. I saw it fuller as I wheeled closer. The house bore semblance to a fashioned soot rock or obsidian ore. There it sat, laid atop a blanket of snow.

The journey through the snow stacks and mountain range was nothing but arduous. Navigating the winter tempests had only been eased upon spotting the manor's extrinsic appearance. Perhaps that was why it had been wrought out from dark wood. It was a gloomy beacon amongst fathoms of white. It was striking against the snow. My geriatric anthropology professor would have once remarked that the estate was a foul omen to be forsaken. That it was a deceptive lure guiding the lost and languid through the snow towards it. Coming from such a city as Arkham, Massachusetts, all the way to the Carrington estate out in the glass wastes of Nova Scotia was galling. The world was quieter up this way.

Truthfully, upon being sent there to scrutinize details of abandonment, I was under the impression that the community was one of welfare and charity. Though, my arrival was far from opportune. I was alone in winter. I had not seen another soul for a while. My automobile whimpered like a wounded wolf as it fell silent. I should have known that such an arrival would mark the first of many misfortunes, out in the frosty wilds.

*

I was convinced that, somehow, the house was calling out for me.

Still, I remained hesitant to accept the estate as being a manor. Nothing but its size proved worthy of such a claim. I had expected cast iron gates surrounding the estate, decorated with gargoyles and wolf snouts. The convenient cobbled road eluded my vision almost entirely. It was buried beneath several feet of snow, I was sure.

I could not and did not spare any time to think of such inconveniences. The cold was assailing my toes and my dead hands were bruising blue.

Quickly, I drew closer. I was suddenly struck by the broad doors, shattered and splintered, a sign of exerted strength and forced entry. Somebody or something had walked snow inside. The doors were black as night. From what I could tell, they had been wrenched and ripped off their steely hinges. No sudden gust could have done this.

The sable wood was slashed with claw marks. Some frenzied beast, it seemed. Perhaps a bear or a lost timber wolf? I could not know for certain then. I recall running my quivering fingers through the slashed grooves. They were larger than any animal I had since considered. The wood shavings were peeling off in a silent wind. They curled away from the doors like a twisting mimicry of the original carpentry. I stepped through the doors. An easy motion, as they had been slacked ajar. I slid through like a cat burglar and walked into the Carrington estate, into the darkness. Snow was closing in.

*

My footfalls echoed in a hollow space.

Black boots punched down to the cool, frost-sodden floorboards. Some seconds passed before my eyesight adjusted to the place, connecting with its darkness. The air was dead in there. I saw a superlative gallery filled with cloth-covered furniture and stacks of canvas paintings. Watercolour faces eyed me, peeking out from behind veils of frost. The gallery itself was far greater than any university classroom or other estate I had ever had the displeasure of visiting. A careening stairwell with exquisite railings swooned up towards the upper floors.

The house was inexplicably large and disturbingly silent. To my left and right were doors, tucked in the shade cast off the overhanging balcony. It stopped the winter glare from streaming in through the windows. Though, I doubt any light or warmth would have proved successful in assaulting the rime. My gaze did not linger there for long.

The winter sun was always early to rise and quick to set. And setting it was. The glare was fading. What little light remained was being stolen away by the sudden threat of night closing in. The gallery became a fading picture of scratchy contours. One of the windows was completely shattered. A tapestry curtain flapped in the howling gale outside. The fabric was shredded, torn, and pulled. The gale found its way through the glass and whistled its deathly rattle through the walls. The Carrington estate found its voice and began to cry.

I needed some light. So I struck a match, which did little to affect the darkness. However, not all was black wood and torn cloth. Dried blood lathered the floorboards and stairwell, gritty paint splashed on a splintered canvas. On the walls around me, I saw the same claw-grooves. They had gashed straight through the plasterboard and wood, uncovering cold cinderblock beneath. The wallpaper covering the interior of the gallery was floral like a willow swamp, and withering. It grimly decorated the solemn gallery with a feigning sense of blooming life. I felt nothing but death in that house. Death and solitude.

I ran my gloved hand down the plaster, caressing its shreds. It crumbled at my touch and the warmth of the match. A quick shoot of trapped air snuffed the firelight out between my forefinger and thumb. Darkness quickly followed. It was clear to me that the cold had found purchase inside the Carrington estate some years ago. The shattered doorway had been broken inwards with no small degree of force. The snow that had carried inside on a winter gale had not travelled upstairs. That much I could ascertain. Despite a gut instinct pleading that I turn around and escape, I started up the stairwell. A black curiosity demanded I investigate.

*

My slow and steady ascent was accompanied by creaking.

The floorboards were weaker upstairs than anywhere else in the estate. The walls were decorated with uncomfortable hanging characters whose faces caught shadows in foul ways. For every corridor I walked through, a small boulevard of doors flanked its edges. It was only upon retrieving my flashlight from my briefcase that I could fully visualize the route ahead. The house was giant and complex. I was certain I could easily become lost here.

I fetched my flashlight. Each step saw it flicker. The cold had wormed its way inside and was doing its worst to seal me in the gloom. My flashlight was freezing up, so I knocked its head against the walls to strike life back into it. The sound of the act echoed and did little to conceal my presence within the estate. Frost fell from the ceiling and sent sibilant whispers through the house until they fell out of earshot. What secrets they shared was unknown to me. I ignored them and carried on.

As was expected, I ventured into every room. Many were barren and empty. Though, not all of them. What I came to find in a sequestered chamber was both extraordinary and harrowing. Some of the rooms I inspected were congruent with the rest of the house's aesthetic. Each one was derelict and neglected.

I investigated a child's quarters. A cradle sat in the corner, a small pile of knickknacks stacked atop a dusty carpet. The wallpaper was reminiscent of the one in the bedroom of my childhood: woodland critters frolicking through sunken willows. The sight made me smile slightly and forget my whereabouts. The window pane in that room was shattered too. A gentle breeze danced through the curtains and licked at my face like thin mountain air.

The night was setting in now and growing stronger. I could see a pearly moon rolling across the sky, bouncing across the guardian mountain range. From this height, I could see lots of the surrounding wilderness that was not shrouded by fog and snowfall. The mountains surrounded the region. The Carrington estate was central and low, like a blackberry rolling around at the bottom of a porcelain pot.

The child's room – congruous with a great many others – was dirtied with scatterings of frozen gore. It was the same substance from the gallery downstairs. My soul felt weary and strained by the thought of what horror scourged these walls. I struggled to comprehend what could have occurred at the estate, and what had become of the Carrington family thereafter. I would investigate further after settling for the night rush. I could not drive into the nearest town, not with the threat of blizzards at the doorstep. I would have to stay the night in the old house. I would face the spirits of the past, the monsters.

*

Later that night, once I had unloaded my papers and other essentials, I rested.

Blue twilight quilted the starless sky. Much of the Carrington estate and surrounding wilderness were plunged into darkness. Fortuitously, I found a candle holder, hoisting it upstairs from the dining room to guide my way through the black. It was an effort to keep the flames alight in the cool. Something wanted me to stay in the dark.

For several hours that evening, I sat in a room that lacked the blood splattering across walls and floorboards that characterised the other rooms. To which I had no complaints. The warmth which emanated from the candlelight was incredibly welcome. It drowned my fingers in heat. Roosting in a croaking old chair, I had sprawled all my legal notes and notices out in front of me to determine the soliciting of the Carrington estate.

For some strange reason, I could not bring myself to press the rigid fountain pen against the parchment. The inkwell rested virgin at the border of the desk's candlelight. I could not think straight. I was still repulsed by the thoughts of what had occurred in the house and what fate had befallen the Carrington family. Dwelling on such thoughts proved harmful. For the rest of that night, I was jumpy and alert to the grim truth that, out here in the blasting white snowstorms, I was utterly alone.

Sceptically, I started to investigate the living quarters. The act felt like an illegal violation of the Carrington family's privacy. But my career and longing for substantial answers demanded it. That was what I told myself to satisfy my moral compass. I started plundering and pilfering through several drawers, desks, and wardrobes, my search continued in the dim light of milky candles.

It was following several instances of stacking envelopes and research notes that I began to scrutinize the loose treasures of my inspection. There were several leather-bound journals hidden under mattresses or false floorboards. This intrigued me greatly. I can assure you, without any hint of untruth, that I was quite flummoxed by what I read.

*

Most peculiar amongst my pickings was a stuffed collection of monographs.

Each page, note, and scroll detailed scratchy sketches of something freakish and grotesque: a creature. The accompanying research notes and annotations detailed a crepuscular creature — similar to a stag or some other wild beast — and how it lurked in the wilderness of the surrounding mountains. The annotations were inky scribbles at best, but something about reading them by candlelight disturbed me greatly.

Against my better instincts, I read on. The thing was not like any animal I had ever encountered. If I were to put it straight, I could only describe it as the terrible by product of lupine and equine breeding.

It wore the gaunt face of an elk. Its mantle of antlers spindled outwards like some withered oak tree rendered leafless by fall. The creature's limbs were long and wrought from ropey muscle. The skin and patchy fur were strapped tightly over the bone. Each paw, foot, and claw sprouted a grizzly ungula or talon.

The creature's mask was most unnerving of all. It was skeletal, with eyeless sockets.

The thing's bony cheeks let loose a series of fleshy tendrils and grippers which fell against its hollow ribcage. I was unsure whether the beast was supposed to have fur. The faded sketch lines had only given the slightest impression of grey skin.

The drawing was horrifying to stare at. I cannot say whether I was staring too long and too intensely at the sketch, but I could swear that, eventually, the drawing started to stare back. Cold sweat trickled down from the tip of my nose and mixed with the melting candle wax on the desk. Wax streamed towards my hand, onto my fingers. The smell of sizzling flesh scented the room. The pain was excruciating. Though, it soon became apparent that it would be the least of my troubles, for I was not alone in the house. Something else entered.

*

If I were to be truly honest with you, I was unsure how long I had read through my findings for.

All the while, strange noises had been whistling through the Carrington estate. The great doors had no way of closing, as I've already told you at length. It was a wonder they still stood at all. Staring at the papers, it was beginning to become clearer what foul fate had befallen the Carrington family, out there in the snow.

My musings were interrupted by a sudden blasting gale. No. Not wind. A shriek. I tore my face up from the writing desk, with little time to brace myself. I fell backwards on my chair, riddled with fright. I fled out from the chamber's doorway and cast my stare up and down the corridor. I warded the blackness away with my dribbling candles. It proved feckless for anything other than illuminating the few feet before me.

I waded out and through the hallway towards the gallery downstairs. My silhouette cast dancing puppets against the aura of the candlelight. Snarling filled the darkness.

Then, I was running. The snow on the floor was not from my boots. And suddenly, the hot breath exhaling at my shoulder was not my own.

I fled for cover, dropping the candelabra to the floor in the wake of my footfalls. I did not make it far from the stairwell before something caught me. I was hoisted outwards through the shadow by long bones that began to puncture, flay, lick, and lash. I kicked. I screamed. I thrust my sharp pen outwards into the eye of an antlered creature, its muzzle dusted with winter snow.

The creature howled.

I ran, or rather limped, out from the Carrington estate until I saw my vehicle in the distance. The automobile was buried under mounds of snow and frost. The ruby strings of my open guts kissed the crystal floor like an oil painting.

The snow was decorated with blood diamonds.

I reached my automobile before my eyes rolled over like a gibbous moon. Darkness closed in around my vision. The last thing I remember from that terrible night was the slashed doors of the frozen Carrington estate closing shut. The glint of icy eyes in its darkness. It was six hours before the snow cleared and I reached the nearest town for shelter and medical assistance. Nobody believed my story about my experiences up in the mountains. They claimed the beast to be a bear or juvenile wolf.

I know otherwise. I know the beast that lurks in the snow. I have seen its eyes and felt its icy claws. And when next you find yourself someplace snowed in and all alone, perhaps you shall feel them too. You will know the Wendigo.

MUDBERRY

A dark December came to the village of Bram.

Midwinter celebrations decorated the streets beneath the boy's round window. Bram was hearty, quaint, and dainty. Many of its buildings stood two-storey tall. Once, they'd mostly been whitewashed cabins. Hardwood and stone buildings bore chimneys of orange brick. Cheap paint peeled off and Bram had become grey. Now, there was an effort to brush Bram into a more festive palette for Christmas. Buckets of pick-and-mix paint occupied people's doorways and littered alley edges. Holly branches and faux robin nests hung from burnished doorknockers. Their pompous faces pouted. Tonight, Christmas had come to Bram again.

The statue of a chubby woman rose from the middle of Bram. She'd been there much longer than any cabin. She cradled a marionette in her arms as though it were a baby. The doll's expression was blank. And its bulbous eyes were discomfortingly human.

The trees around Bram were dusted like upright rolls of roulade. Even the buildings were painted merrily. They were unbothered by the holes in their shingled roofs. The village's insides were exposed like gaping wounds. A draughty breeze drifted inside. Snow covered wardrobes, trunks, and carpets. Puddles of water lapped around burning hearths, where chopped logs crackled merrily and melted the invasive frost.

Bram remembered every child. But December did not. Each year, it disowned a child. This Christmas, the child shivered alone in his bare bedroom. No colour. No ornaments. No merriment. No toys. No loving parents to read him a bedtime noel. He slept in the shadow of dusk. He hoped to escape the evening's boredom whilst merrier children threw snow and balanced carrots outside. Before him, the boredom had been another boy's. And another boy's before him. Before they'd grown old enough to leave for work, buy homes, and have children of their own. Ruben was this boy's name. And he was a boy of eight. Plum and periwinkle coloured his cheeks and chin. Ruben had a busted lip and a constant backache. He'd grown used to the pain. It was beginning to numb. He was clumsy and had the bruises to prove it. He had brown hair, but patches were now missing. Other children did not like or play with Ruben. They thought him odd and disturbed. So Ruben grew up alone instead.

Ruben was one of many discarded children in Bram. He did not have any valuables. Even his candlelit and cobwebbed bedroom was not his own. It belonged to Miss Mildred's Most Merry Home for Unwanted Children, an orphanage. Ruben disliked the bedroom. It'd been dunked in darkness. Clothes birthed limbs and crawled. Mice squeaked in the wardrobe. And a beast growled beneath his bed. Nothing merry ever happened here. But a bed was a bed. No matter how uncomfortable.

*

Ruben had been told that he was a broken toy. And that he should be happy.

Mildred demanded appreciation. Ruben gave Mildred what she wanted. But he'd never called her by one name, Mama. Ruben had a Mama, once, and a Papa too. And they'd loved him dearly like no other. Ruben disliked the celebrations of Christmas. It reminded him of the fire that blazed two Decembers ago. It brought back memories of hoarse screaming and burning meat. It reminded him of his parents' death amongst the flames.

A baked breeze blew through the window again. On it now was roasted chestnut, carved bird meat, cranberry, pork crackling, cocoa spice, blackcurrants, and melted chocolate.

The warm scent wafted over to Ruben, who wriggled beneath a blanket. He was tossing and turning to find a dream. But sleep was lost. Dreams had never been Ruben's answer. Dreams had never made his bed.

Doorbells chimed and pinged endlessly. Hearty voices blasted Christmas carols beneath his window. Men, women, and children were busking for coins. Coins for a charity nobody had ever seen, or heard of. But each Christmas they returned with wider purses and paunch.

Dust caked the ceiling of Ruben's bedroom. It was badly cracked. Dry grime padded his blanket, seeping from above like brown sugar. Another orphan had once told Ruben that all dust was dead skin. And that had kept him up for a week. Ruben came around and coughed.

He hacked. No blood. Not this time. Ruben was a delicate child and prone to disease. This was why he was pale. He had hollow cheeks and a deep, sunken stare. Ruben was a malnourished cherub. He'd once been plump. Grandmother's doing. When she'd died, he'd blubbered. But, in black comedy, Ruben had also dropped his blubber. When Mother died, he'd lost his appetite wholly. Ruben had become weak and drowsy. He was so small.

Mildred found that quite agreeable for her purse and purchasing habits. One less meal bought. Mildred waited for disease to claim him. She'd waited for Ruben to boil in a damp fever and pass in his bed sheets. Mildred used all the extra coins for new powder masks. She hoped to attract moneyed bachelors. She was far too old for such fantasies now.

A girl, Dolores, had told Mildred this once. Dolores had been Ruben's only friend in the orphanage. Now all he had left was the boy behind the wall, Edmund, and a chubby, black spider in his bedroom named Spindleshanks. Ruben still called Dolores "Dolly" when he remembered playing with her in the snow. Dolly had been taken into Mildred's bedroom and punished for her comment. Ruben did not think she'd been adopted by a loving couple. That never happened. But he'd never seen or heard from Dolly again. Nobody had.

Dolly's neighbouring bedroom was empty and had been crimson. Ruben now owned her headboard, chests, boxes and wardrobe. Her dolls and toys were locked inside and Ruben never looked at them. Dolly did not have much.

None of them did.

*

Only a porcelain riding pony remained in Dolly's old room.

Ruben could hear it rocking slowly in the midwinter draughts. He used to despise the noise. Even now, the creak kept him up at night. The difference was that, now, it reminded Ruben of Dolly. Without the pony, Dolly would have been scrubbed from Ruben's memory. She would be just another discarded orphan who had come and gone with Christmas. A child had disappeared from Bram every December for as long as Ruben could remember. Poor old Dolly had merely been the latest. He hated that, but he couldn't change it. It was tradition.

Ruben clambered out of bed and rested his palms on his bony knees. He was dizzy and cold. The round window was pushed wide open. It bore a top layer of snow like icing on a hot fruit cake. Ruben's drapes billowed mildly beside Dolly's old wardrobe. A heavy current pulled them out into the open, winter air. Ruben picked himself up and meandered across the room. Dolly's windowsill used to be lined with sugar. She'd insisted on doing so and had never told Ruben or Miss Mildred why. Ruben's ledge only had dust. No sugar.

He bundled up an armload of cloth and drew them back inside. It was not done lightly. Ruben's lungs emptied. He battled to bridle his breathing.

A night market sprawled throughout Bram's square. The village was lit by ornate gaslights and decorated with bunting. Ruben could see merrymakers browsing the twenty wooden stalls. He spied a butcher's bundle of long, red sausages, a carpenter peddling carved reindeer and chipmunks, and children pulling their parent's hands over towards plush bears. Ruben bowled his eyes over and tiptoed to grab the window edge. He pulled it down and slammed it shut. Air squealed through its gaps like a pig.

Ruben heard a rustle like tinsel. He looked at the lock and noticed something caught between the wall and the window, blown in by the breeze. A piece of parchment flapped outside and remained half-still inside. Ruben pinched the corner of the note and drew it through, into his bedroom. The note was blank. It was the sort of papery material found in old library books at the back of the shelf, untouched for an age or two. Ruben ran his thumb over it. He felt the gritty skin of the sandpaper. He slipped, and the blade of the note slid across his thumb, opening it up. Ruben gasped sharply. He bristled as goosebumps crept up his arm.

The note drifted to the floorboards below.

Ruben pinched his bleeding thumb.

Hot tears welled up in his almond eyes. He was used to pain and it numbed promptly. Blood dribbled down and blemished the parchment. Ruben picked the note back up and headed for bed. Mildred wouldn't take kindly to the mess when next she came to either punish or feed him. Ruben wrapped up his wound in the bed sheets and then hid the note under his pillow. Ruben closed his eyes. And for the first night in many, he began dreaming.

Beneath his head, blood seeped into the note's sandy parchment. The juice curdled and clotted, forming a blushing middle stamp. Inside, it curled and licked around like an ink quill. Ruben's blood spelt one word, one name.

Mudberry.

*

A new day of advent came to Bram. Residents woke from sugar-coated slumbers to balmy mornings and warm breakfasts. In Miss Mildred's Most Merry Home for Unwanted Children, breakfast would be plated up hard and cold. Ruben roused in his springy bed knowing that this morning would be no different from any other.

There was a horrid odour in his bedroom. And he knew it to be dry blood.

Ruben murmured. He waved off the last sleep of the cold night. But Ruben had been warm. How odd. He moaned to keep the company of his dreams. Dreams, he'd been dreaming. He'd napped all through the night without any interruption. Not even once did the slightest hint of black fantasy slither in and unnerve him. Ruben's dreams had detailed a distant Neverland. He'd visited a marvellous theatre, steaming banquets, and a craftsman's workshop. He'd addressed an audience of children his age, each one rosy-cheeked and as pleased to see him as the next. Ruben's drowsiness waned and his aches were on the mend. Perhaps this was the orphan's first taste of a new Christmas spirit. Perhaps it was a spirit which longs to recover the discarded and unwanted from Mildred's clasp and deliver them to a happier place. Perhaps not.

Ruben rose from his bed and the dusty sheets slipped away. He indulged himself in a long stretch and felt relief. In a moment, it was gone. And Ruben was left feeling languid again. He recalled the previous evening. He looked towards the window again and found one of his curtains trapped in the latch. That was right. He remembered the curtain and the parchment.

Ruben examined his thumb to investigate the painful notch in his skin. The memory of the cut remained. A natural lattice of maroon and pink. The nick was hot with the process of healing. Blood dirtied Ruben's sheets and the floorboards beside Dolly's wardrobe. Not a lot. But enough to poke Miss Mildred's ire and prompt her hand to punish him. She called it discipline. Ruben normally wondered whether Mildred had experienced such discipline in her childhood. Maybe that was why she delighted in an orphan's disobedience.

Ruben veered his head and reached underneath his pillow. He needed to know if the note was there and that he'd not imagined all of this. Before he could grab it, Ruben pulled his fingers back. Clanging echoed through the orphanage. Ruben had no clock on his wall. But the graphite sky informed him that the hour hadn't yet passed seven. All the other children in Bram were still sleeping noiselessly. When they woke, they would each rush to a hanging calendar and gulp down advent chocolates wrapped in coloured foil. The unwanted were always woken early for hard-knock chores and productivity. No chocolates for the orphans.

One more clang.

Ruben knew this noise as well as any orphan in the home. Mildred walked down the hallway. She was accompanied by the noisy thrash of pots and pans hitting one another and creaking planks. Ruben could hear her hollering for the children to open their doors. She was at the bottom of Ruben's corridor. She was drawing nearer.

*

'Open up!' Mildred barked. She'd woken up on the wrong side of her bed again. 'Get up you rats! We've got pots that need washing and boards that need scrubbing!'

Unfortunately, Mildred was right. Ruben did indeed have boards that needed scrubbing. And quick. He listened for the wrinkle of bootstrap leather normally held in her grip. One lash for laziness, two lashes for lying, three lashes for disrespect. Dolly's punishment had sounded much, much worse. Ruben's concern for her bloated each new morning without a proper answer.

'Coming, Miss Mildred,' one child shouted.

'Hold on, hold on,' another bumbled. How plucky.

Ruben began making his bed and made for his bedroom door. Footsteps padded back and forth behind it. He hauled the bloodied duvet into a big chest and knocked it down with his elbow. Ruben shut his lids tight, grabbed the handle, and opened his door wide. Pushing a doorstop to hold up and endure its weight, which he by himself couldn't. Ruben opened his eyes. He was level with Mildred's belt. Luckily for him, it was tied about her waist for once.

Ruben gulped hard.

All orphans were doing the same. They posed in their doorways, dishevelled and drowsy. Mildred paced from one end of the corridor to the other. She feigned an expectant cough. In unison, the children managed her welcome like a poor man's choir.

'Good morning, Miss Mildred,' their voices were croaky and diminutive. Mildred beamed at each of them, expecting more. She never needed to ask twice. 'Good morning, Miss Mildred, the orphans chanted once more, louder this time. None of them meant it. Mildred knew it, and it gave her pleasure.

'Better,' Mildred said. 'Breakfast is served downstairs. If any of you were quicker, you may have caught it while it was warm.'

The orphans scattered down the crooked staircase. It was missing steps and had claimed many broken collarbones and dislocated arms. The orphans were careful not to come too close to Mildred. They gave her a wide birth. Ruben's bedroom was hidden in the corner of the hallway. He was the last to come down the corridor. He did not make it to the end.

'Oh, Ruben?' Mildred's voice stopped Ruben dead.

'Yes, Miss Mildred?'

Beads of fever trickled down his cheek to his swollen lip. He thought of what happened the last time he said the wrong thing at the wrong time.

'I heard you up late last night. Don't let it happen again.'

'No, Miss Mildred. I'm very, very sorry.'

Ruben knew what she wanted to hear. He only pleaded that Mildred herself was too tired to consider messing with his emotions so early in the morning. Maybe she too had felt the Christmas spirit. Unlikely as it may be.

'Good, now hurry along. Before the others eat your breakfast.'

'Yes, Miss Mildred.'

She plucked at Ruben's dark hair with dirty nails as he passed her by. Before he ducked and disappeared down the stairs to join his found family. Mildred watched him leave. She had a weak, predatory stare. Like a jackal or stray dog sniffing for meaty scraps.

Mildred turned on Ruben's door handle and looked inside, inspecting meticulously. She sniffed the air and choked a little. She saw nothing unexpected but seemed amused by the chamber's decrepit decor. When pleased, Mildred closed the bedroom door once again.

Ruben's room was still drab, still bare and chill. But the blemishes and stains from the night before had disappeared. Ruben's blood was gone.

*

Ruben did not eat breakfast.

By the time he'd come downstairs the other boys and girls were devouring his share mercilessly. Ruben did not blame them. The orphans were always hungry. The bread had been baked many days ago and was hard. The milk was curdled and thick, more like candle wax. And the silverware they dined with had been left to stew in gunk overnight by Miss Mildred.

Nobody wanted to clean the knives and spoons before Bram's sun had even come up. Not that the sun was keen to during the midwinter months. And so the children ate their breakfasts using them. Daring diseases they would likely not defeat and fail in seeing one of Bram's distant Christmases. And never make New Year's Eve. Ruben normally ate his meals with his hands.

Once the morning meal had passed, Miss Mildred's labours were divided up amongst the children again. That was how Miss Mildred's Most Merry Home for Unwanted Children had become known as the "workhouse" and "pokey". The orphans went about their drudgery to avoid Mildred's mood and belt. Even after the orphanage had been made spotless, they would be expected to head upstairs to clean their bedrooms. However, this was an easily handled chore. None of their rooms were messy because they had no junk to jumble.

Ruben laboured downstairs on the bottom floor.

But he did not do so not alone. A big boy, named Rudolph, was beating couch pillows behind him. The other children called him Rudi, for he was rude. Rudi disliked Ruben. He blasphemed and bullied him when Miss Mildred wasn't around. However, Ruben knew that Mildred would have likely enjoyed this display, at least to an extent.

Ruben had been burdened with sweeping out the fireplace, replacing the chopped logs, and loading up on coal. That part of his job had been basic. The orphanage had an impressive abundance of coal. Ruben believed that Mildred had filled the children's boots with coal the previous Christmas morning. Blaming black-hoofed Krampus for the deed and handing herself an excuse to discipline the orphans deemed naughty enough.

*

One broad sweep of soot and coal choked Ruben.

He'd been kneeling, head ducked beneath the crooked chimney. He reeled back and bashed the back of his skull on the hearth's dome. Ruben burped up a muffled cry of pain and rubbed the bump. The throb made him wince a bit.

'Keep it down!' Rudi barked.

He was arranging Mildred's most beloved pillows. When he turned around and realised that Ruben had indeed hurt himself, he began chuckling. Ruben ignored Rudi and picked his job back up. He did not need a distraction.

'Ruben.'

Ruben heard his name carried on a morning draught. He looked back at Rudi, assuming the boy hoped to annoy him. But Rudi was locked in his chores like the rest of the household. The voice had come from the fireplace. A whisper had come down the chimney's gullet.

The fireplace was damp from melted snow. Ruben took his broom and, with the butt end, knocked on the cold blocks. There was a pregnant pause before the chimney knocked back. A bead dropped down, bouncing off the brickwork and burying itself amidst black coal. Ruben pried the minuscule orb loose and examined it in his palm.

He held a perfectly round bead, decorated like a bauble. The chimney bead was wrapped in strawberry pink foil. The wrapper peeled open down the middle ridge. Ruben noticed a new shade beneath, dark brown. Chocolate, the voice had delivered Ruben one piece of chocolate. Ruben slipped the chocolate into his mouth and let it melt on his tongue. Festive warmth bubbled in his belly and colour returned to his cheeks. It was a natural, healthy colour. Not the dark palette of bruises. Then, many more were delivered.

Ruben heard a noise like hail or ball bearings. He quickly nudged his broom out of the way and pulled back from the hearth. The moment Ruben ducked back under the arch, minding his head, a rainbow shower of chocolate baubles shot down into the pit. Ruben uncovered a hoard, glinting in the ashes. Chocolate gems foiled in lime, jade, mauve, plum, and amber. Ruben reached over to pluck them out like oyster pearls.

'What you got, kid?' Rudi loomed over Ruben's shoulder in an instant. He too was a kid, but he lauded his two years over Ruben like a crown. 'Show me!'

Ruben grabbed a handful before Rudi pushed him aside.

'No, I've got nothing!' Ruben lied. Rudi bullied his way over into the fireplace. 'It's just a bit of chocolate,' Ruben admitted. Rudi did not say anything but began greedily padding his pockets with their weight. 'Please, Rudi!' Ruben pleaded. 'I haven't eaten breakfast, I'm hungry!'

Rudi kicked backwards like an unnerved donkey. His boot ploughed into Ruben's ribs. Ruben fell onto the couch and felt all the air leave his little body.

'Move over, kid!' Rudi ordered. 'Slow then and slow now!'

In the minutes that followed, when Ruben clambered back upstairs to his bedroom, every last chocolate had gone. Rudi had either eaten them whole or pocketed them for the evening hours before bed. And Rudi would pay for that.

*

In a shadowed corner of Miss Mildred's Most Merry Home for Unwanted Children, Ruben heaved open his bedroom door. He did not slam it. Miss Mildred might have been nearby. He was blubbering and fighting to contain a march of tears. Diving onto his hard mattress, Ruben screamed into his pillow. He bunched the material up around his cheeks. He felt the brush of parchment beneath his pillow and raised his head. He'd nearly forgotten the bloody note from the night before. It felt different. It'd changed.

Ruben drew the parchment out to inspect it. No note. Not anymore. He held an envelope. It was much smaller than any post he'd ever seen delivered or received in Bram. A maroon stamp decorated and sealed the envelope. It was slightly gritty, textured like congealed blood. A round doll mask had been pressed and moulded into the wax. Not unlike Dolly's old belongings. The doll appeared happy and charming. One eye winked.

Ruben pried the envelope open, being heedful of not damaging the waxwork. He unfolded the parchment to reveal a word written in dry blood. Ruben read it aloud.

'Mudberry?'

An immediate gale pulled the round window open and snow blasted in. Ruben walked over and shut it again. But the snow glistened in a way it did not outside in Bram. Outside it'd been thick, and fluffy. Here, it twinkled like crushed crystals. Ruben dipped his finger into the powder and brought it to his lips. It buzzed in his mouth like sugar. He'd eaten sugar. Ruben remembered Dolly, reminiscing about her old habit.

Had Dolly asked for sugar? Or had it blown in through her window too? Ruben couldn't find an answer and so he dismissed any questions he had. Not now.

The sun had finally begun rising over Bram. Ruben heard the distant and mirthful chuckle of children his age in their family homes. He imagined what that must be like. He longed to go back to a life of love, a real childhood. Ruben dreamed of building snowmen with carrot noses and button eyes, and scarves wrapped around their fat necks. He dreamed of exploring Bram's Christmas markets and indulging himself in its bountiful celebrations, just for one night. Reality broke the daydream like a mirror. Ruben blinked away the shards. Only a handful of chocolate baubles remained to please his empty belly. Spindleshanks the black spider descended on a wisp of silk from the ceiling and landed atop his bed. Ruben wouldn't sleep, but there was an odd comfort in knowing his arachnid companion was still there with him. And, eventually, when night made its bed and all went silent in Miss Mildred's Most Merry Home for Unwanted Children, dark things came out to play.

*

Rudi's downtrodden bedroom was dark.

He owned more than the other orphans in the home. He'd stolen, lied, and bullied his way into stockpiling an impressive junk pile under his bed. Most impressive by day and unnerving by night, however, were Rudi's toys. He did not doubt that they'd belonged to one hundred children before him, but that did not matter. They belong to him now.

Rudi crouched on his bed, underneath a grey quilt. Like Ruben, Edmund, and old Dolly, Rudi's bedroom was stripped bare of colour and Christmas merriment. However, unlike them, he had no windows. He couldn't see the pretty snowfall dappling Bram or the winter moon smiling in the night sky.

The only brightness in Rudi's bedroom came from a dwindling candle. The flame illuminated prize dolls, dummies, and bears. They stared at Rudi with black, button eyes and painted faces. He'd taken them from many different orphans and had wanted Dolly's after she disappeared. Unfortunately, they'd gone to Ruben instead. Now, they were buried deep in Ruben's inherited wardrobe.

Rudi heard a squeak.

He threw off his bed sheets and looked around. Rudi saw nothing but the toys sleeping in shadows. Many had wooden bodies, arms, and legs. They were dramatically garbed in cardigans and marching band uniforms. Some had instruments. Others had animals.

Generations of hard play had destroyed parts of them. Fluffy, white stuffing protruded out from wounds in the wood and cloth. One doll stood out amongst all the others. Rudi did not recognize it. Certainly not one he'd taken. Perhaps it was a new one. Perhaps it was a present from another orphan in the home. It was a marionette. He had red hair, porcelain white skin, eyes which had been stitched shut, broad hips and a broader grin. Unlike the other toys Rudi owned, this one was moving.

There was no breeze. He rocked backwards and forwards on his haunches like a cat ready to pounce. The golden bells on the buttoned-up coat chimed discordantly. Rudi could hear his wooden creak. He groaned and squealed like a pig. He had a dark red nametag affixed to his collar. The doll was called Mudberry.

Rudi remembered that name.

He knew it somehow. Maybe he'd been one of Dolly's old toys. Rudi turned his back on the doll and reached over for his bedside candle holder. He heard a jingle. When he brought himself back around, Mudberry had gone. He waved his candle around to find the doll. Firelight flooded patches of darkness. He couldn't be seen. From his bed, Rudi looked towards his junk piles and toys.

A squeak came again.

He heard a lock configure and a latch click open. It came from one of the trunks in the corner of his room. In the trunk's thin opening slit, Rudi spied a pair of eyes. No movement. No blinking. They were open wide and looked directly at him on his bed. Two boiled rubies.

A pale mouse tail slithered in beside Mudberry. He barely caught it with his candlelight. Rudi clutched the quilt tight to his chest. The trunk opened a bit more. Something bowled down into the candle's warmth. It was shiny. A bead knocked against a bed leg. Rudi dared to remove his eyes from Mudberry. He looked down, only for a moment or two.

Wrapped in scarlet foil and painted like a bauble, the bead had been identical to those he'd pinched from Ruben. Rudi had a taste for them now. He felt compelled to eat more and more chocolate until he couldn't move.

He clambered down out of bed. His bare feet touched the cold floorboards. Rudi had always been disturbed by the dark. But he never told anyone. He'd had nightmares of a beast dragging him under his bed and devouring him whole. But all Rudi cared for now was the chocolate. He picked it up between two fingers, peeled it open, and popped it between his cheeks. It tasted like Christmas. Rudi hadn't experienced such flavour in years. This morning had been the first. And he hoped this evening wouldn't be the last.

*

Mudberry hadn't moved from inside the trunk.

He stared at Rudi. Again: no movement, no blinking. Rudi was beginning to ponder whether they were Mudberry's eyes. Maybe it was a trick of the light. Besides, he'd seen the doll. His eyes had been closed. He'd been made that way and couldn't be changed. But his eyes looked very human.

Two more chocolates rolled towards Rudi.

The second bead bordered darkness. Rudi paced over and picked one up. He hesitated before the second. The candle flame began dwindling as if being snuffed out by a lick of air or pinched fingers. In Rudi's bedroom, there was neither. The only things in that room were Rudi, Rudi's broken toys, and Mudberry.

He knelt and picked at the second chocolate in orange foil. The bead escaped his fingers. It rolled a bit further into the darkness. It closed in on Mudberry's trunk. Rudi paused. The taste lingered on his palate from before. He knelt in shadow now. And his candle had nearly extinguished. When Rudi finally caught the chocolate bauble, he grinned. He'd not even noticed Mudberry's right eye roll down lazily and beam at him.

Rudi gasped and stumbled backwards. The trunk had opened even more. The eyes were moving. They appeared white and fleshy, like balled-up eels. A hand protruded from the chest. Mudberry had big hands with red sausage fingers and a cupping palm. He held out a handful of chocolates. They'd been peeled slightly to accentuate their seductive aroma. Rudi momentarily stepped back. But Mudberry jangled his hand in a charming gesture. The chocolates jostled and mixed like the colours of a fruit bowl.

Mudberry's eyes looked kinder now. Pink, more inviting than before. He winced, upset that his present had been denied. The doll started sliding back into his heavy trunk before Rudi paced forward a couple of inches. Not two steps into the dark, Mudberry's eyes were alive again with purpose and meaning. But with what intent, Rudi did not know. He hungered even more. His belly hadn't been pleased by Mildred's stoney bread and Ruben's fireplace finds. He needed more. He'd discerned his desire. And so, Mudberry held out more.

Mudberry curled up his fingers, gesturing for the child to approach. Rudi came in close. Mudberry's hand slowly bunched and pulled back inside his holding. Rudi paused. Then he placed a hand on the lock and moved to heave the chest open. He did so.

A howl of trapped air put out his candle. Darkness enveloped him. Rudi looked down into Mudberry's box. He reached down into the trunk. And a gloved hand loped out and grabbed his arm. Rudi did not have time to scream for help and wake the orphanage. He was pulled deep down inside. Rudi did not entirely feel all that happened next. All he knew was claws like rending meat hooks and the mischievous squeaking of hungry mice.

Behind his bedroom wall, Ruben only heard a bump.

*

'Did you hear that, Ruben?'

The whisper belonged to Edmund. Edmund was the boy behind Ruben's wall. He knocked in a rehearsed pattern and Ruben's headboard vibrated. 'Ruben?' Edmund said. 'Are you asleep? Probably, never mind. I'm sorry. I'll be quiet, goodnight!'

If, by chance, Ruben had been asleep, then he'd have been vexed. Vexed that Edmund had robbed him once again of a lovely luxury. But he'd not been. Not heavily. Ruben woke and believed himself to be blind. His room was black tonight, not grey. But for his round window, he would have panicked and fiddled for his bedside candle.

A few moments passed and Ruben's eyes adjusted to the dark.

A blizzard blitzed outside. Bram breathed in a midwinter drift. It'd been very late, or maybe very early. The night was odd like that. Mist seeped through the village streets and licked up at doorways. Bram's lady statue rose from the Christmas mists like a beacon. What neither boy noticed, was that the marionette was gone from her arms. Ruben had always been enamoured with these witching hours. He always felt that he was peeping at the world in its most vulnerable state. And that he shouldn't be awake whilst the rest of Bram slumbered. Ruben knocked his headboard in the same pattern and responded.

'I'm awake,' Ruben mumbled. 'What do you want, Edmund?'

'Didn't hear that?' He repeated.

Edmund sounded concerned. Bram's orphans were no different to homed children in that regard. Nobody liked things going bump in the night. It could be a burglar, a monster, or a strong breeze. Edmund found none of those comforting.

'I heard,' Ruben said, 'probably just an open window.'

He rolled over onto the cooler side of his pillow. He'd stuffed Mudberry's envelope in the case. Ruben felt the parchment crunch under the weight of his cheek. The red wax had stained it from the inside, like blood weeping through hospital bed sheets.

Edmund did not reply immediately.

'Didn't sound like wind,' he said after a few minutes of silence, 'came from Rudi's room. He might've hurt himself.'

'Oh, doesn't sound bad,' Ruben failed to hide his smile. Nobody was there to see it. 'Go back to sleep, Edmund. Miss Mildred might hear us.'

Ruben heard Edmund chuckle behind the wall. He'd said it quietly and had wet his words with mischief. It was only under the cover of nightfall and private conversation that any orphan could get away with such disrespect towards Mildred. No threat of her belt had even passed by any orphan's mind.

*

That night, Edmund and Ruben chatted about very much and very little.

When neither child could sleep, they would talk. And when one stopped, one whispered again. With Dolly gone, they were each other's only remaining solace. And that suited them just fine, all things considered. Edmund dozed off before Ruben. He'd eventually asked a question, and there had been no answer but for a snoring purr. Ruben was disappointed that he'd had to spend the night alone, but glad to know that Edmund was sleeping soundly.

Before long, Ruben was bored again. He'd enjoyed gossiping with Edmund. He'd enjoyed it so much that he'd not even noticed his wardrobe door and what came out of it.

The wardrobe had been opened. Not by Ruben. And he imagined not by Mildred. She detested coming into Ruben's bedroom above all others. It was the most chill and depressing in her entire orphanage. He'd lucked out in that department.

How long had it been open? Ruben hadn't noticed anybody come in. He'd only slept a few winks before Edmund woke him up. Just before the hubbub from Rudi's bedroom beneath him. A horrible thought hit him. He'd also not noticed anybody leave. Perhaps he'd not been as alone as he'd imagined.

Ruben heard clockwork ticking. But he had no clock.

A voice came from Dolly's old wardrobe. And Ruben knew his suspicion to be true. It was a mild voice. It sounded near and far, distant but right beside his ear. It was the same voice from the chimney that morning. The voice that had brought the chocolate.

'Ruben,' the voice was rounded and proper. Heavy and warm like honey or a winter blanket. 'Don't be alarmed, Ruben, my dear boy.'

Ruben moved to scream. But he coughed instead. He'd still got dust in his lungs. He pulled his blanket up high and pressed it against the bridge of his nose. He did not remove his eyes from the wardrobe. He wanted to break away. But couldn't. The hanging clothes moved. And nothing prepared Ruben for what doddered out of the woodwork and into his bedroom.

It was a doll.

*

The coat hangers parted.

Two notched, wooden hands peeled back Ruben's clothes like theatre curtains. A draught billowed through the opening. The hands belonged to a rather short fellow. He'd been plump and made almost entirely of spruce wood. A doll, definitely, but Ruben did not know what kind. He looked part marionette, part ventriloquist dummy, part porcelain doll, and part clown. More than anything, he looked like the snow-dappled statue in the middle of Bram.

He even had dimples, real ones. They made him look sad, but his bright red lips and eyes lit his face with charm. He wore trousers that were pulled up high to his belly and a belt of pure liquorice. The doll paced out into the light with a funny limp. He'd put most of his weight onto a candy cane for balance. A big bowtie adorned his neck and a tall, wide-brimmed hat sat on his head. His nose was a giant, bloody berry. And it leaked sweet juice onto his chocolate brown skin.

'Good evening!'

Ruben put his hands out, pleading with him to be quiet. 'Keep your voice down,' he whispered. The doll frowned. But even his most dramatic frown failed to pull the grin from his lip. He rocked his head and pointed his candy cane across the bedroom towards Ruben on his bed.

'Oh, what's wrong, boy? Why must you be so boring?'

'I'm not boring,' Ruben managed. 'I'm bored. Who're you? What're you doing here?'

'Me?' He said, pointing a big finger at his heart. 'Why, I'm Mudberry. I'm your new toy. Every boy needs a toy, doesn't he? Didn't you get my note?'

Ruben reached under his pillow and took out the envelope. He did not take his eyes off Mudberry, who did not stop smiling at him. He even pouted. The stamp looked like Mudberry. And by chance, it had his name on it too. 'Oh, so you sent this to me?'

'I did. And you signed it. Why, that is how I came to be here, dear boy. Oh, and apologies for the blood. How is the thumb?'

Ruben did not see Mudberry bite his lip. He'd looked down at his wound. The gash had healed like he'd never been pricked.

'Better!' Ruben gasped, keeping his voice down. 'How did you do that?'

'A toy never tells,' Mudberry chuckled, 'but I'm glad you're feeling better.'

'What were you doing in Dolly's old wardrobe?' Ruben said, rubbing his knees and lowering the blanket a bit. He'd come from the wardrobe, no doubt about it. Ruben even slightly recognized him from Dolly's lost and found jumble.

'I've been sleeping,' Mudberry announced. He jabbed out with his cane like a carnival barker addressing an audience. 'Poor Dolly didn't need Mudberry anymore. And so my friends and I decided to take a bit of a nap. You understand, right Ruben? It can get ever so dull around here.'

'Oh, don't I know it.' Ruben despaired. 'So you were one of Dolly's broken toys?'

'Broken?' Mudberry feigned offence and snapped one of his arms the wrong way in jest. 'I'm just as I'm made to be. We were Dolly's. Before her, we'd been another's. People don't play with toys forever, Ruben. One day we are chucked and chopped, thrown off into the nasty place called Throwaway. Just like you were.' Ruben had been building up a smile. But it dropped when Mudberry said that. 'My bad, I apologise. It's been a while, children change.'

'No,' Ruben trailed off. 'You're right.'

'Cheer up! Dolly may not be around anymore, but *we* can still have fun, right? Don't go being bored forever! Come here, come and play.'

Ruben considered Mudberry's offer. But he heard movement downstairs.

'I'd love to, but you best go back in a box. Miss Mildred will hear us.'

'Miss Mildred,' Mudberry scoffed. 'To the north pole with Miss Mildred, I say. Forget her. Forget this sad place and its boxes. Come with me, Ruben. And I will show you a world of wonders. In my home, the Christmas nights surpass all others with their magic. Have my word. You will never be bored again.'

Ruben could hear the clink of iron boots coming back down his corridor. He knew damned well what that meant. He even heard the crinkle of belt leather.

'Ruben?' Miss Mildred barked. Her voice was muffled. 'I warned you about making noise! I know you're awake in there you little rat!'

'That's my queue!' Mudberry straightened.

The marionette paced over and climbed back into the wardrobe.

There, Ruben spotted the arching outline of a door and a golden doorknob. The door was incredibly small. Even Ruben would have to kneel to crawl through. And where could it possibly lead?

Mudberry opened the door and Ruben looked down. There was a long, dusty tunnel littered with toys and clocks. Like an old stocking or sock. The smell of Christmas wafted out, filling the bedroom. There was nothing in that particular scent that Ruben was inclined to dislike. No burning. No memories.

'Well,' Mudberry paused by the door, 'are you coming?'

Ruben hesitated. But any place was better than the orphanage. He clambered out of bed and hurried into the wardrobe. His bedroom door swung open as he did. Miss Mildred bullied her way inside and moved to belt his mattress. She found it empty. She turned at the slam of the wardrobe's door. Mildred opened Dolly's old wardrobe. She pulled the clothes and rails aside and looked down inside.

Mudberry and his dainty passage had vanished.

And Ruben had gone.

*

Moments after the wardrobe door closed behind him, Ruben was alone.

Mudberry had disappeared without a trace. No little boot prints in the dust. No jingle from his golden bells. Ruben knew that the doll couldn't have gone far and that he must have moved directly ahead. For ahead was the only way Ruben or Mudberry could go.

The tunnel was cramped. Ruben began to feel claustrophobic and hot. Nerves weighed him down. But he did not panic or allow his breathing to get out of control. He had not wanted to breathe any dust in by accident. After all, the passage was caked in the stuff.

Ruben snivelled and his eyes watered. He felt itchy and dirty. He continued crawling. The tunnel brimmed with ancient toys and antiques. Poking out from the fabric walls, there had been: pouting grandfather clocks, stuffed animals from a darker age of play, broken mannequins with mismatched limbs, coal lumps, and a dotted trail of sweets which Ruben assumed had dropped out of Mudberry's pockets. They baited him along. He picked each one up and stashed them for breakfast, dinner, and pudding.

Everything glared at Ruben as he crawled on by. Never once did he feel properly alone. But there was no turning back now. Mudberry's door was gone. Besides, Miss Mildred would have been waiting on the other side with her leather belt, ready to discipline him. Then, at the end of the tunnel, Ruben noticed a light. It was purple and orange. Like a sunset. The closer Ruben crawled, the warmer the passage became. It lapped over itself like a tongue over dry lips. He heard Mudberry's voice.

'Come on now, Ruben, we're going to be late.'

Ruben noticed Mudberry's silhouette before it was eaten up by the light.

What did Mudberry mean? How could he be late for something he'd not known about? He'd only just now agreed to come along. Ruben followed him, prompted by the doll's plea. He ventured out of the passageway, first into light, then into darkness. The darkness seemed familiar. Ruben was surrounded by rough wood and cotton once more. He'd entered another wardrobe. He knew this space. It was Dolly's and his. The same wardrobe as before.

How could that be? He had not crawled through the stocking tunnel only to arrive back in his bedroom in Miss Mildred's Most Merry Home for Unwanted Children. No way. Wherever Mudberry had brought him, it was warm. And that was good enough for any orphan in Bram. Ruben spied Mudberry's white and red cane beyond the wardrobe's seams. He'd been waiting for him. Mudberry knocked on the doors, feigning impatience.

'Hurry now, child. We don't have all Christmas,' Mudberry chuckled.

Up until now, Ruben hadn't had any Christmas. Mudberry's words prompted him to draw back the hanging jumpers and jackets and push his way through into the room beyond.

What Ruben saw confused him. He looked around, and behind him too. He gauged every last detail. He had not been led back to

Mildred's old shack by Mudberry but to a bedroom. Ruben knew this place. It was his bedroom from the orphanage, but as it should have been. He could only describe the bedroom as though it belonged to a beloved child. The wooden walls and floorboards were painted the same red as Ruben's blood that had previously been spilt and soaked up by Mudberry's note.

It was wonderful.

*

Ruben stepped into the bedroom. Directly opposite him lay an enormous, king-sized bed.

Ruben immediately wanted to jump on it. A pancake carpet with golden swirls sat in the middle of the room. Mudberry finished painting them on as Ruben entered the bedroom. Gold dust shot from the bottom of his cane like sand and threaded itself into the material. Paper birds swooped down from their nest atop the windowsill. They chirped over Ruben's head and Mudberry swatted them away by waving his wide-brimmed hat. Mudberry was right in front of Ruben. He stumbled to his feet and started plodding around the bedroom.

Everything was clean. The floor had been swept. The knobs had all been polished and all the cobwebs had been bundled up in the corner. Black spiders, like the ones from Ruben's bedroom back home, were weaving eight-sleeved winter coats for their hundred children. Those children slept in powdered egg clumps behind them.

Ruben could hear them whispering to each other. Their mandibles chattered together. He could see their egg sacks pulsating and breathing beside them in the shade. He had surprised himself by not being disturbed by them. But there was no sign of Ruben's spider, Spindleshanks. He would know that spider immediately. And his not being there upset him a bit. Ruben checked himself and then gasped at the enormity of the bedroom.

'This, this is my room!' He called out. Ruben immediately brought his hands to his mouth and his eyes went wide. He had not quite shaken the daunting memory of Mildred back home.

'Don't worry,' Mudberry purred. 'Don't think you have to be so quiet here. Be as loud as you want! Miss Mildred won't hear you. Nobody will!'

Mudberry's smile broadened and a drop of berry juice dripped down from his nose, hitting the carpet. Mudberry rubbed it in with his curled boot. His ankle bells knelled like a cat's collar as he did so. Everything about this place was Christmas and splendour.

'Well, where are we?' Ruben said. He couldn't see his little round window anywhere, despite the presence of a windowsill. That was a touch curious to him.

'We're in a better place!'Mudberry barked. 'Welcome to my home! And this is your new room. Do you like it, Ruben?'

He pivoted and spun around on his heel, gesturing with wooden arms in the open space. Mudberry was only small. Ruben imagined that the room must have felt massive and imposing to him. But Mudberry had been unbothered and didn't much mind.

'I love it!' Ruben cheered.

'Good, why, I just knew you'd love it!'

Unlike Miss Mildred's Most Merry Home for Unwanted Children, which had always been quiet, Mudberry's manor was alive with remote sounds. Ruben could hear movement, liveliness, and cheer downstairs. People were making merry. They sounded young, no older than Ruben. Perhaps he'd not been the first orphan Mudberry had delivered here.

Or maybe he would be the last.

The noise was not all that caught Ruben's attention. He had been snivelling, but when the dust cleared from his nostrils, it was replaced with a wonderful scent. Every flavour he had ever dreamed of wafted up from down the corridor and filled his new bedroom.

'What's that smell?' Ruben asked. 'It's delicious!'

'Oh, how it is,' Mudberry said. 'Perhaps you're feeling hungry? Could you eat?'

'Eat?' Ruben smiled properly for the first time in ages. His eyes twinkled with long-lost childhood mirth. 'I could eat a horse!'

'We don't do that around here,' Mudberry wagged a big finger and smelled the air. His nose-berry inflated like a red balloon and deflated promptly after. He waddled over to the bottom of the door and knocked with the curl of his candy cane. And Mudberry pulled him out on wobbly legs. 'Come along, Ruben, come and meet your new family!'

Ruben chuckled loudly and clambered up to his knees. There was no strain in the movement or ache like there had been back home. Ruben's Christmas spirit basked in the warmth around him and felt merriment like never before.

*

Ruben did not know this place.

He knew its plan. He knew all the twists, turns, corridors and hallways, but it was not Miss Mildred's Most Merry Home for Unwanted Children. Not as he'd known it to be. He was unsure if it was even an orphanage. Mudberry's home looked to be anything but. Everything – and Ruben believed that *everything* – had been painted red and was made of wood. There were no creaky floorboards. No splintered carpentry. Nothing in this new home was bare, and nothing more was any bit boring.

Back home, Bram's orphanage was a cold and crooked building, stone grey and sombre. But here, every passage and protrusion was decorated with bunting, children's drawings, and other festive paraphernalia. Mudberry had to keep ushering Ruben along. He had opened the door into a long and unbalanced hallway. He had stopped every few paces to look all around himself in bewilderment. Mounted clocks smiled at Ruben and Mudberry as they headed down the hallway. In languid voices, they moaned their greetings.

'Good... evening... Ruben!' They sang as one baritone choir.

'Hello,' Ruben replied, confidently waving up towards them.

'How's it hanging?' Mudberry giggled, pointing up with his candy cane.

The hallway erupted with a deep chortle. But it trailed off into a disturbing moan. The clocks blubbered slightly and glassy tears trickled down their ticking hands. Ruben assumed that they had pretended offence, as Mudberry had, and continued after the doll. Eventually, their blubbering dimmed with distance. And Ruben heard new voices murmuring downstairs. Ruben prepared himself for a descent down the spiralled staircase.

When Ruben turned a corner and saw it, he settled and gasped with excitement. Before him, a long and winding slide rolled like a tongue from the second floor down to the bottom. A pleasant aroma drifted up the slide like a newly opened bakery. He'd always wanted to go down one of these. He'd seen the children of Bram sliding down them in parks all year round. However, they'd abandoned them for sloppy hillocks come December.

'Be my guest!' Mudberry prodded Ruben's lower back with his cane.

Ruben did not exactly know how he'd been getting back up the slide should he need to return to his new bedroom. But that was another evening's problem. He'd reserved tonight for fun and fancy. Ruben lowered himself onto the top of the slide and, with one big push, slung himself around the corner and skimmed down out of view.

Ruben did not see Mudberry's broad smile drop.

*

The slide wound down much longer than Ruben had expected. As he slid, it started to feel moist and meaty. All the walls above and beside him did too. When Ruben reached the bottom, the tip of the slide licked upwards. He had not expected Mudberry to already be waiting for him again at the bottom.

'How'd you do that?' Ruben said, climbing off of the slide and padding his clothes down. They were damp now and ever so slightly sticky. 'How'd you get down before me?'

'Don't mind that, Ruben,' Mudberry said, casting the question off. 'Did you enjoy it? Are you still bored?' He rubbed his big hands together like a charlatan hiding a coin.

'No,' Ruben rubbed his belly,' I'm not bored, just a bit hungry.' He could smell food again and sniffed the air like an undergrowth critter. 'What's that smell? It's delicious!'

'Believe me, it is.' Mudberry said. 'Come and see.'

And he did. Ruben and Mudberry headed over into a room where Ruben had thought to find a dingy, grimy kitchen. He had been taken aback to find a dining room. It was ornate and comfortably lit. A massive and round table stood in the middle of the dining room.

Christmas candles and crackers sat amongst faux sprigs of holly and bramble. Plated up, was every food Ruben had ever dreamed of eating and every food he'd never considered. Saliva flooded his mouth and he licked his lips. Ruben saw thickly sliced duck meat, pulled pork and apple sauce, cranberry and onion stuffing, red cabbage, potato dumplings, fruit cake, golden biscuits, wobbly jelly, and above all, a ginormous Christmas pudding.

'Please, take a seat. You are a guest in my home!' Mudberry emphasised.

Ruben had been so caught off guard by the decadent display that he hadn't even introduced himself to the people sitting on wooden stalls around it. He looked up and couldn't believe what he was seeing. Dolls, he had seen dolls. They were all smaller than him but could have passed for children. Like Mudberry, they all were wooden and lavishly painted. Some had porcelain masks. Others had berries on their noses. And some were not even human, but horses and robins. None of them had lips or a mouth to speak with, only the painted impression of one. But still, they chuckled like infants and moved rigidly as if their limbs were attached to puppet strings. Each one had a full plate. And none of them had eaten.

How could they? They were only toys.

*

'They're dolls,' Ruben said. He sounded disappointed. Mudberry noticed. 'I thought there'd be more kids here, like me?'

'Ruben,' Mudberry began, 'there are no other kids like you. You are unique, you know. Look at them. Every doll has his or her special something. They have their unique flavour. Just like human children, delicious! And every one of them is glad you decided to join them for Christmas dinner!'

All of the dining dolls turned their heads. Some in unnatural ways like an ageing owl, to look at Ruben. The paint on their faces chipped and contorted into wide smiles and gleeful squints. One of them pulled out a stool. And Ruben sat beside them. He'd only just been able to reach the table and the feast spread atop it.

Mudberry plucked a small delight that had rolled off the table with the end of his cane. Mudberry had a mouth and was able to eat it. Ruben noticed how sharp splinters folded out of his cheeks at all angles to form teeth. He thought they looked dangerous for a child's doll.

'I'd best be heading off, my boy,' Mudberry yawned, 'I've got some business that needs poking.'

'You're leaving? But we only just got here! I don't want to go!'

Ruben didn't cry but the lilt in his voice certainly threatened tears.

Mudberry giggled again and padded his belly. 'Don't worry, Ruben. I'm not going far, besides, you are in safe hands. You have a friend here who will show you all around your new home! I'm sure you'll find the *new* Bram quite beautiful this time of year.'

Ruben heard moaning.

He looked around the table. Peering through stacks of overcrowded plates and steaming bird breasts, he saw a face, one he knew well, although it'd changed.

Rudolph had grown immeasurably fat. He filled out an entire suit of skin with blubber like a heavy bag of bread sauce. His clothes barely fit him and he had a distant, removed look in his dreary eyes. He did not look healthy. Not that any orphan from back home did. Had Mudberry brought Rudi here too? How long had he been here? Why the horrible Rudi of all the orphans? Why not Edmund?

Ruben was certain his time in Mudberry's paradise was about to be completely ruined.

'Oh no, what're you doing here?' Ruben griped.

Mudberry grinned to himself.

'Ruben... is... Ruben?' Rudi could hardly string a sentence together.

His voice sounded heavy and slow. He sounded like the mounted clocks upstairs. Ruben heard them blubber. Rudi's tongue had turned weighty and had given him slurred speech. Beside him, Ruben recognized two broken dolls. The dummy, Cranberry, and the chubby one, Gumball. They had belonged to Dolly too.

Had Dolly been here before? How else could her toys be here?

'Do excuse him, Ruben,' Mudberry said, 'he's had quite a bit to eat this evening!' Mudberry drew out a handful of chocolate baubles and placed them in Ruben's lap.

'Hey, those are my chocolates!' Ruben cheered.

'Yes, they are. And we couldn't let Rudi here forget that now could we?'

Mudberry paddled around the massive table and prodded Rudi's stomach with his cane. Rudi moaned, not quite in pain, but with no measure of pleasure either. He'd either indulged too much or something was wrong. In a moment he almost did not catch, Ruben saw something wriggle inside Rudi's throat and disappear. Perhaps he had been chewing down the remnants of his dinner.

'Poor Rudi has had a change of heart. Haven't you, Rudi?' Mudberry said. 'Come now, your friend is here! You remember Ruben don't you, Rudi?'

'I remember,' Rudi managed. He smiled, the gesture pushing up his plump cheeks.

'Once you've finished eating, Rudi here is going to show you around the house.' Mudberry straightened his wide-brimmed hat and waddled back over towards the tongue slide. 'Whatever you can dream of, I'm sure it'll be in here somewhere! Just be sure to swing by my workshop at the end of the night!' Mudberry leaned in for a stage whisper. 'It's in the attic.' Mudberry winked then leaned back.

'Oh, okay!' Ruben said.

He started tucking into his dinner. His eyes widened and lit up like crescent moons with delight. When he looked back up from his plate, a few minutes later, he'd gone to speak to Mudberry once more. But the doll had vanished. And the others hadn't spoken. Like before, they'd only giggled. Their coded conversations flourished, but Ruben had sat and eaten in silence. He did not know what to say to a doll.

The only part of the banquet he'd understood had been Rudi, who had moaned his name over and over.

'Rudi, Rudi.'

He had started to put Ruben off his delightful dinner. It had not helped that Ruben had been the only person at dinner eating anything. Then, Rudi moaned another name aloud.

'Ruben. Ruben...'

*

Ruben had started feeling a bit greedy.

Before long, he had become full. Poor Rudi had started to nod off with his eyes wide open. Ruben couldn't see any eyelids, but their wet roll told him he'd been sleepy. His skin had a funky hue to it. He did not look very well. But Ruben knew that gorging on too much food would do that to him. And so, he put down his knife and fork, wiped his lips with a gold-leaf napkin, and scooted himself off the wooden stool.

The dolls turned their heads and watched him. He walked around the table towards Rudi and prodded his bloated belly to wake him up.

'Hey, Rudi, wake up!' Ruben said. He had to wait a moment before Rudi's eyes rolled back down and beamed directly into him. 'Oh, good, you're up! Come on, Mudberry said we can go look around! We've got to be back at his workshop by the end of the night though.'

'Mudberry, Ruben?'

'Yes, hello, Rudi,' Ruben said. 'Come on, we don't want to miss anything.'

Rudi heaved himself off his stool and landed with a big thud in front of Ruben. He had always been taller, but now he had become much, much wider. His lips began to twitch as if moved by puppet strings, and he drew a big smile. Ruben saw another wriggle, this time beginning around his cheekbones and bedding up about his brow. He heard a squeak like a mouse from his mouth. What was wrong with him?

'I'll... show you... around... our... new home,' Rudi drawled. 'My treat... Ruben!'

Ruben couldn't quite believe that this was Rudi. Nothing of the bullying boy from back home seemed to remain here. 'Oh, umm, thank you, Rudi! Lead the way!' Ruben said.

The dining dolls began to cheer and giggle again, wishing the orphans well and good on their night exploring Mudberry's home. When both orphans had wandered off out of sight, all cheer and merriment in the house waned. The dolls that had been present went quiet once again. They all went dormant, winding down like broken clockwork. All their ticking died. Each painted expression dropped. Ruben's banquet blackened like burnt wood. And in a moment, became sawdust. When the door before Ruben opened, it did so to the sound of squeaking. And the hungry chatter of a hundred white mice.

Ruben never knew what would become of him in Mudberry's house. Back home in Bram, nobody ever knew what had become of him either. Ruben merely became another one of December's missing children, a child, like Dolly, who was remembered only for their disappearance.

But Mudberry remembered. Mudberry remembered well. He knew that next year, another boy would be waiting for him, as Dolly had done the previous midwinter. The name of the orphan boy behind the bedroom wall was Edmund.

And Edmund would endure a very merry Christmas indeed.

THROWAWAY

'What is this place?'

It started with a toss, cast off into the gloom. Into a place that smelled of everything and nothing at all. There was a tang of stale sweat in the trapped air. Yet, the elf toy, Joker, only found dust, skin flakes, and the colourful sheet-wings of twitching insects. Then, he felt his wooden boot knock against the heft of something else. Another toy. That one was not moving anymore. It was dead and still. Joker caught his breath. 'What's happening?'

Then, he noticed more. There were too many of them there with him. Toys he had never greeted or known since his time in the child's life lay in the black without life or reason. Their time had been spent. Their games had been fulfilled. Their playtime was finally over.

They were the Unwanted. A grim understanding shot through Joker's clockwork heart, a heart ticking and ticking and ticking. Joker's playtime was over too. Now, he found himself in that cluttered, labyrinthine world where old toys go. Joker had roused in another world.

This was the world of Throwaway.

The clarity that came after that was frightening. Joker had not thought to find himself there for many, many years to come. After all, he was only thirteen. An unlucky number for any toy, of course, but Joker's owner, the boy Peter, was only recently turning through his teenage years. He could not have outgrown Joker *that* quickly. Joker was not only a toy for children. Not anymore, anyway. How could this be? No. Not here. Not in Throwaway. This was all just a terrible collection of thoughts and fantasies. Not really happening.

This was not real.

'Not real,' Joker urged, pressing his fingers to his temples. 'Not real at all!'

When Joker reopened his eyes, nothing in the world around him had changed. It was real. Joker was in Throwaway. Peter no longer wanted to play with him.

Joker stood, hauling himself up to his feet with a creak and a clack. The toy was tall and lithe. He wore a fitted suit of white and green diamonds over black-lace tights. He straightened out his frilly shirt, dusted off his exaggerated shoulders, curled his pointed elf boots like witch ring fingers, and combed through the wild rag of green hair sprouting from his skull. That same vivid jade garnished his giant brows and the eyes painted underneath.

For once in his lifetime, Joker felt his painted smile chipping away.

He flicked at the rickety buttons and tinny chimes lining his little waistcoat. They echoed out, too high a pitch to be pleasant, and then faded into nothing. That was the only sound left in Throwaway with him. It echoed out and off until it left him in silence again.

'Why?' Joker continued. 'What have I done to get here? I was a fine toy to own!'

Joker started to pace back and forth, to and fro. There was no immediate route through the darkness to follow. Throwaway first appeared to him as a great and dusty tunnel. The only light came from tiny globules that drifted overhead like dust motes. The tunnel's ceiling was a grave for fireflies. They were the only enchanting thing the tunnel offered up.

The rest of the fabric walls were latticed with cobwebs and grime. Joker took in the webs from all the spiders, counting the ones that were catching things and eating their gooey innards. The ones that felt rather large in the tunnel compared to Peter's room. At the end of that tunnel, Joker could see the way out. There it was: Peter's bedroom. Always just out of reach to return to. Round, pale faces with smiling clock hands greeted Joker as he found them in the murk. With every other step, Joker tripped up on something, the springy entrails of a slinky dog. It was foul in Throwaway, foul, cold, and lonely. And Joker had not been lonely in a very long time.

Joker trembled at the terrific chill. Toys did not get goosebumps. They did not feel heat or cool as their owners did. Yet, in Throwaway, Joker suddenly felt all too real. He felt vulnerable. Joker had not thought to worry about the true value of life until he woke in Throwaway. Now, he felt danger lurking around every cotton corner, spying from the shadows. When he searched through those very shadows, he found no malice, only grief. For what he found there infected his clockwork heart with rusty terror.

The toys that slept in the shadows were out of use and bereft of joy. Their spirit and colour faded in equal measure. Many were missing eyes, buttons, and limbs. Their hearty paintwork was flaking away and crunched under the light weight of Joker's feet. Little clouds of sleep sugar went up with each step. This was a tunnel of corpses. A teddy bear with once-fluffy fur now lay crunchy and disembowelled of tufts. A slinky dog had been laid to rest beside it, curled up without an owner to walk it around its room. It was missing its front left paw, and had likely limped over there, accepting its fate.

Joker watched them ruefully. There were others too. Though, he did not have the heart to look at any of them for fear of what he may find. All he heard was a Victorian rocking horse gently creaking back and forth as if stirred by a gust. And yet, there was no air for it to do so.

'For all the places a toy could find itself,' Joker started, 'this was not topping the list.'

Joker leaned backwards against something large and tough. He sank down to his knees and scratched his itchy nose. His nail brought away the white paint. He had only just entered Throwaway, and he was already starting to rot and fall apart.

Joker turned around and felt the harsh, leathery texture against his back. It was a big boot. It was Joker's boot. At least that had been cast away with him. Joker's boot: his home. That brought a smile to an otherwise sour face. 'At least I've got you with me, right?'

'You're late for tea.'

Joker stood up to attention with that interruption. This new voice was tired and raspy. Clearly, from one utter, the toy had spent too much time breathing in Throwaway's still air. Then, it chortled. Joker looked around frantically, turning his back to everything in a whirling motion. He squinted into the gloom of the tunnel, ahead and behind, front and back. He saw nothing. 'What's that? Who's there? Show yourself!'

Then, a toy appeared. A strange, dark green silhouette, with an overcoat, a faux top hat with a price tag still attached, and a lacklustre uniform hidden beneath its patchwork jacket. Joker could tell that jacket was not his, not originally. It had been found down here in Throwaway or robbed from another toy's corpse. It was a toy, of sorts, likely in its formative years. It had a big nose and a big frown that constantly twitched as if wanting to grin but having forgotten how to. It touched the lip of its numbered top hat in greeting.

'Who are you? What are you?' Joker fretted.

'You're like the rest of us now, Joker,' the strange toy stated. 'Forgotten, thrown away. Let me welcome you to your new home, for as long as you shall know it. Follow, a tea? There's plenty of it. And it's not often we get guests in from up top!'

'No, thank you,' Joker said quickly. 'Why do you know my name?'

'We've been watching you for quite a while, friend. We're happy to have you for tea.'

'Really? Well, I'm not going to stay here. I'm getting back to Peter's room, one way or the other. Nothing's going to stop me, not you, not tea, nothing.'

'You're not going anywhere.' The toy with the hat took a step closer. The lines in its face were wrinkled and filled with grime. This toy was far older than any Joker had ever known.

'Who are you? What are you?'

'Nobody, not really. To think I once belonged to Peter's father. Hatter, that's what he used to call me. Without him, I have no name. I am nothing to anyone. It happened to me, you see, went mad. It happened to them too. We're all mad in Throwaway.' The Mad Hatter gestured towards the ravaged toys cluttering the tunnel around them. 'There's little point fighting it. Anyway, what's life without a little strangeness?'

'What are you talking about?' Joker questioned. 'I'm not going to wait down here to rot, go mad, or worse! Certainly not with you for company!'

'You have no choice,' the Mad Hatter said. 'Neither did I, neither did *they*. That's what happens to us toys. Our children get older, they lose interest. They stop caring for their toys. It appears that your Peter has stopped caring for you. So *we* will care for you instead.'

'I won't hear it,' Joker covered his ears. 'You're crazy! I'm getting out of here. You're not to follow.'

'You know, for a Joker, you're awfully unfunny. A riddle for the wary, Joker: there are no comforts in Throwaway. Don't go looking for them.'

'You're out of your mind,' Joker groaned.

'We're toys,' the Mad Hatter chuckled wryly, 'we're made for fantasy.'

There was no point in sticking around to argue with the Mad Hatter or for Joker to lament his predicament. Joker knew that. He was not only a witty toy; he was also a smart toy. Joker fetched out his old bindle, a sack on a stick, from a pile of forgotten keepsakes. Then, he fetched the giant leather shoe that shrunk down to fit at his waist when he touched it. He felt lucky that it had been thrown out with him. With it, Joker put one foot in front of the other and started through the fabric tunnel into the fouler, creepier regions of Throwaway.

'I'll find you again!' The Mad Hatter shouted out after him, his voice rattling along the gossamer walls. 'Be sure to stop by for tea!' Joker did not turn back. 'Don't chase the rabbit...'

Joker was gone into the gloom. He would walk the world of Throwaway until the very end. Forever searching for a child who no longer wanted him and a future fit for fantasy.

For that is the fate of toys.

RODENTS

Thomas Herbert. That was his name. A man with nothing left to live for.

Cheer and joy ran from him with the night. His troubles started a few years ago. Three or four, he could not properly remember. Now, Thomas was sixty-six. He was no longer the young, strong man people had known. He had worked as a cultivator and farmhand in the town of Thatching. The den of thatched huts was sleepy and small, candle-lit too. Nobody visited Thatching. They only ever passed through.

Except for Thomas.

Thomas had no roof over his head. He had no family. Although, his homelessness carried one benefit. He could find a hidden beauty in the town that others could not. He enjoyed everything that came in autumn's footsteps. The naked trees dropped their burned leaves to the ground along with dark chestnuts. The smell of red apple pie wafted from the bakery along with steaming ground coffee beans. He could even pinch a chopped log to set alight in the dry undergrowth in the wheat fields for warmth. There was nothing else Thomas loved about this life. But he had that. And that was all he needed.

Nobody seemed to mind Thomas's living there. He was a ghost. Not even an intrusive one worth banishing. He lit no fire tonight, however. Only a harvest moon gave Thomas Herbert light.

*

To live was a cruel punishment.

Knowing that your childhood would never leave, but it would never live again. Now look at him: homeless, collapsed in an old barn, dirty bottle in hand, grumbling about his better days. Thomas Herbert's plunge into hopelessness was acknowledged by all of Thatching. When he passed, it would be the only legacy he left behind, a stain. Buried in the earth.

He had no children. No lover. No animal companion to sleep by his headstone on a cold autumn night. He was an empty husk. The warmth in his hungry belly was beginning to chill tonight. Thomas reeked of alcohol. His grizzled face and beard were darkened by cigarette ash and chimney soot. He took what jobs he could now. Money never bought him happiness. He had stopped working now. All he did at night was lay down. He plundered crates for scraps of meat and crumbs of bread. Then, he waited for the reaper to come knocking.

He still waited.

Thomas had to be careful where he stood, bowed, and knelt. The task was hard enough on his body. It was even harder with alcohol in his blood. In the barn around him, equipment rested upon hanging hammocks. All were covered with white cobwebs.

Thomas found sickles, scythes, gourds, and hooked chains. The barn rafters were a gallows jungle of frayed rope and child choppers. Moonlight split the thatched roof. It lit the dusty air like bone powder. Nonetheless, it was quiet here. No people. Thomas would be gone come the morning. Nothing but his pathetic stench would remain.

The homeless man climbed over heaps of junk. He brushed patterned cobwebs from the path ahead. He took a swig from the bottle's chunky lip. Bronze whiskey slid down his throat too quickly and Thomas vomited the drink up. An admixture puddle of alcohol, bile, and spit mixed on the barn floor. Thomas wiped his upper lip of phlegm and grit. He cleared his throat with a growl and shot out the remaining ichor into a hay bale next to him.

Here, Thomas was out of sight of the police. They had inquisitive flashlights and sniffer hounds. And he whipped up quite the pungent smell for them. He would welcome an arrest.

At least that would find him a bed for the night.

*

Thomas looked around the barn. Then, he cleared a depression in one of the hay bales.

That would keep him warm enough throughout the night. He slept easily in harsh conditions. When sleep eventually found him, it was numbing. Nothing moved in his dreams. He simply slept without concern, nightmare, terror, or picture. He had not slept so perfectly in some time. Perhaps his life was starting to get better. Only now.

Thomas awoke a couple of hours later. It was still night. Something unexplained and unseen had nipped him and his senses tickled him awake. Thomas did not know what it was. He looked over to his whiskey bottle. It was dry now. He had not remembered drinking all of it. Maybe that was why he had fallen asleep so precariously. He had done so with a spell of dizziness. An instant hurt jetted through his boot and into his toenail. It was hot and stinging.

Thomas squealed and sat up, looking around. He heard something jitter and chatter in the darkness of the barn. The hanging hooks swayed in a hidden breeze. Thomas cursed before launching the whiskey bottle in the direction of the disturbance. It smashed into a hundred pieces and reflected the yellow moonlight. Then, Thomas began to feel a new pumping inside him.

His foot was beginning to throb through his boot. The pain came from nowhere, piercing and gnawing like a lance of nibbling pinpricks. Thomas could feel hot bile rising in his throat again. The veins in his neck were constricting like lazy corn snakes.

Thomas curled over onto his side, laying foetal there on the cold barn floor. His body was beginning to shake. He had never felt the presence of old bones. However, now, they were starting to rattle like flutes and drumsticks. Agony washed over the homeless drunk like gutter waste. Thomas felt the pain moving now from his boot.

He could no longer move.

But he could feel.

*

Pain climbed up his baggy trouser leg with little feet and jagged nails.

Thomas managed to lug his hand up to his face to shield it from the oncoming threat. His hand was heavier than before. Pain tweaked on his knuckle veins. A rat — a heavy, chunky, black rat — was nibbling at his hand and sucking up his juices.

Thomas shrieked, gargling saliva, bile, and worse. The rat squeaked in response before Thomas threw it across the room. He used his free hand to attempt an escape. There was nowhere for him to go now. Thomas tried screaming, but he was too far from Thatching for anyone to hear his plight. He had spent a lifetime keeping hidden. Now he would suffer it.

Something trickled up his thigh: something hairy that scratched with each footstep. Then, the same sensation travelled up the other trouser leg too.

Teeth and claws began to anchor themselves into the pale meat of Thomas's thighs and knees. Their weapons sank straight down to his feeble bones and peeled away his skin. Thomas's baggy trousers were filling up with more of them. They were blocking out the golden moonlight seeping through the hinges of the barn door.

Thomas could not move. He was frozen by panic and viral infection in an instant. The infection was quick. The process of what happened next was slow, too slow. The colony began with the outer bits. These were the appetizing layers. Thomas's skin came away. Then, they burrowed through his cheeks and into his mouth to fetch his tongue and tonsils. The scurrying beasts then claimed his eyes. Pain numbed his mind and body. Thomas lay there as the rodents' banquet. Blind, deaf, and dumb.

Thomas died alone. Nobody would mourn him. He knew that in his final moments. He had once believed that — when his time came — life would flash before his eyes. He had been lied to. He saw nothing, nothing but blackness and the yellow flash of rat teeth.

A morning later, Thomas Herbert was not found by the farmer.

Only a pile of bones remained.

THE TROLL PAINTER

This is the tale of a great man.

A man who painted trolls and other things. In the dark and unforgiving wilderness of Småland, Jönköping, a great artist once lived. To many others, he is one of their greatest inspirations, full of colour, haunting darkness, and root fears. He still lives today through literature, poetry, music, and paintings. You may find that you too find the same haunting beauty in the dark forests of Småland. This man was known by one title above all others.

The Troll Painter.

The Troll Painter was never afraid of the gloomy forests, even though they would come to engulf him, in the end. The Troll Painter was accepted by the enchanting woodlands of Småland, just as you may be. Yet, once he tried to leave and forsake it, he died. Now others walk where he once walked. Others create where he once created.

Are you prepared to hear the tragic tale of the Troll Painter? Or are you frightened of what awaits you in the dark?

*

The Troll Painter's life ended in the most tragic of ways. Though, in his brief life, he created wondrous art, the likes of which are still renowned today. He is still known as one of the finest artists in Småland. His brush strokes and colour had a rare grace, a quality all of its own. There was life in his art. It breathed. The Troll Painter was always well-dressed and always smoking his pipe. Yet, the most intriguing thing about him was his instinctual commitment to the forest. Its nature was his nature.

Its life was his life. His death...

The Troll Painter loved to spend time in the darkest, deepest woods. It was there that he met the trolls. The Troll Painter was born in Taberg, a quaint town in the heart of Småland, at the foot of a great lake. From a young age, he showed great interest and talent in art. And when he travelled to the nearest city to pursue his career, the

Troll Painter met the love of his life, Esther.

Esther was nearly as talented an artist as the Troll Painter, who was instantly captivated by her radiant beauty and fell madly in love with her. She evoked in him the feelings of fairytale princesses, damsels, and fair ladies in lakes. Yet, Esther and the Troll Painter were very different. The Troll Painter was lured into the deep and dark forests and the forgotten mysteries of nature. Esther adored the city, the bustle, and the noise of happy families chattering away under gas-lit streetlights. But most of all, Esther loved the sea. She loved water, a grim irony. Before the pair got married, Esther dwelt in the city whilst the Troll Painter lived quietly in his forgotten forests. They communicated through handwritten letters, stamped with the wax face of a fat green troll. There was little doubt how much the pair loved and cared for one another. Esther wanted to marry the Troll Painter. Yet, Esther did not want to live in the forest. She thought it a dark, dangerous, and unholy place. In their letter exchanges, the Troll Painter tried convincing Esther to come and stay and live in the woods with him. It was clear to Esther that the Troll Painter would never leave. Nothing could tear him away from it. He was bound to it. He was a part of it. Every part of him was connected to the forest.

Just as it was to him.

*

Finally, Esther settled and made her choice. They got married and Esther came to the forest with everything she owned. Together, they travelled a lot. The Troll Painter was grateful that his career had started to blossom and flower for real. It was rumoured that the Troll Painter had once stated that he truly saw everything he painted with his own eyes. This was a curious quote, for what it was that he painted was truly fantastical.

Trolls. Giants. Tooth Fairies. Goblyns. Sirens. Brownies. Pixies. Sprites. Witches. Hags. Crones. Stolen Children.

The Troll Painter became renowned as the greatest painter of fairytale creatures, characters, and magical lands. You may recognize some of his creatures lurking in the forests, peeking out from behind trees or winking above the waterline. Though, by the time you notice them, they are already gone. Though, be assured, they can still see you. They are always there, watching.

The Troll Painter's paintings were everywhere. His cute and magical critters appeared in children's books, in dark literature, and even in theatre productions from towns to cities. The Troll Painter painted down everything that appeared in his mind's eye. Or that he encountered in the forests. The whole of Småland loved him for it. And eventually, he came to love one thing greater than the forest.

The Troll Painter and his wife, Esther, had a child.

For many years, the Troll Painter lived out his finest and most comfortable dreams in the forest with his family. Though, it did not last forever. The forests promised the Troll Painter greatness. Yet, it demanded the full commitment of his heart and spirit in return. It asked for the Troll Painter's complete loyalty. The dark forests and black lakes of Småland were a seductive mistress that he could not oppose. It gave the Troll Painter everything that he could have ever wanted. Yet, if he ever thought about leaving it, it was prepared to take everything from him in turn. The forest was a cruel and unfair thing. That was true.

Esther was unhappy living in the forest with the Troll Painter. She did not like the endless trees and the way the sun rarely rose above them. It was always dark. And it was always quiet. She thought it a lonely place full of things that wanted to harm her and their young child. The Troll Painter, however, rarely came home from the forest. Sometimes, he would roam it for days at a time. Esther wanted their family to return to the city to live the life she wanted. Even though she knew it was something her husband would reject.

The Troll Painter had one reason above all others to roam the forest. That reason had a name. It, or rather he, was called Litté. Litté was a troll child. But Litté was different from the rest of the people in the forest, for Litté possessed sun eyes. He could live happily in the forest and mountains as a troll, and also amongst the humans in their towns, cities, cottages, and huts. Litté was not just another fanciful figment of the Troll Painter's imagination. Litté was real. Litté was his spirit, his connection to nature and to the forest itself.

The Troll Painter identified deeply with Litté. Like the troll child, one part of the Troll Painter belonged to humanity and the other belonged to the forest. Both of them had one foot in each life. And neither of them would fit in fully in one or the other, or decide on which path of life to pursue forever more. They needed both. The Troll Painter needed both. He could not live without the forest, or without Litté.

Esther wanted to move to the city to start painting again, painting the things she wanted to. But as time went on, the Troll Painter became increasingly upset with the decision facing him. He knew what decision he would have to make. For his family's future and happiness, the Troll Painter would have to leave the forest behind and move to the city. The Troll Painter would have to leave little Litté alone in the dark with the trolls. But whilst the family waited for their new home in the city to be built, they remained in the forest, a forest which had started growing darker. As though the forest were upset with him and his choice, warning him, threatening him never to leave it or forsake its trust. The Troll Painter's mind grew darker still.

Darker, and darker, and darker. Until all his thoughts and art turned black.

*

When the Troll Painter spoke to his friends and colleagues about the troll boy, Litté, they each assumed he was speaking in metaphors and fantastical terms related to his artistry. After all, there were no such things as trolls. Not really. Or so people thought.

Yet, one day, something immeasurably strange happened.

The Troll Painter went for one last walk around the forests with one of his closest friends, a few days before the Troll Painter died. The friend claimed that, all the way, Litté the troll boy was following them, hiding behind the rocks around them. He stated that the troll boy appeared regrettably sad and longing. And that the Troll Painter was full of grief, guilt, and shame. The Troll Painter told his friend that he felt too bound to Litté and that, for both theirs and his family's sake, they needed to part, at least for a time. That was a lie.

That was why the Troll Painter had agreed to move to the city with Esther and their newborn son. Upon hearing this, Litté looked up at the Troll Painter with troubled green eyes, as though he knew something the Troll Painter did not about what lay ahead. After that, the Troll Painter went silent. The friend said his goodbyes and then Litté pulled the Troll Painter in close for one final hug. And at that point, the friend knew that their embrace would last a lifetime and forever after.

There are those in Småland who claim that the Troll Painter knew he was going to die soon after that last meeting. The Troll Painter himself may have feared for his life when faced with leaving the forest for good. Others, friends closest to the Troll Painter, claim that the artist had been quite ill and tired for several months. And that death was coming no matter what.

After that, the Troll Painter was left without inspiration or life. He was always upset. Nothing lightened his mood or brought him cheer. He only ever thought of Litté. He only ever thought of the forest. When the Troll Painter had met with a friend for the last time, he had turned to him and thanked him for everything they had ever done together. He had thanked him for the best and worst times, and more. The Troll Painter told him how much he meant to him and how he wished him nothing but the best for the future. The Troll Painter's friend appeared very unnerved by their final meeting. He felt as though the Troll Painter was talking to him for the last time. And that they would not ever see each other again. Of course, he was right.

Other people said that the Troll Painter's sixth sense, the one he had always possessed, had gotten far deeper and more intense near the end. All that is known with certainty is that the Troll Painter returned from his last walk through the forest to tell Esther that he wanted to take the rail to the city. They had originally planned to travel by boat, but the Troll Painter had a foul feeling about sailing the lake. Yet, Esther insisted that they travel by boat, for there had been a tragic railway accident three months before.

At long last, the Troll Painter agreed to take the boat. But the terrible feeling he had looking out across the lake never left him.

In Småland, there was a truly giant lake. They call it Vättern. It is there still, if you wish to visit it. The giant lake was so large that, standing on the pebbled shore not knowing the water was fresh, it could have easily been mistaken for the sea. No land or shore could be seen on the other side. Only dark water.

The vessel the Troll Painter, Esther, and their child boarded was called *GOOD FLOAT*. An unfortunate name in light of events to unfold. In the late evening, the Troll Painter's family boarded the boat and set off, leaving the forests behind for good. A storm was brewing in the night and the Troll Painter was growing increasingly nervous. He talked to the captain of *GOOD FLOAT*, who assured him everything was under control.

The *GOOD FLOAT* was fitted with lifeboats, jackets, and everything else that made it safe. At that point, the Troll Painter's mind might have been at rest, and he might even have felt hopeful for his family, hopeful that, at last, they could live happily ever after. And yet, there was no denying that the Troll Painter felt sorrowful for leaving Litté.

In truth, nobody ever found out what the Troll Painter was thinking or feeling. Three hours later, as the storm was thrashing out, the *GOOD FLOAT* was turned over and plunged into darkness. A few minutes after three o'clock in the morning, on Easter Sunday, as the night was at its blackest, *GOOD FLOAT* disappeared into the lake to the wailing of a sad choir. The great lake swallowed the boat. And nobody aboard survived.

A few days later, the wreckage of *GOOD FLOAT* was recovered from the bottom of the lake. It was a huge undertaking, a spectacle for all of Småland to witness first-hand or read about. People flocked to Småland to watch the recovery. The Troll Painter, Esther, and their newborn baby's bodies were found and identified. Esther and her baby were taken away, to be buried in the city with the rest of her family.

The Troll Painter was returned home. He was buried in the forest. Some of his oldest friends said that whilst visiting his grave, they had caught sight of the small troll boy, Litté, laying flowers atop the tombstone before disappearing back into the darkness of the forest. To this day, the Troll Painter is remembered by the fair folk as Småland's greatest creative, and a true friend of the forest.

Many years later, it is our turn to roam the forests as the Troll Painter once did. In a letter to his friend, the Troll Painter once wrote, 'Our time is short. Our lives aren't frequent. I often think of the people who came before me. And I often think about the people who will come in the years after I am gone. But, most of all, I think about my paintings and the forests. I think of Litté in the trees. I think of the great, mossy stone sitting next to me. It will likely look the same a few hundred years from now when we are dust. And so, I patted it on the back, and told it to say hello to whoever is good enough to sit here in the future.'

Now, we must sit in our own forests. If we listen, we may hear the Troll Painter's voice through the stones. The voices may ask questions. 'What are you writing today? What are you painting? Please don't go.'

And for now, the reply must be, 'I am writing about trolls. I am writing about fairytales and forgotten things.'

Everything is connected in the forests of Småland and the world beyond. Deep and dark things flow together beneath the earth in roots or tides in strong currents. The very same currents which dragged the Troll Painter down to his eternal reward. When things are created from the forest – stories, art, or music – they are created with the heart and spirit of the Troll Painter and the voices he left in the stones. Perhaps one of these voices belongs to Litté, the troll boy. Perhaps he is still out there, all grown up. Or perhaps not.

And yet, there is darkness in this truth. It often comes to a point where you travel so far into the rooted woods and deep forests that you will not be permitted to return home, just like the Troll Painter was. The secrets revealed to those who wander through the trees are not suitable for everyone. You must be ready to see, hear, and learn it. Otherwise, you can never go back. Once seen, the invisible things will remain with you forever.

The Troll Painter's kobolds, goblyns, fairies, and troll boys were painted in watercolours with playful glee and humour. That was how he had seen them first-hand. For they were real, and he had seen them. Each of his canvases depicts characters both cute and creepy; the works are as enchanting as they are frightening, truly capturing the spirit of the deep dark forests. In the end, the Troll Painter never wanted to leave the forest. When he did, it refused to let him go. And now, with his body buried beneath the earth and the roots cradling his corpse in gentle repose, the Troll Painter's life is given over to the forest forever. Go now, walk there.

You will feel him right there with you.

And maybe, you will find Litté there too.

NO WAY OUT

Thick trees and tangled walls rose from the ground beyond the castle. It was a labyrinth. The hedge maze was a great and vast network of connected paths. Each of them was laden with the foulest creatures the world could offer. Threads of serpent roots and knotted vines wormed over one another beneath the maze's junctions. The old cobblestone road that had led up towards the forsaken fortress was now overgrown and lost to the touch of time.

Years later, footsteps fell onto the moss and dark cress of that path. For, unto the hedge maze, the lost and forlorn Tristan had entered. Tristan was a stranger in a strange land, a wanderer in unfounded territory, a lover now lost and full of grief. He was tall, lithe, and strong. There was nothing soft about Tristan but for his face. He had a youthful face and a gentle stare that would harden with the rushing memories of those now lost to him. What he wore was what he always wore. A dark leather jerkin, threaded trousers, knee-high waders with pointed toes, and a tattered cloak of the finest green that slept over his shoulders and warded rain from his skull. That was what he always wore. The hood was always up.

Only the flicker of trouble and curiosity in Tristan's jade eyes gave light to the face beneath the cowl. Other than that, the hint of shoulder-length black hair fell out from the cloth. At his waist, his left wrist rested on the twisting hilt of his only sword. It lay there, sheathed in mottled pinewood, waiting for its master to draw its course. And there, carefully wrapped away in his satchel, lay an urn. The container was malachite, and a silver adornment of antlers was grooved into its colour. Tristan carried his past with him, even now. Even into this dark and terrible place, this forsaken labyrinth. His footfalls fell gently across the mossy cobbles, for Tristan was a ranger, of a certain type. He knew the truest character of the quiet movement. He knew when to wait. And he knew when to go. There were others with him in the hedge maze that night. And night it was, for dusk had been pushed away into the clouds. The purple and gold were spirited off from the firmament.

Currently, the world above them was black and cool. There were no stars. There was no moon. Only tired clouds trailed across the night sky. Tristan moved amongst his companions. There were fourteen of them. Tristan was the fifteenth. Fourteen friends and swords swore for one stranger. For that was what Tristan was to them and to all others. He was a stranger. The man in charge of their retinue was named Finnegan. Finnegan wore grey clothes and a silver ring shirt. These men had no colours that they had sworn their honour to. They acted only in favour of others' fair giving. And that was what Tristan had promised them, in exchange for their support and guidance through the hedge maze. In truth, there were not fifteen of them in total.

No. Not quite. There were sixteen. Yet, the sixteenth character of the travelling cohort was kept out of sight. It kept close to Tristan, under the green cloth of its owner's torn cloak. It watched intently, peeking out between rips in the fabric. The others had not seen it, not yet. It was Tristan's secret. Their current path through the labyrinth gave way to a wrong turning. Thereafter, the turning gave way to ruins. It opened into a toppled and ruined outpost tucked away in the vegetation. The ruins were quilted with lichen and thorns. The remnants of statues were littered about the glen in which it rested.

The faces on the stones were upset. Some frowned in grim acceptance. Others' mouths were agape with fright and fretful warning. Tristan watched them all for movement. It would not have been the first time a statue had come to life around him. The cohort quested through the ruins of the hedge maze. They could see the tower of dark stone rising up from the labyrinth's heart. Though, where from they could find it, they did not know. Fountains of shattered stone rose into sight from the tangle. Much of their masonry and stonework had been trampled down into the undergrowth from years of previous travellers seeking refuge or ruin in the hedge maze. Filthy rainwater wept out from the breaks in the stone and transformed the ground beneath their feet into a quagmire. They could not move quietly now. Each of the retinue stomped and squelched as they felt things slither around their ankles. Whether they were vines or serpents masquerading as one, they could not be certain. It was not raining, not anymore. It had been wise of Tristan to wait until the rains had passed. However, the threat of them still lingered in the clouds ahead. The prospect of their flooding lay around for all to notice.

Toppled pillars lay in the flood. They jutted out from the morass. Their marble bodies were tainted green from algae. Reeds and weeds hung from them too. They clung to each of the ruined stacks like strands of greasy hair. None had entered or worshipped in this clearing for generations gone by. That was clear to Tristan as he surveyed the ruined statuary. Tristan stepped forward, wading. There was nothing clumsy about his movements. Though, the same could not be said for his cohort. They lashed and thrashed about the weeds gathering up to their knees. The pungent reek of the algae became far more noticeable as it drifted towards them in floats. A number of them went ahead, lifting their torches aloft so as not to ignite anything close to the water's surface. Their embers took off and away into the night in little stacks of smoke.

In the darkness, the light of their torches cast them each as gaunt and amber phantoms. Finnegan went up after his men and gestured for Tristan to follow them. None of the sellswords wanted to be in the hedge maze, let alone after dark. And Finnegan would not keep them there any longer than was necessary. Their task was to navigate the stranger through the labyrinth towards the tower. That was all that mattered. Though, none had ever found their way to reaching it. After that, and prompt payment for their efforts, Tristan was none of their concern. A quick gust of wind rushed through the flooded statuary. Some torches went out completely. Others struggled as their flames were tugged away. The darkness grew stronger, thicker. And they were all made entirely aware of the coming chill.

Then, the uncomfortable quiet was shattered.

A grating cry shot out from atop one of the wet stones. One of the retinue — a younger boy — turned to face his friends and the stranger with them. They all turned back with faces white with terror. A twisted and sharp arrow pierced his throat. The boy gurgled and spat before his eyes rolled over, and he toppled from the stone. He splashed down into the quagmire and floated up on his face. The sellswords gathered, forming rank.

'Curse it, goblyns!' Finnegan cried. With that, all hopes of stealth and passing without trace were forgone. 'Gather up, all of you,' he ordered, 'form together, tight! If the goblyns trap you here, you won't see tomorrow!'

Finnegan's warning was met with prompt returns of 'yes, Sir' and 'right'. They waded through the ruins, careful not to raise their heads too high above the stones of the statuary. There were things far worse than goblyns lurking in the tangled walls. But they had not yet reared their ugly heads. Only one truth mattered to them now. The retinue was no longer alone. The guarantee of a goblyns ambush was suddenly imminent.

Finnegan's sellswords were not veteran warriors or heroes. They were not adventurers or questing men. They were working men with convenient access to steel. And their whereabouts had been convenient to Tristan when first he had met them in the nearest tavern. Now, he felt grief in having brought them into the labyrinth.

Nonetheless, they followed Finnegan without hesitation. They splashed over into a tight-knit formation and drew their swords with a scrape of unsheathed steel and fourteen — no, thirteen — flashes of worn-out silver. Then, the walls of the hedge maze began to rustle and shift. Twigs began snapping and the fresh squelch of smaller footfalls reeled through the dark. Something struck out from the turning ahead. One of the sellswords was grabbed around his throat by something far smaller and yet far stronger than he. Finnegan thrashed out with his shortsword and, with a flourishing strike, cleft the attacker's fist free from its forearm. Tristan listened for a terrific screech of pain and found a flash of fangs like flat knives grin behind it.

Finnegan grabbed his man and pulled him back into formation. His shortsword was filthy with thick, dark green juices. It was wet with goblyn blood. The reek filling the air was fouler now, fouler than it had been when first they had entered the flooded statuary. The sellswords bunched together with Tristan at their centre and quested further into the hedge maze. The quick and tight turns of the labyrinth quickly saw their formation break apart into strands and trails. With the greater lot of their torches extinguished, they could not see a thing. The clash of blades with teeth rang out from somewhere Tristan could not tell nor see.

Something sharp whipped past Tristan's left ear and tore a sheet of cloth from his cowl. Dark hair tumbled out as he turned to face the attacker. In an instant, knives were flying out from the foggy vegetation towards Tristan, Finnegan, and their cohort. Another man fell to the ground with a deathly thud. Three little knives protruded from his spine. The retinue turned in every direction in fear. Some had already vanished into the fog and the walls of the labyrinth. Their number was rapidly dwindling. Soon thereafter, the formation was no more. And there would be no defending the ambush.

So frightened were they that they did not pay attention to what lay above them, the tiny figures crouching atop the maze, scuttling closer along the tangle. Tristan saw them. He counted them up quickly. Though, nothing certain could be found in their number. Tristan turned to Finnegan, reaching a gloved hand out to his shoulder.

'Our time's up,' Tristan said sternly. 'There are thirty goblyns. They've found us. It's too late to turn back. We *have* to continue.' Finnegan nodded by way of reply and wiped his shortsword clean of goblyn blood.

The night came alive with the wicked chatter of laughter. Another flat knife and rush of teeth flew out from the fog. Finnegan thrashed it away with the face of his shortsword and hurled its little body away into the hedge. Before he reached down to skewer its stomach with the point of his weapon, it scurried away with a chortle. 'Take pity,' Finnegan cursed, 'we can't take thirty. For every goblyn we slay, three more appear from the fog. What're we going to do?'

'Threat not,' Tristan stated.

The stranger slipped through the fog and took the cloth from his head. His jade eyes lit up in the shroud. Tristan stepped over the still-twitching corpse of the nearest goblyn. He ground his heel into its ankle until it stopped. Then, he waited. He watched for the little contours and outlines rummaging through the fog. Three more appeared. Tristan reached into his cloak and thrashed his arm out again with a sweeping gesture. Three dark thorns, each one long as a quill and razor-sharp shot out with a throw. Each one found their mark in the eye and skull of a sneaking goblyn. Tristan reached into his cloak again at the sight of another crawling through the tangle. He flicked the thorn out with cerebral precision towards it. It whistled through the empty air until it found its mark. Tristan and Finnegan both heard the squeal, pant, and gurgle that followed.

Then, the quiet returned.

'Ha!' Finnegan cried. 'They flee!'

'No,' Tristan said firmly. 'They gather. They've run out of knives and arrows. Now they only have one option left to them.'

'What's that then?' Finnegan returned, feigning confidence.

'Teeth,' Tristan said.

*

'Can't see anything in this fog!'

Finnegan swatted away the branches that curled out from the labyrinth walls like fingers. Then, he turned to slicing them away with his shortsword and brushing them from the floor with his boot. Finnegan was still searching for the cobbles that once lay somewhere this way. Those cobbles guaranteed navigation and safe passage to the tower at the heart of the hedge maze. However, his hopes of finding it were entirely unfounded. And he was starting to question whether there was a path, or if the stranger, Tristan, had strung him up on a fool's errand. There were only six of them left now: four sellswords, Finnegan, and Tristan himself. The last of their cohort still lingered beneath Tristan's cloak, terrified of what dangers were unfolding around them.

Tristan paused at the complaints from Finnegan and his men. Though he had spent much of his life in gloomy forests and by dark lakes, Tristan was aware that his retinue's eyes were not as accustomed to the dark. He himself admitted that it was becoming overly difficult to find one's way in the reeling fog around them. He winced and regretted that there was only one course of action. If he were to reach what lay ahead, for better or for worse, they needed light. If it were light that they needed, then it was light they would have.

Tristan crouched down, half-vanishing into the quilt of fog. He slung the satchel from his shoulder – under his armpit – and started rummaging through his rations, crating supplies, and the rest of his essentials.

'What're you doing?' Finnegan urged. He did not spare many glances for the stranger crouching before him. The torches around them were going out, and the rest of the men were backing up to their position on the path. Finnegan could still see those swatting away grasping hands and dirty fingers from the labyrinth walls. There was a scream and cry of anguish as another one of their cohorts was dragged away into the fog and opened up with grates of wicked teeth. The goblyns chattered in the fog, satisfying their frenzied hunger.

'We haven't got time for—'

'Grant me this,' Tristan interrupted. It took Finnegan a moment to realize that the stranger was not talking to him or to anyone else present. Rather, to nobody that they could see. Tristan tore a cloth covering away from a dark green container. It was malachite, a vase or urn, and it was more ornate than anything Finnegan had ever seen. It appeared priceless. Intricate grooves of thorns and leaves and antlers traced through its exterior in streams of mithril silver. Tristan's eyes remained shut. And Finnegan was starting to worry at his disassociation with their current whereabouts. Tristan unsealed the urn, took off one of his gloves, and reached into it. Grey and black ashes streamed through his fingers like sand from an hourglass. He pressed the lid shut tight once again. Then, he spirited the container away once again into his cloak and stood.

'What's that, tell me!' Finnegan demanded.

'Quiet,' Tristan stated. His sternness caught Finnegan off-guard. And he quickly noticed the way his gentle stare had become cold and unforgiving. 'If it is light you want, then it is light you will get. Forgive me.'

Tristan strode out in front of the remaining sellswords towards a curtain of fog. He held his hand out and began to sprinkle the ashes into the air. Whilst doing so, the stranger started chanting something that none of the others present could translate. It was no language that they understood or had ever heard in their lifetimes. Tristan continued to chant as the shapes charged through the fog towards him. He felt his companion twitch and clutch at his chest beneath his cloak. Tristan could see them now. The goblyns leapt off from the fallen statues, swung from vines, and crouched atop branches. Their eyes were alight with hunger and wicked intent. They were all wearing dark red caps and long hoods. Their smiles stretched from ear to pointed ear.

Then, his eyes opened with a glare and flare of glittering emerald. The ashes ignited with fiery zeal and took to the air as lime witch lights, illuminating the path ahead and clearing the fog from their vicinity. Finnegan and his cohort covered their eyes before focusing once more.

They only caught glimpses of what followed.

Tristan flung his cloak about his chest and thrashed out with three thrown thorns at the goblyns. Each thorn found its target to a greater or lesser extent. They reeled back in injury and temporarily stayed from their conflict. Tristan ran in to greet them. A thorn hit a goblyn that struck out from above. It landed with a thud at Finnegan's feet, face full of thorny protrusions. A second leapt for Tristan directly, mouth wide open. Tristan parried to its side and let loose a series of thorns down the creature's throat. They exploded out the other end in a shower of green juices and dark offal. The goblyns had conceived their encounter with an element of stealth to their advantage. Yet, that boon had been robbed of them. Goblyns could not fight without dirty subterfuge. Thereafter, the cluster of goblyns retreated from their game into the fog and the unknown.

Finnegan noticed one final attacker approaching Tristan from behind whilst the stranger fought off a fray of others. He clambered up and thrust his shortsword into the goblyn's ribs. It writhed on the sellsword's steel. Then, it slowed, tired, and died there. Poisonous ichor spilt down the length of Finnegan's blade and wet the hilt. He tugged his sword free with a curse and spat on the goblyn's corpse. The acrid stench of goblyn flesh was repugnant. Finnegan wafted the smell away then turned to what was left of the gathering.

Tristan was returning to him and the three men that remained.

'That's all of them?' Finnegan grinned.

'For now,' Tristan nodded. 'The rest won't fight on even footing. Not even in their labyrinth.' Tristan started along the path again. Finnegan was taken aback at the disregard with which the stranger held the conflict. He stepped over the corpses of goblyns and sellswords alike without paying them any attention.

'Wait there,' Finnegan urged. Tristan stopped. 'What was that? I saw what I saw.'

'That's sorcery,' one of the men said. 'There ain't anything natural about it.'

'It's quite natural,' Tristan returned. 'What would you know of sorcery?'

The men looked at one another as though none of them dared to strike the ire of the stranger with his strange magics. 'Tell me,' Finnegan finally voiced. 'You some sort of warlock?'

'Not quite,' Tristan said truthfully. 'But I'm not your enemy. You have nothing to fear from me tonight.'

'And the thorns?' Finnegan said again after Tristan figured the topic concluded.

'*That,*' he began, 'is nothing of your concern.'

'Fine then, have it your way,' Finnegan chortled and spat out a tooth. 'Keep your secrets.'

Tristan did not maintain his conversation with Finnegan and the sellswords. Nor did he continue to stare at them. His gaze had softened yet again and he pulled the lip of his hood back to touch his brow. 'Let's continue. You don't want to wait around here much longer. There's no knowing when the goblyns will return.'

What remained of Tristan's retinue followed him thereafter.

The labyrinth stretched on forever. And they would spend their final few hours there trapped. Trapped alone with a stranger from a strange land and the strange magics he brought with him. The truth of it, Tristan and his retinue founded another rumour of heroes lost in the hedge maze. They were another story. A warning not to enter the goblyn labyrinth.

They never found their way out.

There was no way out...

ABOUT THE AUTHOR

Toby Crabbe is an internationally published author of horror fiction and dark fantasy. A graduate of Creative & Professional Writing from the University of Wolverhampton, his short stories have featured in anthologies published by Black Hare Press, Thin Veil Press, Crumps Barn Studio, and Poe Boy Publishing.

Much of his writing has been collected in hardback, paperback, and digital formats. He continues to create dark tales out of rural Telford and Wrekin, England. Toby is a former student of fellow horror writer and Poe Girl Publishing author R. M. Francis.

THE THINGS THOUGHTS FEAR is his debut anthology that collects his most frightening horror and fantasy fiction into one volume in what makes for a terrific and gothic read. Ranging from quiet folk horror to haunting ghost stories, it will raise the question. What do you fear?

Toby signed with Poe Girl Publishing in February of 2024.

'To learn what we fear is to learn who we are.'
GUILLERMO DEL TORO

'Fear is a place where you just tell the truth.'
CLIVE BARKER

'Fear is contagious. You can catch it.'
NEIL GAIMAN

'You have to make the dark side genuinely appealing.'
RAMSEY CAMPBELL

'If I cannot inspire love, I will cause fear.'
MARY SHELLEY

'There's a fine line between paralyzing dread and galvanizing fright.'
JAMES HERBERT

Printed in Great Britain
by Amazon

48366893R00145